BULL BALLS

A Dante Passoni Adventure

by Rafael Ferraro

Volume One

Copyright 2010 Rafael Ferraro

PART I

London
1989

CHAPTER ONE

Contemptible, thought Nils Laar, waiting for his flight. Just three days ago his photograph and an oversimplified article on his work had appeared in every serious newspaper in the world: "South African physicist Nils Laar, 37, was awarded the Nobel Prize for Physics yesterday in Stockholm. By incorporating gravity and the nuclear forces into the general theory of relativity, Professor Laar achieved a goal that had eluded Albert Einstein for the last half century of his life. In so doing, he proved that . . . "

Yet here he stood, the greatest mind of the century, in line at Heathrow Airport with his wife and two young sons, as incognito as the traveling fools around him.

Laar knew that this bizarre fact could not be explained by his appearance, for he was no ordinary looking man. At six feet two inches, with straight blond hair parted in the center, a prominent beak and piercing blue eyes, he was a striking presence.

Still, no one in the entire city of London recognized him. So it had been during his two days of museum visits and shopping; so it had been his entire life.

They did not recognize him because they could not bear the truth. Which was that men were *not* created equal, and that one man in particular was superior to the rest. They had excluded him from the human community because their tiny minds and laughable theories could not explain his existence.

They had made his life miserable. They had made him angry. They should not have treated him in this fashion. But they had; and now they were going to pay.

An irritating voice rasped in his ears. "Hey, man, you got the time?"

Laar let his icy stare linger on the face of the bearded young

American in line behind him.

"Ten minutes after ten."

"Thanks, buddy."

The American hesitated an instant, as if he had belatedly recognized the illustrious physicist. But no, apparently not. He resumed digging through his rucksack; and Nils Laar turned back toward the ticket counter.

In little more than two hours, he would be gone. Why not admit it now? He had secretly wished for an orgy of popular adulation before checking out of this life and into another.

It was not to be.

The agent put Laar's luggage on the scale, looked at his first-class tickets and asked him if he had a seating preference

Nils Laar said he didn't. He gathered up his tickets and led his family to the boarding area for NTR Flight 31 to Rome.

*   *   *

One of his two tattered leather carry-on bags contained a device that was well-hidden inside the case of his portable radio. He could operate the device, which he had built himself and called "the Mongoose," by feeding it codes from his altered digital watch.

The Mongoose had the capacity to override the automatic piloting system of any American-made jetliner. By programming it in advance, Laar could actually fly the airplane in which he was traveling. And he could do this without the knowledge of the pilots *or* the air controllers on the ground. The Mongoose's powerful signals sent false data to the cockpit and the tracking stations along the flight path, causing all instruments in the aircraft and on the ground to register the values he chose.

Laar had begun construction of his device in 1985, shortly after he had arranged for the "disappearance" of Arlin Gattwater. He had been testing it for almost a year, steering international flights on which he was a passenger up to 50 miles from their flight plans and adjusting their altitude by as much as 20,000 feet. These experiments he carried out at night or on those rare daytime flights when the overcast towered above the jetliner's cruising altitude. No one in the cockpit or on the ground had ever noticed the massive detours.

His second carry-on bag contained the basics he needed to get himself to a Fiat stashed in the parking lot of a church near Courmayeur, Italy. These were an ultralight nylon parafoil, a thermal body suit, a pair of infrared goggles and a makeup kit which, given his lifelong curse of anonymity, he doubted he would need.

He looked out the window. At their present altitude, just announced as 31,000 feet, the 727 was in the clouds. He glanced at his special watch, which also told time. Four minutes after midnight. They had been in the air an hour and a half. The moment had come to take over the aircraft's controls.

A rush of exhilaration welled in his gut, the exhilaration of birth, he thought. His new life was about to begin.

He drained his Seven Up, kissed his overweight Dutch wife and excused himself to go to the toilet. He did not bother to look at his sleeping sons. Perhaps there was a time when he had loved them. But they now belonged to his past, for which he felt no nostalgia.

He opened the overhead compartment and took down his second bag, leaving the bag which contained the Mongoose undisturbed. In the toilet, he locked the door and opened a tiny panel on his watch. Beneath it was a miniature keyboard.

Using the tip of a ballpoint pen, he punched in a nine-digit code. This activated the Mongoose. He entered another code, which transferred the aircraft's position, altitude and speed from the cockpit instruments into the Mongoose's memory bank.

A green light flashed on his watch, indicating that the 727 was now somewhere inside the circle covered by his preprogrammed flight plan. He transmitted a final code, which locked the plane on the course he had set for it.

On the face of his watch, a new number replaced the hour: 11:53, eleven minutes, 53 seconds and counting backwards.

He would come out of the john at impact minus 53 seconds, and jump precisely at impact minus 20.

The descent of the aircraft would be gradual, the turn very wide until the last 19 seconds, when the plane would veer sharply to the left. He doubted the pilots would notice anything wrong until then.

And if they did happen to notice before the final veering? Well, what could he say? It would certainly make *their* final moments more interesting. They would radio air control with a bizarre report: our instruments show us on course, but visually it is evident that we are losing altitude.

Air control would study the radar screens and tell them to relax, RELAX, must be some sort of optical illusion. Impossible that you've strayed. We're watching you. You're splitting your air corridor right up the middle.

It would be even more interesting for the pilots, thought Nils Laar, if they came out from under the overcast at 16,000 feet and saw the peaks of the high Alps rushing beneath their wings.

He enjoyed imagining things. He could see their faces as they hauled back on the controls and found them locked. Coming down, Mont Blanc looming just ahead and to the left, drifting left, DRIFTING LEFT!

Frantic words to air control, calm reassurances that all was well while their instruments remained stuck on 30,000 feet and they hurtled at 568 miles an hour toward the gap between Mont Blanc and Mont Maudit . . .

They were going to make it, Thank the Lord, they were just going to sneak by!

Jubilation.

A reprieve.

Time to get the controls unlocked and shut off the automatic pilot. Automatic pilot! No sir, never gonna use that mother again. It's gonna be the stick from now till retirement.

Then the last wild turn into the mountain, the dizzy 3-D approach of massive rock walls, the pathetic cries of men no longer able to delude themselves.

*　*　*

Nine minutes, eleven seconds and counting backwards. 9:11-9:10-9:09.

Out the tiny window, Nils Laar saw gray. Still bloody overcast. Too bad.

Well, you couldn't have everything. Clothes off, thermal suit on, not much room to work. Not much room, but not much work to do either. Trivial, actually. Lot's of time.

He'd shave his head in the sink, he decided, while he waited for the minutes to pass. Shave his head, then put his clothes back on over the wonderfully thin thermal suit.

Not likely he'd encounter anyone when he landed, much less anyone who'd recognize him. But you never knew. Edward Teller might be vacationing in Courmayeur, out watching the night as he liked to do. Teller was one of the few living humans who *would* recognize him. "Hello, Professor Laar, fancy meeting you here. I thought I read you were on your way to Rome."

He put down his shears and razor and glanced at his bald dome in the mirror. Kristus, he hardly recognized himself! He could forget Teller and the make-up. He'd get out of Courmayeur fast. They'd hear about the crash soon after it happened, might even see the glow of the inferno coming round Mont Blanc, turning its summit into a ghostly silhouette.

Yes, it would be better to be in Turin as early as possible, ensconced in the hotel room for which he already had the key.

Turtle neck and tweed jacket on, a little tight over the thermal suit, no problem; parafoil on, its broad straps pulled snug around his shoulders.

2:17-2:16-2:15 . . . Tatters of mist rushed by the window.

Then . . . he hardly believed his eyes. They came out under the overcast just as they had in his vision! What a sight! More magnificent even than he'd imagined it! Peaks sailing past beneath the wing, cold and silent, alabaster shark's teeth aglow in the steel-gray night.

More clouds down lower, he sees them filling up the valleys, great languid shrouds. They're flying between two cloud layers. God in all His malevolence is opening up His sky to give the sorry pilots one last look. God is taunting them! God, a being who knows how to have fun.

And he is right there with God, partaking of the fun. He is about to jump. Farewell, Nils Laar. It's been an unpleasant life but the next one will be better.

A knock at the toilet door.

1:29-1:28-1:27 . . .

"Occupied," he growls. His voice sounds strange to him, but not so strange *she* doesn't know it's her husband.

"Nils, darling, Kes is feeling ill. Take him in there with you."

A moment of hesitation.

1:09-1:08-1:07 . . .

"All right."

He is being born, he sees his shaved head pushing out the toilet entrance like the head of an infant coming down the birth canal, sees everything just before it happens, always has, always will.

He adjusts his infrared goggles, checks the hood of his thermal suit to make sure he can pull it up at the last moment.

:53. He yanks on the handle, the door opens inward. His wife's jaw sags, his son's eyes grow wide with fear. He doesn't know them, he is someone else.

He steps out, shoves them both into the toilet, hears them fall.

He turns down the aisle, flattening an old man and a kid on his way to the emergency exit at the rear of the plane. Thirty rows of seats, a few dozen yards, American football. Used to watch it on occasion while teaching at U.C.L.A. Professor at age 21, back in the days when he still tried to be social. Never saw the point of the game till now.

He scores his first TD, stops in front of the exit. Hood up. He grips the door lever as the Mongoose unlocks it, glances at his watch.

:29. Must wait. Must be exactly :20. All preprogrammed, all done by computer. At :21 his sailing body will not make it over the Col de Brenva, the ridge between Mont Blanc and Mont Maudit. At :19 he will whistle into Mont Blanc just behind the plane.

Two men are coming at him, heroes. Over the furor unleashed by his violent passage, he can hear his wife screaming.

"Stay back!" he yells at the footballers. "You'll be sucked out!"

The men listen, stop, grab on to seat backs. He yanks down the emergency lever. :21-:20!

He plunges into the icy roar, remembering his first jump when he was a teenager, remembering the 200-odd HALO jumps of his obligatory military service, HALO – high-altitude-low-opening.

He bends into the maximum track position, body stiff and spine slightly curved to give him the shape of a loose comma, arms at his sides, hands open and palms forward, toes pointed like a diver about to go off the high board.

The roar and brute force of wind at 568 miles an hour are incredible. He feels the power of God, the scale on which He plays His games.

For an instant the flight of his body parallels the flight of the plane. Then the wall of air tearing and clutching at his jacket and shoving against his parafoil pack slows him. He falls away.

The 727 makes a sudden sharp turn to the left. He watches, spellbound, as it slams into the impassive face of Mont Blanc a few hundred yards from where he rips through space, watches it explode in a blinding flash.

He is suddenly liking the American sports he disdained as Nils Laar. He is now a projectile, a baseball. He is a Home Run, cracked into center field.

His forward speed is decreasing, and the flat arc of his trajectory is warping into a steep descent. But he clears the centerfield wall, the knife edge of rock connecting two great peaks, the border between France and Italy.

Clouds engulf him, the layer hugging the ground. His infrared goggles pick up the lights of Courmayeur, nestled behind Mont Blanc to the south and east.

He extends his left arm a couple inches, shifting his course 20 degrees. He is right on target.

He stares at his watch, which is now an altimeter. At 1400 feet above the ground, he makes a sudden move from the maximum track position to the spread eagle, thrusting his arms up and out, parting his legs and bending his knees.

His body goes vertical, head up. At 700 feet, he pulls the rip cord. At 400 feet, the parafoil gives his chest and shoulders a firm, friendly jerk.

Perfect, perfect. But what's this looming under him? Some sort of a heated pond! Anxiety nearly chokes him. He fights the cords, steers, barely makes it over the water.

He lands in a snow bank, heart still pounding from the pond passage, sheds the pack which held the parafoil and turns it inside out. It becomes a small soft bag, new carry-on luggage.

He field packs his parafoil, puts away his infrared goggles, tucks his body suit's black hood beneath the collar of his turtle neck and heads for his stashed car.

Minutes later he is speeding toward Turin, cursing the Fiat's defective heater.

Near Florence, Italy
September 2006

CHAPTER TWO

Some things you never grew tired of, thought Dante Passoni, waking to a fine Sunday morning in Fiesole. He stretched, breathed in the smells of freshly baked bread and espresso, smiled at the bright clear Italian voices rising from the square. Kids were arguing over a bicycle, the baker was trying to seduce Signora Pavese, spirited shouts from a gathering of old men mingled with the toll of ancient chimes.

Dante propped himself up on big down pillows and gave precise instructions to the computer microphone built into the night stand beside his bed. The slats of his antique wooden shutters pivoted open.

From the top of the medieval bell tower which housed his flat, he took in the view of Florence in the valley below. Through the soft haze he could see the Duomo, the Palazzo Vecchio, the Uffizi Museum where his father had served as curator. He thought of his distinguished ancestors going all the way back to the Medicis, and could almost feel their presence.

Dante Passoni loved the very old and the very new. Everything in between he considered wasteland. He believed that a synthesis between the very old and the very new generated extraordinary vision, believed it to be the secret of his success as owner of CRC, Italy's most dynamic high-tech corporation.

He spoke again to his computer, requesting Vivaldi's Concerto in D Major, Number 43. Lights flickered and needles jumped on the face of a sleek amplifier. The room filled with joyous flute and violin music. He switched on the intercom and spoke with his butler, a modern-day Sancho Panza, in the kitchen 300 feet below. "Luigi, I'd like my breakfast now."

"Right away, Signore," responded a testy voice. "By the

way, your Uncle Vittorio just phoned. He wants you to join him for lunch at Villa Maseto. He says he has a project he wants to discuss with you. I told him you were sleeping and would get back to him when you woke up."

"It looks like a nice day for a drive, Luigi. Ring him back and tell him we'll be there. And have him set a place for Kiyo."

"Yes, Signore. Anything else?"

"Warm up the Lamborghini."

* * *

Dante stepped into the courtyard behind his bell tower and took a big breath of the cool morning air.

Luigi was seated behind the wheel of his dark blue Lamborghini Murcièlo, checking the things one checked before a drive: oil pressure, turbo boost, oil temperature. He took a swipe at the dash with his dust cloth and got out.

Dante was pleased to see that his butler had trimmed his Van Dyke and put on a fine white silk shirt.

"How does she look, Luigi?"

"Everything *perfetto*, Signore."

"Excellent." Dante slide into the driver's seat. "We're due in Rome in an hour. Let's go."

He waited for Luigi to get in, then hit the gas. The low, powerful car lurched into the alley, roared across the square and hurtled down the Via San Domenico toward Florence. They made a twentieth-first century dash through the center of Dante's city, tires squealing on cobbled streets, gray stone facades and carved wooden doors flying past in a dizzy blur. Pigeon flocks exploded in the air, and frightened tourists scurried for cover.

Italy, how Dante loved it! It was the only modern country on earth not yet castrated by do-gooders.

They screeched up the Autostrada entry ramp and accelerated to 160 miles an hour, Dante's Sunday cruising speed. While Luigi dozed to the steady growl of the engine, Dante maneuvered deftly around sputtering Fiats and listing peasant trucks. Whenever both lanes slowed, he used the shoulders, braking only as a last resort.

Near Orvieto, he saw a dense white cloud billowing over the highway. He flipped on his fog lights, driving lights and radar. "Luigi, wake up. What the devil is that?"

His butler blinked into the sunshine. "Must be the Cavour Talcum Powder shipment to Naples. A tragedy, Signore. If all that talc blows out, the bucks down there won't be able to get into their jeans. An entire subculture will be destroyed."

Dante was not amused: driving was serious business. Some kind of a chemical transporter had sprung a leak. He'd best get around it before the carabinieri closed the road. He pulled on to the left shoulder, his speedometer still stuck at a leisurely 160. "How does it look, Luigi?"

His butler scratched his Van Dyke and studied the little radar screen on the dash. "You can make it if you hurry."

Dante pressed the accelerator to the floor. He strained to see the guard rail as they entered the swirling cloud. They rocketed past the leaking transporter at 190 miles an hour and swung back into the left lane just in time to miss a bridge abutment.

Dante's reflexes were good: he was glad he had taken time for his morning espresso.

He eased down to cruising speed and loosened his grip on the wheel, hoping for a long stretch of clear road. But when they crested the next hill, he saw an enormous traffic jam looming on the horizon. He cursed under his breath.

"The hyberbolic horn, Signore?" asked Luigi.

"I'm afraid it's no use. Look at that chaos, would you? Those Fiats are like weeds. They've overrun the shoulders."

"And the mess probably goes all the way to Rome, Signore. The Pope is blessing adulterers today."

"We should have taken the helicopter."

"We should always take the helicopter, Signore. A shame you're addicted to your car. I know a good alternative route if you don't mind secondary roads."

"Anything's better than this."

They left the autostrada and began a tortuous journey down narrow two-lanes, twisting through a landscape of ancient villages, medieval castles and smoky terraced vineyards whose grapes would soon be ready for harvest. Dante, who liked to be punctual, called Kiyo on his voice-activated car phone to let her know he was running late.

"We're picking *her* up?" asked Luigi incredulously. "She's is Rome. Why couldn't she just meet us at Vittorio's?"

"Luigi, there are some security arrangements I wish to discuss with her before lunch."

"So how do *I* get to Vittorio's from her hotel?"

"A taxi, Luigi. It won't kill you."

"A taxi!" The butler shook his head. "It's just not fair, Signore. All these years I've been your competent and trusted servant. She came from Japan as an industrial spy. She could have destroyed your company. What if she had not switched sides? What if she had run off with all your secrets? She's the one who should be taking the taxi."

"Luigi, please. You are an excellent helicopter pilot, and as such you are indispensable to me. But I must say, at times you can be a real pain in the hindquarters."

* * *

"Well, Dante," said Kiyo in perfect Italian, "it's a good thing you sent me to Rome. There is not one plot to destroy you; there are four."

He glanced over at the brilliant oriental beauty he had made his security director. A man on a bicycle hauling a cartload of zucchini cut in front of him, forcing him to swerve.

"*Four* plots? Really? And you were able to document

these?"

"Yes. IBM can't compete with you so they want to discredit you. The Mafia doesn't like your enlightened brand of capitalism so they want to eliminate you. And the Japanese believe they can sink your Russian deal by raising questions about your morals."

"That makes three, Kiyo. What's the fourth?"

"Graziella Calvino. She believes your Uncle Vittorio has a plan for saving Venice. She fears you and he will conspire to keep Altel away from the lucrative contracts that will be handed out. She also thinks you stole the Russian deal from her. She's been calling you nasty things in public."

"Such as?"

"Bull Balls," said Kiyo reluctantly.

"What's so bad about that?"

"You are missing the point. I think you should stop sleeping with her. It leaves you much too vulnerable."

Dante tapped his horn as they roared past Luigi's taxi. His butler responded with an obscene gesture that looked like a bird pecking at the windshield.

"Kiyo," he said, "CRC and Altel have always had a competitive business relationship. I know Graziella Calvino well and consider her a difficult but honorable woman. If there really is a Save Venice Movement in the making, I shall reassure her that CRC has no intention of interfering with her company's right to bid on all related projects. As for the physical side of our relationship, I stopped sleeping with her three years ago. She was taking too much of my time – not to mention my energy."

* * *

Uncle Vittorio came out to the gate wearing a floppy panama and a white summer suit. His face glowed deep bronze, and a warm friendly fire burned in his eyes. He approached with weightless elegance and introduced himself to Kiyo.

Dante said, "Uncle Vittorio is the younger brother of my

deceased father. He was an influential member of the Italian Senate for over two decades. But politics has been only a small part of his rich and varied life. Not so, Uncle?"

"Ah, Dante, don't embarrass me in front of your lovely friend."

Kiyo said, "I'm very pleased to meet you, Signor Passoni."

"The pleasure is mine, my dear. Tell me, Dante, is *she* your ex-spy from Sony?"

"She is indeed, Uncle."

"Fascinating. And what, my dear, have you learned from us? What would you have advised your superiors if you hadn't switched sides?"

"To drink more red wine. To spend four hours each day at lunch. To drive 200 miles an hour, and to avoid monogamy like a dread disease."

Uncle Vittorio laughed heartily and took Kiyo by the arm. "Well, you must have been a good spy. You've certainly divined the secret of the Passonis' success. I trust you won't betray us."

"Never."

Dante watched the way his uncle kissed Kiyo on the cheek. He could see that Vittorio, at 60, was far from finished with women – or they with him.

Luigi arrived, grumbling about the rude cabbie. He greeted Kiyo and Vittorio, ignored Dante and lifted his nose toward the garden for an olfactory preview of the meal. His spirits soared when he caught a whiff of porcini mushrooms.

The tables, beneath colorful canopies, were set with crystal, silver and hand-embroidered linen. Servants balancing trays of drinks moved among the guests, careful not to bump the spry grand folks or trip over the hordes of children playing at their legs.

Dante made the rounds, greeting his many relatives. Then he sat with Kiyo, Luigi and Vittorio at a secluded table ringed with hedges.

Uncle Vittorio raised his aperitif glass. "*Salute.* Welcome to Maseto, welcome all of you. I hope, Dante, that your purist heart does not object to the liberties I've taken with lunch."

"As long as there are no hamburgers, Uncle."

Vittorio laughed, the crows feet crinkling around his eyes. "No, my boy, I've stopped short of that. But I wanted to display for you a spirit of acceptance and compromise. So I have taken from the sea and the earth, and I have mixed our many wonderful regional cuisines. You see, Dante, the dawn of a New Italy is at hand, an Italy which rises above petty conflict to serve the good of humanity. I know you like symbols. Our meal today is a symbol of the New Italy."

"So when does your symbol leave the kitchen?" asked Luigi, who hadn't had time to eat breakfast.

"Luigi, please," said Dante. "Uncle Vittorio wishes to speak of his plan for saving Venice."

"Yes, you are right, my dear nephew. I want to speak of my plan. After twenty years of defeat in the Senate, it is time to take another approach to the rescue of Venice. The New Italy is coming as surely as the sun rises – but, regrettably, She is not yet here. Rather than waiting on Her arrival, I have decided to direct my efforts abroad. But enough seriousness for now, my friends. We'll talk after lunch. Your butler is hungry, Dante. I can hear his stomach rumbling all the way over here."

Uncle Vittorio clapped his hands and called for food.

* * *

The lunch arrived. There was salty prosciutto and succulent melon; cold chunks of lobster in light green olive oil; linguine with porcini mushrooms and fettucine with white truffles; tuna with capers and stuffed swordfish; a mixed grill of lamb, pork, wild boar, Florentine steak, chicken, pheasant, and quail; salads and cheeses; ripe fruits; an airy zabaglione and a tart gelato.

After the meal, the waiter removed the thicket of wine

bottles and brought espresso. The sun was low in the cypress trees and a lilting afternoon breeze blew from the south.

Vittorio thickened his coffee with three heaping spoonfuls of sugar and resumed his discussion of the topic so close to his heart.

"Yes, my dear friends, I am going to redirect my efforts at saving Venice. I've decided to found an International Commission that will raise its funds from the plundering rich."

"From whom?"

"I am speaking, Dante, of the world's largest corporations. Here in my garden I shall entertain their directors. I shall convince them one by one of the necessity of contributing to the survival of our Queen City. Like a good Passoni, I have set my sights high. My goal is to raise sixty billion US dollars."

"Sixty billion dollars!" exclaimed Kiyo. "Will it really cost that much to rescue Venice?"

"I'm afraid so, my dear. First of all, we must devise a way to control the high waters from the Adriatic. Then we must stop the sinking of the hundred islands on which the city is built. We must repair the damage to art and architecture caused by centuries of neglect. And we must stop the pollution coming from the huge industries on the mainland. This will all be very expensive."

Dante folded his napkin and shifted in his chair. "What makes you think, Uncle, that the big international corporations give a damn about Venice?"

"Oh, I don't think they do, not for a moment. The Senate, I assure you, cured me of any naïveté that might have afflicted me. My strategy is to make sure that these rogues cannot afford *not* to contribute. I plan to lead them into a war of images against each other. The losers of this war will lose market shares and profits – and *that* they do care about."

He smiled warmly, then continued. "And if I might whisper a secret to you, my dear friends, Siemens and Toyota have already pledged several billion each. Do you honestly think that IBM,

General Motors and the others can afford to refuse me? It would be like refusing UNICEF. It would be a devastating blow to their corporate image, a blow that could prove fatal."

"Bravo, Uncle" said Dante. "Bravo. I believe you're really on to something. You might actually pull it off. You are truly a great philanthropist."

"No, my dear boy, I am no more a philanthropist than these corporations. I love Venice, that's all. I am doing this for my own satisfaction. There is only one true philanthropist left in the world, and you know who he is."

"I assume, Uncle, that you're speaking of the South African, Pieter Godessohn?"

"Of course, of course."

"*He* might be a good for a few billion. Have you contacted him yet?"

"Oh, yes. The moment I had my idea. In fact, he was the very first. It was strange, Dante, how cool he was to me on the phone. I remembered him as quite the gregarious type."

"What did he say?"

"That saving Venice was an upper-class concern unworthy of his democratic ideals. I tried to convince him that the loss of man's most beautiful artifact would ring out round the world like a death knell of civilization. He was unmoved."

"Well, Uncle, he can afford to say No: he doesn't have the public image problems of your corporate candidates. I'd like you to put my pledge of a half billion from CRC in the pot. We'll double that amount if the Russian deal goes through. Now, Luigi, warm up the car. We're due in Milan for dinner."

"Milan! But, Signore, Milan is four hundred fifty – "

"Luigi, please."

Venice
November 2006

CHAPTER THREE

An ill wind came off the Adriatic, the scirocco. Heavy dark clouds rushed past Santa Maria della Salute's majestic white dome. Rain fell in horizontal sheets. On the ribboned surface of the Grand Canal black gondolas yanked at their moorings. Wet pigeons huddled in flocks beneath ancient gables and dripping marble statues. Already the Piazza San Marco lay under several feet of water – and the tide was still rising. The season's first storm had struck with a vengeance.

Several miles inland, the rain lashed the slender barred windows of Giorgio Puzzo's villa. The atmosphere inside was close, the air too heavy for the central dehumidification system to dry.

"Bring me another coffee," Puzzo ordered.

Gina walked quietly to the kitchen. She turned on the espresso machine, which was the type used in bars, a large stainless steel box covered with nozzles, gauges and intricate tubing. It reminded her of Giorgio Puzzo's refinery on the shore of the Venetian Lagoon, the place to which her life had been wed since he had brought her to Italy as a young girl.

The machine had been getting a lot of use lately. She knew this was a sign that Giorgio was under pressure. Whenever he became tense he supplemented his benzedrine and cocaine habits with huge doses of caffeine.

She pumped four long handles with ivory knobs, filling his mug with a liquid as thick and black as the crude that came in on the tankers.

Puzzo tasted the espresso. He raised his small bloodshot eyes and glared at her. "Water," he hissed. "Dirty water. You didn't make it strong enough. You're worthless." He drained his mug in one swallow and fell silent.

Gina returned to her cleaning. She dusted the black marble dogs guarding the front door. When she noticed that lint from her rag had remained on the beasts' heads, she lifted her skirt and wiped it away.

She gasped, she should have known. She had done something to displease him.

He rose from his chair as if he were going to strike her, fulminating about her filthy Arab habits. "Don't touch my statues with your dress," he rasped.

She bowed her head and apologized. He slumped back in his chair, exhausted by his outburst.

Gina returned to her dusting. She had been with him ever since she was 11 years old. Now she was 23 and he was 50. She should, she thought, have become accustomed to his foul moods by now. But she hadn't. If anything, his yelling and constant criticism upset her more than when she was a child.

The telephone rang. Puzzo answered. "What? The Donatello's docking today? In this weather? I see."

He hung up and gave Gina a rare smile. "Get ready," he said. "We're expected at the tanker port."

* * *

The black Mercedes limousine eased out the spiked villa gate and turned on to a narrow road. They drove through the farming village of Noale, where a few peasants walked among the puddles.

Gina sat with Puzzo in the passenger compartment, looking at the village so she didn't have to watch him inject a full syringe of benzedrine into his arm. As soon as he put away the needle, she heard him snort his cocaine. His words, so sparse until now, came in torrents.

"So tell me, Gina, what will it be like to see your father again? Do you look forward to it? Or do you feel like spitting in his face?"

They came to the industrial suburb of Mestre. She watched the prefab tenements glide by the window. "Why do you ask me such things, Giorgio? You know Kamin Aziz is not my father."

"Well, he was your stepfather. Aren't you angry with him for giving you to me like some trinket?"

Gina bowed her head and pushed her blue-black hair away from her eyes. "I am not angry at anyone, Giorgio. I was an unwanted child. I am grateful for what I have."

* * *

Armed guards opened a huge iron and concrete gate, and the Mercedes entered the refinery. It was four o'clock in the afternoon, and nearly dark. Towering distillation columns touched the clouds, the odor of sulfur fell with the rain. Orange flames danced against the overcast and shimmered on the cold aluminum skin of a thousand pipes. In the distance, shrouded in mist, Gina could see her stepfather's tanker, the Donatello.

They drove above the mud on elevated concrete service roads, a network of miniature highways. At the administration building, a utility van and a small bus with blackened windows joined them. The procession continued on to the tanker port, stopping beside the Donatello's freshly painted hull.

Sheik Kamin Aziz emerged from the ship's innards, a giant heap of flesh wobbling beneath his elegant robes. He wore a red-checked khaffiyeh held in place by a thick gold band. He still looked as he had in Gina's earliest memories.

Gold was everywhere. It was woven into the cloth of his robes and dangled from his wrists; it circled his fat fingers and snaked through his sandals. She wasn't surprised. She knew he had so much gold he stored it in blocks too heavy to lift.

He waddled down the gangplank, his progress slow beneath the canopy. He fussed with his robes, sidestepped puddles, scolded his overanxious servants.

His harem followed at 20 paces, six young beauties draped in white and turquoise silk. Gina could have been one of them. She supposed her life was preferable.

Behind the girls came the first wave of his entourage, bearing sacks of couscous, slaughtered lambs and musical instruments wrapped against the rain.

The Sheik made his way to the rear door of the limousine beneath umbrellas held by his servants. He heaved his great bulk inside, filling the Mercedes with exotic fragrances sweetened by the dampness. Gina watched Puzzo momentarily vanish beneath the great man's embrace, then resurface muttering greetings in Arabic.

"Ah, my friend," the Sheik said, "you have lost still more weight. Are you ill? Do not worry. I have come well-stocked. We shall fatten you up."

"My health is fine, Kamin Aziz. I assume you've brought me help in dealing with this powerful new Commission."

"Ah, yes, my friend. The Commission will not see the light of day. The Presence has been very specific about how we achieve this."

The Sheik's appraising eyes turned to Gina. "Ah, Dalelah, you have become a beautiful woman. Tell me, how old are you now? Sixteen?"

"She's twenty-three," Puzzo said. "She goes by the name of Gina here. Don't compliment her. It makes her vain."

"Yes, yes, simply magnificent," said the Sheik. "If I had known what was to come, Giorgio, perhaps I would have offered you a block of gold instead of this child. But it is very good she is here, and very good she has turned out so desirable. If she passes the examination ordered by the Presence, she will be of great use to us."

"Gina? She can't even dust a room properly."

They drove away from the docks and looped around behind the petrochemical plant. Gina felt a shudder of dread. Something ominous hung in the air, like the stench of sulfur from the refinery.

She glanced out her window. In the distance, across the Lagoon, she saw the foggy skyline of Venice. The view made her heart ache with longing for all the beautiful things destiny had denied her.

* * *

By nightfall, the new concrete building at the center of the complex, built to house imported workers not registered with the authorities, wailed to the rhythms of middle-eastern music. The dining room had been cleared of tables and chairs and strewn with colorful cushions.

Gina sat with Puzzo and the Sheik, trying to ignore the dozens of Pakistani engineers who had been living in isolation for months.

Waiters from the Sheik's kitchen staff, wearing tall red hats, served perfectly seasoned lamb, piles of couscous and brimming goblets of Algerian wine. Soon the musicians broke into a frenzied number, announcing the arrival of the belly dancers.

The Sheik patted Puzzo on the back. He licked his lips, which glistened with lamb fat, and lit his opium pipe. For a moment he watched with reverent calm as the belly dancers strained and shivered in front of him. And then, to Gina's dismay, he stood and began grinding out lascivious gyrations of his own. His jewelry jingled, and his huffing rose like the pant of a steam engine.

He was about to lay a hand on one of the dancer's thighs when Puzzo grabbed him by the wrist. "Dammit, Kamin Aziz, I want to know what's going on. I want to know *now*. We can celebrate later. Let's go where we can talk."

The Sheik's bell-shaped face bent into a smile. "Very well, my friend. If you must know now, go to Room Seven. And bring Dalelah with you, yes? I'll be along shortly."

* * *

"My name is Manfred Strasser," said the blond giant who

met them at the door. His pale blue eyes were set far apart, and his legs bulged like tree trunks. "I have been sent to help you with your mission." He escorted them into the room.

"What mission?" grumbled Puzzo irritably.

"I don't know yet," said Manfred, smiling at Gina.

"What do you mean, you don't know?" Puzzo barked.

"He does not know, my friend," said the Sheik, waddling into the room. "Giorgio, I must remark once more that you do not look well. I am worried about you. Have you forgotten what I told you when you worked with us in Yemen?"

"What was that, Kamin Aziz?"

"A man, my friend, is like a tent. He has four main stakes – gold, food, women and laughter. If all of these stakes are not in place, he cannot stand up to the winds of life.

"Now, my friend, I know that you have nearly as much gold as I. But you are not eating. This means that you have pulled up the stake of food. I have heard no laughter from you – very dangerous. And from the way you behaved with the belly dancers, I see that you have given up sex. My dear Giorgio! You have let yourself become a tent with only one stake. The slightest breeze will blow you away. This is not good. So much depends on you."

"I'll stake myself better, Kamin Aziz, as soon as we solve the problem of the International Commission. They plan to start snooping here in three weeks!"

"Very well, my friend, we'll solve it quickly. Then I shall supervise your recovery."

The Sheik put the bag he was carrying on the bed and patted it. "I have brought a Pandora's box of gifts. These gifts will help all three of you in the coming days."

He rummaged through the bag's contents and pulled out an odd-looking gun. "This is for you, Manfred."

The giant grunted and accepted the gun with a smile, turning it over and over in his hands. "A Taser!"

"Yes, yes," the Sheik said, "a Taser. It is a very useful gun, Giorgio. It is like your Christian God. It strikes down the wicked with bolts of lightning. But unlike your God, it does not kill or maim. Anyone who is shot can later rise from the dead – like your Jesus. This gun will be very good for Manfred. We do not want him leaving a trail of bullet holes and broken necks."

The Sheik dug in his bag and handed Puzzo a doll, a young girl dressed in traditional Saudi robes. "For you, my friend, to help you combat the stress of living with only one stake."

Puzzo frowned. "What am I supposed do with this?"

"Do not look at her with such scorn, my friend. She is made of cocaine. Undress her. Sniff her. You will like her."

Puzzo squeezed the doll's little finger. Gina watched it crumble into a fine white powder, which he immediately snorted. The Sheik, she thought, must not know of Giorgio's drug problem. More cocaine wasn't going to help keep *his* tent up.

"And for you, Dalelah, the loveliest gift of all." The Sheik held up a diaphanous white silk dress embroidered in beige, so light it trembled in the turbulence of his breath. "Go and try it on, my child. We would all like to see you in it."

Gina stared past the mountainous bulk of the Sheik at the drawn red curtains, her heart beating wildly. Revulsion churned in her stomach. She would look almost naked in that dress.

"Thank you," she murmured. "Thank you, Kamin Aziz. I shall try it on later."

The Sheik let out a booming laugh. "Do not be frightened, my child. We only wish to *see* you in your new dress. It is a very beautiful dress. Manfred, escort her to the bathroom."

The blond giant started toward her.

To her great relief, Puzzo intervened. "What do you want from her, Kamin Aziz?"

"Ah, my friend, I see that you wish to protect your personal property. This is a good sign. It demonstrates that you are not entirely unstaked. Do not worry. I must see her in the dress, that is all. Orders from the Presence. No harm will come to her. You have my word. Dalelah, please go put on your gift. Otherwise I will have to ask Manfred to help you."

"Go on, Gina," Puzzo said. "You heard Kamin Aziz. No one will harm you."

In the bathroom, Gina felt more naked with the dress on than with it off. She looked in the mirror and closed her eyes. What was she to do? She couldn't go out there like this. The lines of her body were clearly visible through the silk!

Manfred began knocking, the Sheik called to her. She wished she knew how to say No, but she didn't. She held her breath and turned the knob.

"Ah, yes, truly magnificent," the Sheik said, taking her by the arm and leading her across the room. "Now be still, Dalelah. That's it, that's it. Lean up against the wall. I must conduct a few observations to be sure you are as healthy as you look. Turn around. Ah, yes, very good. Now turn toward me once more, my child. Giorgio, look at her. She appears very innocent, very shy – you know, my friend, almost like a virgin. Yet she drips with the Essence of Woman. She cannot help herself. She is ripe, she is delicious, no man in his right mind could resist her."

Johannesburg, South Africa
November 2006

CHAPTER FOUR

Word of the Philanthropist's generosity had spread to the ends of the earth. Now, after 14 years spent helping the needy, Pieter Godessohn was inundated by a never-ending torrent of requests for aid.

These requests came from every imaginable cause, and from every corner of the globe: from earthquake victims in Turkey, women's groups in Alabama and relief organizations in central Africa. They came from the giants of charity, UNICEF and the Christian Children's Fund, from the United Way and the Swedish Council for Birth Control in the Third World. They came from many thousands of legitimate unknowns, from the Rainbow Coalition for the Homeless in Newcastle and Mothers of Methadone-Dependent Teenagers in Amsterdam.

And they came from multitudes of ingenious quacks in search of a quick way to get rich.

The immense foundation had once been a one-man enterprise. No longer. On the eighth floor of the Philanthropist's downtown Johannesburg office building, armies of highly principled employees worked in neat cubicles, partitioned by glass and stretching endlessly along the windowed walls.

Here the requests arrived in the form of letters, telephone calls, faxes, E-mail transmissions and personal visits. They were condensed to basics by the staff and sent on for review.

The Philanthropist's office was also on the eighth floor, smack in its center, thick-walled and windowless, like a big misplaced cube.

He could have chosen any floor of the skyscraper for his office: after all, he owned the building. But he preferred to be near his employees – those devoted young people whose hearts, as he liked to say, were in the right place, who would have worked for the cause *gratuit* if this had been necessary.

It was not necessary: the Philanthropist was the wealthiest man in South Africa. No matter how much he gave to charity, his great fortune continued to swell.

From nine in the morning until noon, he sat in his deep leather armchair perusing his staff's condensed reports. With his uncanny ability to spot real need, he made his godlike decisions, casting aside unworthy requests and scribbling in his loopy, gregarious hand the amounts to be given to those who merited help.

His instructions traveled up to the top floor in pneumatically propelled cylinders – a quaint, old-fashioned system he refused to do away with. There, another staff made arrangements for the dispersal of funds.

When such things as account numbers and currency preferences had been established, the data traveled back down to the Philanthropist, who gave the final payment orders to one of his seven banks.

But the Philanthropist did a lot more than render judgment on requests for aid. From two in the afternoon until late at night, he actively sought out causes and individuals attempting to serve the good of humanity.

This was "Help the U.S.A. Month."

A shelter for battered women in Omaha, none of whose directors has ever heard of Pieter Godessohn, receives a phone call out of the blue – and a grant of $500,000. An alliance of handicapped veterans which has been fighting for years to get the City of Phoenix to install wheelchair lifts in its buses suddenly discovers that the city has been given an entire fleet of spanking new buses with the most advanced lifts installed at the factory – compliments of the Philanthropist. The founder of a tiny hospice for black AIDS victims in Seattle, on the day his lease on the hospice's humble dwelling is to be canceled, learns that he has become the dwelling's new owner – thanks to its purchase on his behalf by a white South African.

And so it goes from one country to the next, from one end of the globe to the other, a great outpouring of capital and heart, a charitable work of epic proportion.

* * *

The Philanthropist's past – the version he gave to the press and his half dozen biographers – was fascinating. In the course of his 54 years, he claimed to have had three identities: Peetai, Pieter Godessohn and Arlin Gattwater.

When he was 13 years old, his existence had still not been recorded in the public registry of any nation. He did not make his "official" appearance until 1966, when British Safari guide W. W. Cartwright came upon him living with a native tribe in what is now Zimbabwe. The youth, through Cartwright's intervention, was taken from the tribe and placed in an orphanage in Pretoria.

Soon thereafter, Jan Viljoen, a tenacious Dutch journalist, having read about the white youth who had emerged from the bush speaking only a tribal dialect, took it upon himself to unravel the lad's bizarre saga and find out who he really was.

The journalist managed to trace the boy's roots to Paul and Maria Godessohn, a young missionary couple who had left Holland for southwest Africa in 1948. The Godessohns were murdered in a native uprising some years later. News of their deaths did not reach Holland until 1953.

The missionaries who filed the police report mentioned rumors that Maria Godessohn had given birth to a son while serving in the bush. It was presumed that the infant had perished with his mother and father.

The journalist's investigative work clearly indicated that the son had not perished but had been spared and taken in by the natives. Dutch authorities, accepting Viljoen's conclusions, granted the boy Dutch citizenship and gave him the name Pieter Godessohn in place of his tribal name, "Peetai." Soon thereafter, a well-off bourgeois family in The Hague applied for adoption rights, which were granted.

Pieter Godessohn's crisp new official papers were sent to the orphanage in South Africa, along with rail and steamer tickets and instructions that he be returned to the Netherlands, where his legal guardians awaited him.

But the attempt to repatriate young Pieter Godessohn went awry. On the day set for his departure he mysteriously vanished, taking with him his passport and few possessions. He was thought to have returned to the tribe that had raised him.

A half-hearted search for the boy was mounted by the local authorities. But it ended abruptly when the rainy season came and washed away all hope of finding him.

* * *

Pieter Godessohn did not reappear until 1991, a quarter of a century later, when he showed up in court in Johannesburg, self-assured, worldly and fluent in half a dozen languages. He had come out of obscurity, he said, to contest the will of South Africa's recently deceased racist billionaire, C.P. Wittersand.

Wittersand had left his vast fortune, which included seven banks and a sprawling empire of gold and diamond mines, to the Order of White Knights, citing in his will the "absence of any living blood relations, to whom my estate would otherwise have gone."

During the sensational four-month trial, Godessohn, who represented himself, was able to establish that Paul and Maria Godessohn had in fact been relatives of Wittersand. But attorneys for the Order, the most renowned trial lawyers in the country, challenged the identity of the man claiming to be Pieter Godessohn.

The trial grew messy, the crowds of spectators became rowdy. Was Godessohn for real – or a brilliant impostor out to snare one of the world's largest fortunes? The courtroom, in the second month of the trial, became so boisterous the press and public had to be excluded.

To prove his identity, Godessohn placed in evidence his official Dutch passport, 25 years old, expired, but still in good shape.

He took and passed eleven lie-detector tests. He produced scores of witnesses who claimed to have known him as Arlin Gattwater, the identity he told the court he had assumed at age 16, when he left his tribe for the second time.

And why had he lied about his name at this point? the judge wanted to know. Why had he not used the name Godessohn which, after all, was his legal name?

"Because, your Honor, I had already gone through the humiliation of being a curiosity in a strange, new world. At the orphanage, I felt like an animal on display in the zoo. When I left my tribe for the second time, I knew what to expect. I did not want to be the same curious 'Pieter Godessohn.' I wanted a fresh start. I wanted to blend in, to be as unobtrusive as foliage in the jungle, or dust on a jeep."

The judge listened, thoughtful and impassive, as the days passed and the attorneys for the Order of White Knights grew weary.

"So you assumed the name Arlin Gattwater after you left the tribe? Is this your testimony, Mr. Godessohn?"

"Yes, your Honor. I would like to tell the court exactly how this came to pass."

"Objection!"

"Overruled. Go ahead please."

"Thank you, your Honor."

Godessohn, calm and convincing, explained how he had made his way north to Kenya, where a kindly, aging English couple, the Gattwaters, believed his fabricated story of a plane crash, of dead parents, of his own amnesia and months spent wandering in the bush.

The Gattwaters took him in and became so fond of him that they made arrangements for his adoption. Palms were greased, a common practice back then, certain questions were conveniently omitted by the authorities – and Pieter Godessohn became their son, Arlin Gattwater.

When they died within a year of each other, he was already living in Britain, a good student in a special school for "late bloomers" in Kent. They left him all they had, enough for him to survive until he graduated.

The records, subpoenaed from Kenya and Britain, bore all of this out.

He told the court how he worked for a few years in England, then moved to the continent in search of more satisfying employment. Several years later in Holland – and very much to his surprise – Gattwater-Godessohn learned that his real mother, Maria Godessohn, had been a relative of the infamous South African racist, C.P. Wittersand.

He forgot about Wittersand, whose principles he detested. He continued to work for relief groups and – given his own strange past – became increasing involved with the problems of the Third World.

In 1985 he returned to the heart of Africa, hoping to understand as a man what he had experienced as a boy. He told the court how he came up against the raw horror of human suffering at its most basic level, how he encountered famine and war, disease and poverty. He lived in constant frustration, unable to be of any help because of his lack of funds. He became engrossed with native life and disillusioned with the relief organizations for which he worked. Little by little, he lost contact with European friends and employers.

Then, in the spring of 1991, he saw an article in a two-week-old Durban newspaper reporting the death of C. P. Wittersand. That was when he – Gattwater-Godessohn – got the idea to come out of isolation and research the old man's will. Because of its fortunate wording, he decided to come forward with his real identity, Pieter Godessohn, and claim what was lawfully his.

So much money left to an evil cause.

So much money to help the world's oppressed if he, Pieter Godessohn, won his case.

Which he did, to the shock of the public and the conservative establishment.

For many months after the trial, influential voices lamented the court's decision. Godessohn was an impostor, they said, no matter how righteous his present work, that of a philanthropist, made him appear.

But with time those voices subsided. Godessohn's apolitical brand of charity helped South Africa's image abroad. He gradually became a hero of the right and the left, of the rich and the poor, of Blacks and Whites and Indians.

The voices of doubt subsided.

Then the voices died out altogether.

But the voices had been right. The Philanthropist Pieter Godessohn was an impostor. He was not Peetai, the boy who had been born to Dutch missionaries and correctly identified as the son of Paul and Maria Godessohn.

The real Peetai, who was also the real Pieter Godessohn, had thrown away his passport on the way back to his tribe.

The Philanthropist, at that time a boy of 13 himself, had found the document quite by chance while hunting in the bush and placed it in a safe deposit box in Johannesburg. A precocious teenager shunned by his peers, he was intrigued even then by the idea of leaving this life for another.

The Philanthropist had tracked down the real Peetai, whom he found still living with his tribe, in 1984 – and made sure that no one, white or black, would ever see him again.

Nor was the Philanthropist Arlin Gattwater, although plastic surgery, steroids and body building had given him a near perfect resemblance to the man of that name. Gattwater was no more. The Philanthropist had arranged for him to make his final peace with Africa in the spring of 1986.

Rome
November 2006

CHAPTER FIVE

It was a gala in the finest Roman tradition, and it was all in his honor. Uncle Vittorio felt as if he were gliding rather than walking, freed from gravity by his soaring sense of achievement. He moved among haughty film stars and shrewd international financiers, powerful politicians and smug cardinals, addressing them like family.

They were in the courtyard of the Medici Villa, standing among the sycamore and cypress trees. A string quartet played exuberantly on the terrace, and waiters in black tuxes filtered like ballet dancers among the guests.

Scrolls of high cloud glowed pink on the edges of the falling night. Though it was autumn, a warm breeze blew up from the South, so warm the glittering event had spilled outdoors.

Uncle Vittorio let the sensuous breeze push him toward Lina Lazzarino, Italy's most beautiful screen actress. She was arguing a point of law with the Minister of Justice, who was having trouble keeping his eyes off the V of her low-cut gown.

"*Buona sera*, Vittorio," said Lina, embracing the Savior of Venice. "I've been waiting all evening to see you."

The two men shook hands.

Lina said, "You, Vittorio, are a miracle worker. Minister, just have a look around you. Pietro of the Greens is laughing at something the Leader of the National Alliance has said! And how about that old Communist, Ammintore. I don't believe my eyes. He's actually having a conversation with his archrival, Cardinal Giotti. Vittorio, darling, you have shown our strife-riddled nation the meaning of brotherly love. You have given us an example we can believe in. The New Italy has been born at last, and you are Her undisputed father."

"Yes, yes," mumbled the Minister of Justice. "I must say all of this is quite amazing. Perhaps we should think of Vittorio as our Gandhi."

"Baah," scoffed Lina. "What a pathetic analogy! Poor Gandhi was celibate. One should find another with whom to compare our virile hero."

Virile is right, thought Vittorio, gazing at the fabulous females within eyesight. Which one would he choose for the most special night of his life? Lina herself? Or Stefania, Fiorella or Laura? There were so many, one more beautiful than the next.

He knew just making the choice should be an enticing bit of foreplay. But Vittorio found himself on the verge of boredom. He suddenly realized why: at one time or another he had slept with every woman at his gala.

Momentarily distraught, he excused himself and walked toward the villa to pay his respects to the hardworking armies in the kitchen, pausing briefly when the Pope made an appearance on the balcony.

He entered a service door and wove a weightless course down a corridor crammed with waiters, chauffeurs and butlers. Soon he was surrounded by hearty laughter, raw emotion and earthy wit.

Uncle Vittorio felt at home with the common folk; he felt at home everywhere. He saw Luigi waving and walked over to greet him. "A damn shame, my boy, that our Dante could not be here tonight. Those Russians are taking up too much of his time with their inefficiency."

"Yes, Signor Vittorio, they certainly are. I know he tried very hard to make it back. He's leaving Moscow early tomorrow morning."

"Well, that's good. We've all missed him. Did he at least send that delightful security director of his?"

"She went with him to Russia. He sent me instead."

"I see. Well, Luigi, do enjoy yourself. There are plenty of fine looking ladies here."

"One in particular," said Luigi, nodding. "The one standing by herself in the corner. She came to meet you, but her name did not appear on the guest list. The guards wouldn't let her out of the kitchen."

Uncle Vittorio smiled. "She *is* something. I'm glad she didn't let the absence of an invitation deter her. Excuse me for a moment, my boy."

* * *

When he walked up to her, she held a bouquet out to him. Uncle Vittorio was too spellbound to take it. She backed off as if he had rebuffed her. He formed words of reassurance with his lips, fearing she was about to flee. But he did not dare whisper them, for she looked as though the slightest hiss of air through his teeth would send her scurrying into the crowd.

She averted her eyes. A blush the first color of dawn spread across her cheeks. Again she offered him the flowers.

This time he took them.

Without the bouquet, she looked almost naked. She was very dark, from the South, he thought. Her hair was raven, so black it was nearly blue. She wore a simple dress of diaphanous white silk which clung nicely to her body.

He felt his old heart beating faster. There was something almost girlish about her, a litheness and innocence he sorely missed in women over twenty-five. He put her age at nineteen. Most certainly a girl from the land.

Ah, but these peasant maidens ripen early, he thought, ripen while they are still in full bloom. They were without doubt the finest fruits of Italy.

She was stupendous. Of all the women who could be his tonight, he wanted only her . . .

"Senator Passoni," she said in a voice so soft he could

scarcely hear, "I am a simple worker from a village near Venice. It has caused me great hardship to come, but I had to see you. I had to tell you how I feel. You have saved our city, and you have done so without robbing the simple people of their dignity. Your Commission does not turn our city into a playground for the rich. It provides the funds to clean up the industries we depend on for our livelihood. You have understood us. You have given us hope for the future. You are a great man. I . . . I want to express my gratitude."

He stepped closer. She bowed her head, and her straight black hair fell forward over her eyes. He brushed it back and gave her a tender kiss on the cheek.

Her perfume was nothing he recognized, though he knew them all. It carried the scent of ripe melons and shaded gardens and orchards steaming in the sun.

She took his hand in both of hers. "Signore," she whispered. "Senatore . . . will you be with me tonight?"

He did not answer, for his answer was clear.

"I must go now," she said. "It must be later. I have a father and a *fidanzato*. I cannot be seen in public with you. They would – "

Vittorio held a finger to her full, moist lips. "I quite understand. Have you come with a car?"

"Yes, my brother's Fiat. It is a shameful wreck."

"Find us a place where you will be comfortable. Meet me atop Monte Mario at midnight. There's an old tomb just past the summit. Do you know the way?"

"I shall inquire, I shall find it. I must go now."

"The hours until I see you again will pass too slowly," he said, and that was the truth.

* * *

Uncle Vittorio glanced at his watch: ten to midnight. He had had Luigi fly him up here, no other way to escape the press.

Now he was alone.

He leaned against a rock wall two millennia old. He would wait here, he thought. It was a fine spot from which to enjoy the view.

Below stretched the lights of Rome, glittering under a slender crescent moon. The stars were out. Light was everywhere and yet the night was dark.

He ran his fingers over the wall, and its decrepitude made him think of early Rome. That was the beginning, the distant past. Then came Venice, which he had saved for the future.

History, he thought, was like a magical web of human actions spreading across time. He was a strand in that great web, crossing other strands, flowing with them for a moment or a year, leaving his mark on them as they did on him. Those stones beneath his fingers were the past. The girl he had just met and her unborn children were the future.

Vittorio waited, sandwiched comfortably between layers of time, until the whine of a tiny engine took his breath away.

She parked the Fiat across the narrow road. She got out and stood perfectly still, silhouetted by the city lights. The moon gave a hint of gloss to her black hair and highlighted the curves of her body beneath her softly glowing silk dress.

The dress, he thought, had to go. In his mind, he raised her arms, slid it over her head and let it fall limply to the pavement, leaving her naked.

He was on fire as he imagined himself taking her on the spot. And why not, why shouldn't he do just that, with Rome so magnificent below and the heavens watching benevolently from above?

He walked to her. She fell into his arms and returned his kiss. But when he let his hand venture beneath her dress, she stopped him. "Wait," she whispered. "Please wait."

"Of course, my dear. Shall we stay for a moment and enjoy

the view?"

She did not answer.

Vittorio took her gently by the arm and walked with her to the old stone wall. He turned her so that her back was against his chest and they were both facing the city. He wrapped her in his arms and leaned against the wall for support. "It's beautiful, Rome," he said. "Beautiful, isn't it?"

"Yes."

He kissed her neck, touched her breasts with his hands, held her tightly to him. Her shoulder blades cut into his ribs, the stones of the wall pressed into his buttocks. Again he ventured beneath her dress.

"No, not here," she repeated. "I have found a place. A modest hotel in Orte."

"What's your name?" asked Vittorio. "You are the loveliest creature on earth and I don't even know your name."

"Gina," she whispered. "Please, let's go."

*   *   *

Uncle Vittorio drove, cramped and happy behind the wheel. They left the city and sputtered down vacant country roads. He closed the canvas sun roof to keep his panama from blowing out and stroked Gina's cheek with his fingers.

He thought he felt a tear, though it might have been a drop of night, and he groped for her hand. It was soft, not the hand of a worker. He wondered idly why it was so soft. "What is your work?" he asked.

She looked down. He watched her hair spill forward in a gesture he had already come to love. "We make wicker baskets," she said. "My family has done this work for many generations."

Wicker baskets, soft hands. She was so beautiful they did not let her work. That would be the secret of her soft hands. Still, her life could not be easy.

He felt a twinge of guilt over his villas and limos, his wine cellars and worldwide contacts. But he knew that without these things his gift to Gina and to humanity would have been impossible: Venice could not have been rescued by a commoner.

"Will I see you again after tonight?" he asked. "I want very much to see you again."

"Let us think only of tonight," Gina said, her voice sweet but sad. "It is too difficult for me to think beyond."

Uncle Vittorio pulled her close and kissed her. The road zigzagged up the mountainside to Orte. A few lights twinkled on the steep terraced hills, but Rome had sunk beneath the horizon.

They drove through an opening in the medieval town wall, bumped down a narrow alley and parked in the deserted town square.

Water trickled from an ancient fountain, the music of eternity. Wrought iron benches and squat trees cast their weak shadows across the cobblestones.

He led her to the door of the Hotel Lazio while she dug in her purse for the key.

November, thought Vittorio. Not tourist season. The hotel looked empty.

Inside their room, Gina lit a candle. He saw flowers, a simple offering of cheese and fruit, a bottle of spumante.

She stopped in front of the frail shuttered door to the balcony, looking very tense.

Uncle Vittorio believed he understood. She was young and timid, perhaps even a virgin. He would have to allow her the time and space to relax. He opened the wine, sampled the cheeses, asked her to peel an apple for him.

At last she came and sat on the bed. The room was warm, but she shivered when he took her in his arms.

"Here, help me get this thing off," he said. "We'll climb under the covers so you're not cold."

She removed his tie, unable to look at him. He took off his

shirt and guided her fingers across his chest. She seemed to be stalling, focusing all of her attention on his medallion, untangling the fat gold chain from his chest hair. She looked at it in the flickering light of the candle.

Yes, of course she would be intrigued by it, he thought: the fine gold work depicted the skyline of Venice, a city she loved as much as he.

The medallion, Vittorio told her with quiet pride, had been his gift to himself when he had reached his goal of 60 billion in pledges from abroad.

Gina seemed moved. She shed a tear; this time there could be no mistaking it.

Perhaps, thought Uncle Vittorio, perhaps it was not such a good idea to proceed slowly after all. She seemed to be coming unglued, to be losing her nerve. Perhaps he should take her now before the magic moment passed forever.

He lifted her dress over her head, and she did not resist. He helped her shed her underwear, then got out of his trousers and held her in his arms.

Ah, she was young, so very young. There were knots of tension beneath her silken skin, and he felt very bad for her. It would take hours to instruct her in the pleasures of love. That was not a problem. He enjoyed teaching, and he could go on for hours if need be. His member had been tanned to cowhide by 40 years of daily activity.

Suddenly she slunk away from him like a dog expecting a beating. He tried interpret what he saw, but her expression was inscrutable.

And then he felt someone behind him seize the chain around his neck and twist it ferociously.

* * *

Gina slid backwards off the bed, pulling the sheet with her. She cowered in the corner.

Vittorio fought wildly. The bed shook and groaned. She forced herself to look. Manfred, the blond giant, was tightening the chain around Vittorio's neck with such force that the medallion of Venice cut into the waddled flesh beneath his chin.

No! This could not be happening! Please, God, may the gold chain break!

It did not, it was too fat.

They had promised her he would not be harmed. They had told her the meeting was to be a friendly chat about the Commission's treatment of the refinery.

They had lied to her!

A horrible gurgling sound filled the room. Nausea swept over Gina and made her retch. She had led him into a trap! He was the only man in 23 years who had ever treated her kindly, and he was being strangled to death because of her!

She tried to make herself move, to come to Vittorio's aid, but the weight of her past paralyzed her.

The gurgling became eerie, otherworldly, rising in her ears to a horrible crescendo.

She would never be able to live with herself. She buried her face in the sheet. More hideous noises filled the room.

And then came silence, the heavy silence of death.

Sounds returned, slowly at first.

She heard the fountain trickling lazily in the square.

She heard a train whistle somewhere far off in the night.

And she heard Manfred telling her that if she wasn't dressed in 30 seconds he'd kill her, too.

CHAPTER SIX

Dante's office occupied the top floor of the ultramodern skyscraper that towered over CRC's main administrative complex near Genoa. On very clear days the snow-capped peaks of the Alps were visible to the north and east. To the south stretched the azure Mediterranean.

The design of the office had been the subject of much controversy and highbrow party conversation ever since *La Stampa* ran a special feature on it. Dante, who usually ignored the coverage he received in the press, read the article one night after a wild argument with Graziella Calvino, hoping it would help him sleep.

It did: Passoni Watchers were no nearer understanding him than they had been a decade ago. Not one of the journalists or architects allowed into his sanctum sanctorum thought to speculate that the room's ambiance might help Dante find the delicate balance of spirit and intellect needed to slay dragons like IBM, Siemens and Sony; not one noticed the energy-giving synthesis of the very old and the very new.

The office was a vast uninterrupted space bounded by soaring, asymmetric walls of glass and marble. A stunning array of variously canted skylights covered the ceiling. The movement of the sun and clouds generated invigorating changes in the day lit interior.

Atria were everywhere, filled with the exotic flora of faraway continents. Original Raphaels and Fra Angelicos adorned the segments of wall which were not glass, and Renaissance sculptures stood around like casual visitors. Above the statues and atria hung a large brightly colored Calder mobile, a reminder that in Dante Passoni's world earnestness and caprice were two sides of the same coin.

The desk, not quite in the center of the office, was bare except for a computer keyboard and two flat-screen monitors. There were no files, telephones or computers anywhere in sight.

* * *

It was the morning after Uncle Vittorio's gala. Dante had been back from Moscow for less than an hour, but he was already hard at work. He had just finished sending out his weekly directives to his division chiefs all around the world. Now it was time to raise the capital for the biggest project yet undertaken by CRC, his Russian venture.

He typed a lengthy code on his keyboard, placing a call to Japan on his private telephone system. It was dinner time there, all offices were closed. But the leaders of Japanese industry and finance found Dante's telephone system so useful that they had installed it in their own homes. Dante had explicit instructions to drop in after business hours.

On the monitor to his left appeared the face of Shojiro Nikawa's lovely young daughter. Dante chatted with her casually while he waited for her father, the President of the Dai-Ichi Bank of Tokyo, to come in from his garden. Twenty minutes later, a deal securing the entire 14-billion dollar loan package needed for the Russian venture had been hammered out, transmitted and signed.

Nikawa asked only one favor in return for the gargantuan loan: that Dante give a piece of the Russian microchip contract to his father-in-law, Tanaka, Chief Executive Officer of Hiroshima Semi-Conductor.

Dante accepted this arrangement, for he knew that Tanaka had copied CRC's new microchip design and therefore produced a good product. The small loss to CRC he would simply consider interest on the corporate loan.

When his call reached Tanaka, the old man was supervising the preparation of a sushi banquet, intervening autocratically with his knife and berating his flustered chefs. Tanaka agreed to the billion-dollar minideal without looking up from a tour de force of precision slicing.

Seeing so much food on his monitor made Dante hungry –

not for sushi and neatly splayed little vegetables, but for the specialties of his native land. He was stuffed like a plundering Cossack from a week in Russia; stuffed but not satisfied.

He phoned his favorite restaurant, Da Marino in Genoa, and went over the day's offerings with Chef Bosisio. Finding them excellent, he reserved a table for himself and another table for a small team of his security people.

His lunch agenda set, Dante rang up the Russian Minister of Foreign Trade. He was put through at once, as he knew he would be. Dante Passoni enjoyed greater respect in Moscow these days than the American President.

"Vosnyvich here."

"Good day, Minister. This is Passoni in Genoa. I have good news. CRC has raised the capital we need to move ahead."

"Most impressive, Signor Passoni."

Dante settled back in his comfortable leather sling chair, glanced at his watch and began to map out his plans for getting the enormous project off the ground without bureaucratic delays. Minister Vosnyvich, an enlightened technocrat, evidently liked what he heard: he gave Dante the green light to begin immediate construction of phase one, a state-of-the-art robotics plant near Gorky.

Another coup for CRC, one of many this year.

Stretching his legs, Dante typed a shorter code on the keyboard, his last serious item of business before lunch. CRC communications satellite 4D, in geosynchronous orbit 25,000 miles above his office, relayed his call to the Lamborghini garage a few hundred yards down the road.

A narrow set of buttocks in rough gray pants materialized on the screen. His mechanic, Franco, was draped over the side of the Lamborghini, his head deep in the engine compartment. Dante shouted his greetings above the shriek of the engine.

When Franco finally heard him, he swiveled and looked up,

his hair a tangled black mass and his smile a mouthful of crooked teeth.

"Hey, Signor Passoni, welcome home. Madonna, you're going to like what I did to your car."

"Franco, did you repair my starter?"

"Signor Passoni, I ask you, what is a starter? A piece of carbon steel, a couple of brushes. How can a man of genius like myself devote his short time on earth to something as boring as starters? I worked on your turbocharger instead. Wait till you drive her."

"Franco, I know you're a genius of the motor, but the turbo was not malfunctioning. The starter, on the other hand, left me stranded five times last month."

"Five times. That's nothing, Signor Passoni. You should hear what happened to Signor Bertolli."

Dante realized his attempts to have his starter repaired in Italy were futile. Italians built the best engines and turbochargers in the world, but they did not care about starters. He would put his German division of CRC on a custom job – and make sure he had Luigi with him at all times until the new unit was installed.

"I'm very upset with you, Franco. Bring the car to CRC. And leave it idling, please. Good-bye."

"Good-bye, Signor Passoni. Once you're on the road, you'll forgive me."

Dante dialed Luigi. "I'm driving to Genoa for lunch," he told his butler. "I'd like you to accompany me in the helicopter in case I have mechanical problems with my car. It seems Franco got a bit carried away. Can you meet me above Pontedecime in ten minutes?"

"Certainly, Signore."

*   *   *

After the gloom of Russia, Dante was breathing the exuberant air of Italy. He ran his Franco-tuned Lamborghini up to

7,000 rpm and 180 miles an hour in fifth, shifted into sixth and jammed the gas pedal to the floor.

He rocketed past a group of carabinieri tending a radar trap. His rear camera photographed them and projected their imagine on to his monitor. Staring open-mouthed at his car, they reminded him of medieval horsemen lost in the twentieth-first century. Dante laughed: he would be halfway to his antipasto before they thought to radio ahead.

"Hey, Signore, slow down!" cried Luigi, who was flying along at 1,000 feet just ahead of the car.

Dante reached over to the speaker on the dash and turned down the volume. "What is it, Luigi?"

"Something on the road a couple of miles ahead. I'll get my telescope on it. Holy Madonna, Signore, looks like tomatoes. A whole truckload!"

"Thank you, Luigi."

Dante braked, eased around the obstruction and returned to full throttle. He overtook a Porsche on the right, darted through a knot of slow-moving trucks and focused his attention on two large Mercedes. One of the Mercedes was trying to pass, but the other kept speeding up. Dante looked in vain for an opening: there were trucks parked on the right shoulder, and a Fiat was stalled on the left.

"Luigi, how fast are they going?"

"Let me get the laser on them. Almost parked, Signore. A sickly hundred forty miles an hour."

"How does the center strip look?"

"Madonna, Signore, you can't do that. We had rain here the other day."

Dante conducted a quick visual check of the grass: no sign of mud. He cut his speed and pulled on to the median. The traction was good. He hit the gas, hurtled past the feuding Teutons and bounced back on to the pavement spewing dirt and grass.

A tunnel loomed ahead, a black hole in the steep green mountain. Luigi took on altitude. Smiling to himself, Dante flicked on his radar and driving lights. "Time me, please."

"Careful, Signore. There could be something else on the road in there."

Still accelerating, Dante hit the blackness at 200 miles an hour. He experienced a rush of exhilaration he got only from the sport of tunnel driving, but this tunnel was far too short. It seemed as if he had scarcely entered when he burst out the other end into the dazzling blue midday.

"Eleven point two three seven four seconds," reported Luigi. "Exit speed, two hundred nineteen point seven miles an hour."

Dante announced the figures to his computer and nodded with satisfaction. His fastest blast to date through this particular tunnel. That starter dunce, Franco, *had* worked wonders with the turbocharger. Dante made a mental note to call him after lunch.

"Luigi, what is the state of the toll plaza?"

"Crowded, Signore, really jammed. The adulterers must be back from Rome."

"Any closed gates?"

"Let me sight through my scope. Yes, as a matter of fact, Number Four."

"Keep it that way."

"Done, Signore."

The helicopter darted ahead and swooped low over the masses of cars waiting in unstable lines to pass through the toll gates. "Hold your positions!" Luigi ordered through the hyperbolic horn, his voice amplified to an earsplitting shout Dante could hear a mile away. "Drivers, hold your positions. An emergency vehicle is approaching."

Luigi hit his siren switch, and a sound like the arrival of a thousand ambulances shook the earth. Dante could see drivers who were preparing to switch lanes freeze in their seats, stricken by the fear of God.

He spoke a carefully researched license number, that of the President of the Republic. The number appeared instantly on his license plates, a simple precaution against the high-speed cameras the government had installed to identify tollgate crashers.

He roared into the gigantic traffic jam, howled between long lines of waiting cars and shot through the gate with the large red light blazing above it.

When he entered the city, Dante called Kiyo to let her know he would be arriving several minutes early.

*   *   *

Ristorante Da Marino was on a busy thoroughfare facing the harbor, and the staff had taken advantage of the fine weather to set up linen-bedecked tables on the sidewalk. Diners lunched on pasta and seafood, accompanied by the music of Italy: the frantic honking of automobile horns, the high-pitched whine of Vespas, the heated arguments and joyous laughter of passersby. Luigi hovered 600 feet above the harbor, the clatter of his helicopter lost in the great cacophony of noise.

Dante sipped a Campari soda while he perused an article in the newspaper on last night's gala in Rome. It was entitled "A Triumph for Vittorio Passoni."

He looked up in time to see another Italian triumph in the making. A very English-looking tourist in khaki shorts was leading his homely wife along a seam in the sidewalk chaos. The man, for reasons Dante could not even begin to discern, had a superior smirk on his face. His spindly alabaster legs flashed like lawn mower blades in the golden sunlight.

The couple was being followed by two teenagers on a Vespa. The kids wore dark sunglasses and jeans so tight they could only have been gotten into with the aid of Cavour Talcum Powder. Their shirts were open to the navel, and big gold medallions bounced on their still hairless chests.

The driver of the Vespa pulled close to curbside and slowed, raising a flat board and bringing it down squarely on top of the woman's gray bun. The passenger snatched her purse and tucked it to his stomach. The scooter reared up in a perfect wheelie, swerved into the traffic and disappeared around the corner with a deafening buzz.

Another normal day in Genoa. Dante ordered lunch.

* * *

During his second seafood course, Dante saw something he did not like. Graziella Calvino's red Ferrari was coming toward him, cutting a swath across six busy lanes of traffic.

The car screeched to a stop on the sidewalk in front of Giovanni's tobacco shop. Graziella, who looked more like a movie star than a corporate executive, leaped out. She stood tall and defiant, her chestnut hair waving in the breeze.

When she spotted Dante, she threw back her head and marched to his table with swaying hips and clacking heels. She sat down, took off her sunglasses and glared at him.

"It was rotten of you, Bull Balls. The Moscow idea was mine from the start. You stole it!"

"Calm down, Graziella, I did no such thing. It's hardly my fault if Vosnyvich chose CRC over Altel. Would you care to join me for lunch?"

"Give me a large break," she hissed, sliding his plate to the other side of the table. "It's you who's going to join me, Passoni. We're partners in abstinence until you give me my fair share of the Russian deal."

Kiyo appeared at table side, looking upset.

"It's all right," Dante said. "I don't believe I'm in danger. Graziella and I will work it out."

Kiyo leaned down and whispered in his ear. "Dante, don't be ridiculous. I'm not worried about *her*. Fendi from the *Corriere* just called headquarters. He's heard a rumor that your Uncle

Vittorio was murdered. I thought you should know."

Fendi! He had reliable sources at the police. Dante sat for a moment in stunned silence. Then he leaped to his feet and ran through the inside of the restaurant toward the back alley, where his car was parked.

Graziella charged after him, her breasts bouncing wildly and her dress swishing over platters of food.

Dante jumped into his Lamborghini and turned the key. NOTHING!

"Luigi!" he shouted into the mike. "Luigi, get down here! My starter is dead."

"I thought you had Franco fix it."

"Just get down here! Hurry!"

Dante watched in disbelief as Graziella took off one of her heels and began pummeling his highly polished hood. "You're not going to get away with this," she screamed. "Oh, no, Bull Balls, not this time. You wouldn't do this to a male competitor. We're going to settle this here and now. Open the door or I'll bash your windows in."

The helicopter appeared above the narrow alley.

"Get down here," Dante shouted. "She's turning my car to scrap."

"I can't, Signore, I can't. I have a thirty foot blade sweep and the alley's only six feet wide."

"Drop the rope ladder. I'll come out the sun roof."

"You're done, Passoni!" shouted Graziella. "Hear me? Done. The world is going to learn what a snake you are!"

Dante lowered his window a crack. "Shut up."

The ladder tumbled earthward. Dante opened his sun roof, grabbed it and let Luigi's electric winch hoist him up to the helicopter. Luigi helped him inside.

"Signore, what in the name of the – "

"Go! Fly! The bell tower in Fiesole."

* * *

Working from the terminal in his flat, Dante cracked the main police computer in Rome. A horrible feeling welled up inside him when he learned that the rumor was true.

Luigi entered with coffee. "Madonna, Signore, what's wrong? You look terrible."

"Uncle Vittorio is dead. He was strangled early this morning in a small hotel in Orte."

"But . . . this cannot be. I saw him just last night. I helicoptered him to the top of Monte Mario after the gala."

"You *what?*"

"He asked me to help him, Signore. He had a date. The press was swarming around his limousine. The girl did not want to be seen."

"Who was the girl?"

"I don't know. She came to the Villa Medici to present him with a bouquet of gardenias. She was not on the guest list. The guards wouldn't let her leave the cooks' and servants' quarters. But then Vittorio came down to compliment the kitchen staff. He saw her . . . and he was taken with her."

"But who *was* she? What did Uncle Vittorio tell you during the helicopter ride?"

"He didn't know her name, Signore. He said she was a stranger, a farm girl from a village near Venice."

"He was a fool to go with her."

"Don't judge him harshly, Signore. You did not see her. I assure you, Jesus Christ himself could not have resisted such temptation."

Dante put a hand to his forehead and closed his eyes. For a moment, he thought he would be sick. "All right, Luigi, fuel the chopper. We'll fly to Orte. Perhaps we can turn up some helpful clues before the carabinieri muddy the waters forever."

CHAPTER SEVEN

At noon the Philanthropist left his office and took his private elevator nine stories down to his private gym. The doors opened on an immense room filled with free weights, sophisticated conditioning equipment, punching bags and a full-sized boxing ring. He greeted the gym's three black attendants and instructed them to set the machines to maximum resistance. A few minutes later, he came out of the dressing room wearing shorts, tennis shoes and a tank top.

"Korean boxing today, Mr. Godessohn?" an attendant asked.
"Tomorrow, Ken. Mr. Haak is in Durban."
"Lucky for Mr. Haak."
Godessohn smiled. "Perhaps."

He penciled a check mark on his chart: this was workout number 4,227 since he had begun his vigorous exercise and body building program in 1989.

He took his resting pulse with a thick hand on his wrist and an eye on the wall clock: 41.

He stepped on the scales and moved the weight a notch: 229 pounds, all muscle. At 54 years of age, Pieter Godessohn felt better than he had at 20. He was living proof, he thought, of the benefits of the anabolic steroid program he had developed for himself.

He stretched thoroughly and ran through three quick sets on the Nautilus machines. He bench pressed 425 pounds half a dozen times, then climbed on the exercise bike and pedaled five miles at an average speed of 23 miles an hour. He jumped rope for nine minutes, scorched the treadmill for another 20, then moved on to more interesting things.

Standing in front of the heavy bag, he took a deep breath, hunched his great shoulders and crossed his forearms in front of his stomach. Then he stepped forward and thrust out his chest in an explosion of raw power. His sternum struck the bag like a huge piston and sent it careening on its rope.

The attendant who was watching clapped his hands. "Never nobody had a chest blow like that, boss."

"It's taken a long time to perfect, John."

"Well, you got it perfected now. That chest of yours could kill someone."

"I'm very careful in the ring, John. I have been sparring with Mr. Haak for three years. As you know, I've never injured him."

"You're a good man, boss. You're a very good man."

Godessohn toweled off his great bald dome and took his pulse again: 102. He remembered the days when it had soared to 190 at the slightest provocation. Things had changed in the last decade and a half.

He pummeled the low bag with a ferocious barrage of sidekicks, stepped into the ring for five minutes of karate forms and five minutes of shadow boxing and, satisfied his strength and endurance were still on the increase, he went off to the shower.

* * *

In the southern hemisphere, summer was rapidly approaching. By one thirty that afternoon, the mercury in Johannesburg had climbed to 94 degrees. Godessohn broke into a sweat walking from his air-conditioned gym to the air-conditioned pub across the street.

At his table, he used his handkerchief to daub the perspiration from the top of his head. When he cooled down, he motioned to the waiter. "Good day, Willem."

"Good day, Mr. Godessohn. Would you like me to go over our specials with you?"

"I should think not, Willem. Bring me a large plate of bobotie."

"To drink, sir?"

"A pint of lager. And I'd like to look at this morning's *Star*."

"Yes, sir."

Godessohn ate, aware of the stillness around him – a stillness interrupted only by the ruffle and flutter of turning pages.

They recognized him now – his fellow diners, his countrymen, the entire human herd.

They were a contemptible lot, he thought, frightened to chat with one another in his presence. They reminded him of mice huddled at a safe distance watching a lion devour his carrion.

What were they afraid of now? Generosity? Yes, of course. They were afraid of anything bigger than themselves. He wanted to sneer. Instead, he smiled and tipped his massive dome, as if to say, "You may speak now."

The news item he hoped to find was on page three. He read while he chewed:

MOVEMENT TO SAVE VENICE FEARED DEAD
Rome. (AND)

> In the aftermath of Senator Vittorio Passoni's murder, participants in the Italian statesman's $60-billion international effort to rescue Venice have revoked their pledges of monetary support until circumstances surrounding the homicide can be clarified.
>
> It is widely believed here that the death of Senator Passoni, who was instrumental in securing commitments for the enormous amounts of capital needed to save the city from ruin, will make future Italian efforts to solicit money abroad difficult if not impossible.
>
> Mistrust of Italian institutions has always run high in the industrialized world. Senator Passoni's initial success with his International Commission for the Rescue of Venice was seen

by many as a consequence of his ability to overcome this mistrust, to convince potential foreign contributors that the dawn of a "New Italy" was at hand – and that their help in saving the troubled city, unlike previous ventures, would yield tangible results.

Now, with the death of Senator Passoni and a Vesuvian outburst of accusations and counteraccusations threatening to render this chaotic Mediterranean democracy ungovernable, foreign leaders and businessmen have been unable to contain their frustration.

"Perhaps," said William Johnson, Chief Executive Officer of IBM and a previous supporter of the Save Venice Movement, "we should have learned our lesson from Mussolini. We're dealing with opera on a national scale here. If the Italians cannot put their own house in order, funding from the outside is not going to help them. Senator Passoni's death, tragic though it was, prevented my company and others from pouring billions of dollars down a bottomless pit."

Hypotheses abound as to who might have been responsible for Senator Passoni's murder, but . . .

Godessohn had read enough. Work conditions in Venice were normal again. His enterprise need not be delayed.

* * *

Back in his office, Godessohn settled into his deep leather armchair and called on the intercom for his right-hand man, computer genius Vihari Hivali. He unlocked the door with a remote control unit.

Vihari, a 34-year-old South African of Indian descent, came

in wearing a tan summer suit and a maroon turban. He was brisk and friendly, with a permanent smile on his nut-brown face.

"You wish, Mr. Godessohn?"

"I wish, Vihari, to reward you for ten years of loyal and competent service."

"Why, sir, thank you very much for the kind thought, but it is certainly not necessary for you to do more than you have already done. My salary, sir, is more than adequate and I am most content to – "

"Vihari, ten years is a long time to serve a single cause and a single boss. Sit down, please."

The Indian took his place, as he did each afternoon, at his large mahogany desk, one of two in Godessohn's office.

"Well, sir, what type of reward do you have in mind?"

"As you know, Vihari, I have no family. You have become a son to me, more in some respects. When I die, it is my wish that you inherit all that is mine. Everything, Vihari – my banks, my buildings, my mines and, of course, my philanthropic empire."

"But, sir . . . but – "

"Shhh. Allow me to finish. I'm going to require only two things of you in return. I shall ask you to sign an oath of unconditional loyalty to me. For the duration of my life, you must agree to obey any and all of my orders, whatever they may be and however distasteful you may find them.

"Second, I am going to require that you bind yourself legally to continue my philanthropic work and, as your resources grow, to expand its scope."

Godessohn reached in his drawer and pulled out a fat document. "Well, Vihari, what is your decision? Do you wish to become the sole heir of Pieter Godessohn?"

"Why, sir! I am . . . speechless. I . . . I am most honored. Honored, highly flattered, wholly gratified. Yes, sir, of course I wish to become your heir. I tell you, you could not reward me in a more meaningful fashion. But, sir, is this not a bit early to speak of your . . . death? Is something wrong? Are you ill?"

Godessohn laughed and tossed the document on Vihari's desk. "No, I am not ill. I expect to be around for many years. But one never knows, does one? I'm being prudent, Vihari, that's all. I should have done this years ago. It would be a tragedy far greater than my death if the Wittersand fortune were returned to the State.

"Now, Vihari, at the end of the signed and notarized will, you will find in writing the two conditions which I have posed. Please sign above your name if you accept these. Any problems?"

"No sir, absolutely not. I would follow your orders in any case, and I share totally your philanthropic objectives."

Vihari signed the document and passed it back to Godessohn, who deposited it in a small safe. The two men shook hands and embraced. The Indian had tears in his eyes.

"Now, now, Vihari, let us not be moved unduly by sentiment. We have work to do. Get me the map of Chicago up there, please."

"At once, sir."

Vihari adjusted his turban and selected the manual he had written labeled "Cities of North America." He propped the manual on a special reading stand and leaned over his computer keyboard, poised like a pianist beginning a concert. He typed, gently and swiftly, and soon a giant electronic map of the Chicago area appeared on the office's 40-foot screen.

The map, one of Vihari's more recent creations, resembled a work of modern art. The urban area was divided into hundreds of neighborhoods whose boundaries Vihari had drawn according to a complex formula.

The formula, which he called a "philanthrograph," was based on per capita income, unemployment rates, education levels, indices of child abuse, frequency of incarceration, percentage female heads of household, and 76 other variables.

Each neighborhood was numbered and color-coded to reflect its standing on Vihari's scale of urban well-being. The colors ranged from bright, cheery blues near the top of the scale to dingy grays, which Vihari called "the tenement drabs," near the bottom.

Godessohn pushed with his tongue at an aggravating scrap of bobotie that had remained lodged between an incisor and molar. He gestured to a very gray area on the South Side.

"Let's have a look at forty-four, Vihari."

"Statistics or pictures, sir?"

"Names. I know what the place looks like and I can see from your choice of color that the statistics are bleak."

"Right away, sir." Vihari turned a page in his manual with a hand as soft and slender as a girl's. He typed. His beautiful map faded, and with it the boyish gleam in his eyes.

Seconds later, the entire screen turned "tenement drab." A list of organizations and individuals trying to help Neighborhood 44 appeared in white block letters on the gloomy backdrop, accompanied by addresses and telephone numbers.

Godessohn glanced at the row of large round clocks on the wall adjacent to the map. "It's six thirty in the morning over there," he said. "Let's wake a few of these people up, shall we, Vihari? How a person responds to an offer of help at six thirty in the morning tells me a lot about the seriousness he attaches to his cause."

"I couldn't agree more, sir. Whom shall I dial."

"Try the home number of Roosevelt Washington. You see him there near the bottom of the list, the Head of the Coalition to Save the South Side Projects."

* * *

Roosevelt Washington sounded drunk. His girlfriend was high and said she didn't appreciate the prank. Someone else got on the line and told Godessohn that if he was for real, she'd rather see the whole South Side go up in smoke than accept money from a honky racist pretending to be a liberal.

Godessohn looked sadly at Vihari, who had been listening to the conversation on his own extension.

The Indian shook his head in commiseration. Godessohn took a deep breath and instructed his heir apparent to dial another number.

And so it went until five o'clock, the end of the work day, when Godessohn ritually came out of his office to preside over the departure of his employees.

When everyone else had left, Godessohn handed Vihari a slip of paper. "The combination to the safe," he said. "If something happens to me, do not wait for others to find the will."

"I . . . sir, I am so moved. I . . . thank you, sir, thank you . . ."

"That's enough, Vihari. You could go on thanking me for the next quarter century. That would get a bit tiresome, wouldn't it? You're going to inherit three hundred billion dollars. I'm going to die with the knowledge that my life's work is in good hands. In my book, that's an even exchange."

"But, sir – "

"Shhh. I don't want you to mention the matter again – to me or to anyone else – until the day comes for you to take it to the magistrate. And now, Vihari, five o'clock has come and gone. Have a safe drive home."

Godessohn escorted his man to the employees' elevator, shook his hand and gave him a fatherly pat on the shoulder.

As soon as the doors shut on Vihari's smile, Godessohn walked down the long, carpeted aisles of the eighth floor, looking into the glass cubicles in search of a rare employee who might have fallen asleep at his desk.

No one today.

He checked the restrooms, Men's and Women's.

No one.

He stood for a few minutes at the great plate glass window that looked out on the downtown, waiting until he saw Vihari's white Morris Minor emerge from the parking garage and drive off. Then he returned to his office and surrendered himself to his work – his real work.

*   *   *

Godessohn sat down at the second mahogany desk, the one not used by Vihari, and hammered at his own keyboard.

He did not need manuals. He had a photographic memory.

The color-coded map of Chicago vanished from the gigantic screen. Godessohn typed, not softly like Vihari, but with a vicious arrhythmic banging that sent tremors down the stout legs of his desk.

A new, furiously executed set of commands produced another map, this one depicting the Western Hemisphere. The map was a dynamic model which illustrated the interaction among four sets of variables: sea temperatures, air temperatures, wind currents and precipitation rates.

The Philanthropist had needed three years to gather the data to construct his model. Now, while he awaited the conclusion of his Venice enterprise, he enjoyed playing with it.

Colors returned, rich and dazzling. There were colored contour lines snaking around oceans, showing him water temperatures at a glance. Land masses became colored quilts, and the superimposed wind patterns resembled great swirling strokes of a painter's brush.

He chose a month: July.

A day: the fourth.

Colors changed, some just a shade, some drastically. He focused his attention on the north center of the United States, then let his eyes move south from Chicago to the Gulf, west to the Rockies and east to the Appalachians.

The Bread Basket of a nation, of a world. The entire area

glowed a soft hazy green, overlain with gray and ivory streaks, the moisture-bearing winds.

A farming paradise.

His eyes shot to the South Pacific, his strong fingers returned to the keyboard. He found the great localized heat island on the surface of the South Pacific, El Niño.

Manipulating his model, he raised the surface temperature of the ocean in that area, already set to represent a bad El Niño year, by increments of a tenth of a degree. Global warming was on the march.

At an increase of one point four degrees, projecting 20 days into the future, changes started to happen far to the north and east; at one point eight degrees, these changes became radical, devastating.

His mind was charging ahead now, ripping through obstacles like a diamond-tipped augur through sandstone.

It was the mind of Nils Laar, the brilliant South African physicist who went down on NTR Flight 31, London to Rome, when it slammed into the side of Mont Blanc in 1989.

Nils Laar, the best mind ever produced by South Africa, his death a few days after he received the Nobel Prize for Physics even now, some 17 years later, painfully remembered by his country's scientific establishment.

His eyes are back on the central United States. He chooses a date, August 11.

The land, which was soft green from earlier flooding, is now crimson; the gray and ivory wind currents are parched yellow, like the desert sun.

He smiles, types some more, wants to see hard figures.

Stupendous! Average temperatures between the Rockies and the Appalachians soar 27 degrees; average rainfall drops to zero. Other areas of the globe aren't much affected. It's the American bread basket that will take the brunt of his blitz.

He thinks ahead, imagines. By nine o'clock in the morning, August 11, the tar on Roosevelt Washington's roof begins to boil. The demand for electricity generated by millions of overworked air conditioners forces the city's power plants to cut back. The situation rapidly deteriorates. By noon it is 122 degrees in the shade. Roosevelt Washington helps his aging mother and young son into the Chevy, starts the engine and turns on the air conditioning. They enjoy 71 seconds of relief before his engine seizes. Where now? Into Lake Michigan?

Roosevelt, you fool. You should have taken the money I offered you for the Projects. *Taken* it, stolen it, bought yourself a place in cool misty Sweden . . .

But the real disaster, thinks Godessohn, will not be the hundreds of thousands of personal tragedies like Washington's. It will be drought, a drought so savage it will make the dust bowl of the Thirties look like an oasis.

One point eight degrees of temperature elevation in a small patch of the South Pacific – that's all it takes to transform the Bread Basket of the United States into another Sahara!

That's all it takes to wipe out American agricultural production for the next half century!

The Philanthropist sees it all in advance, always has, always will. The Superpower turns to him for help. How he enjoys these little ironies!

He will be gracious, he will try his best. But, as he will explain, there isn't much one man can do to save a dying nation.

This time around, the Americans will beg the lowly Russians for grain.

They won't be able to get enough.

They'll try to steal from the destitute countries of Latin America.

They won't be able to get enough.

They'll turn to Western Europe, to Africa and Asia.

They won't be able to get enough.

Perhaps they will go to war, hurling themselves into campaigns of conquest provoked by hunger and frustration. They'll talk differently about human rights, these talkative Americans. Interesting – it will be very interesting to watch them trying to cope.

Godessohn has had his fill of earthquakes. He has netted 30,000 lives in Armenia, 40,000 in Iran, 100,000 in Pakistan. Small potatoes in backward regions. He is pleased that he has settled on climate for his next round of "entertainments." Climate promises so much more . . .

He built for 20 years like few in the history of the human race had built before him. He made breakthroughs in science that changed the way men thought about their universe. And through it all he was shunned, ignored, excluded.

He wasted a couple of years making the transition to a new identity, that of a big jovial Friend of Mankind. But he is no Friend of Mankind. He has devoted his life to punishing the sorry ingrates of his past.

He works with the complicity of Nature, his only friend. He destroys on a scale matched by nothing short of modern war. Best of all, he is just hitting his stride, just getting started with his apocalyptic campaign of revenge.

And he is learning each day what he suspected as a boy: that it is more fun to destroy than to build.

So let Man go on whimpering about the dangers of modern science; he intends to enjoy them.

Let Man go on theorizing about the demons to which we have given birth; he intends to unleash them.

These are the objectives that Nils Laar, alias Pieter Godessohn, has set down for himself.

He has chosen his second calling wisely. Ever since NTR Flight 31 went down, he has been enjoying the hell out of life.

CHAPTER EIGHT

For the last week, Kiyo and Luigi had been searching the farm country around Venice for the mysterious girl with whom Uncle Vittorio had had his fatal tryst. It was their lack of success that had given Luigi the idea to hold a fake beauty contest.

This rainy November morning, they sat with cameras and tripods sipping cappuccino in a cafe in the small village of Noale. Kiyo looked up from her cup. "Luigi, are you sure you've chosen the right place?"

"Positive," he whispered. "See that man who just came in? He's the baker."

"The baker?"

"Yes. In Italy, the baker knows more about the women of his village than anyone else – except the priest. You'll see."

Luigi bounded to his feet and accosted the surly bald man in the white apron. "Signore, allow me to offer you a coffee. And perhaps you would like a drink as well?"

The baker flicked his wrist as though swatting at a fly and continued to the bar. "Espresso and grappa," he said. "This guy with the Jesus beard gets the bill."

"Yes, that's right, it's on me."

"And for yourself, Signore?" the bartender asked.

"Grappa," said Luigi, who hated grappa. He stopped a safe distance down the counter. Bakers were an unpredictable lot, and this one looked mean.

"So what's this all about?" the baker growled. "What d'you want from me?"

"Signore," Luigi said, "myself and my companion are photo journalists for the new magazine, *Form and Content*. We have been sent into the countryside to find and photograph the most beautiful woman in Italy."

The butcher and the barber, who were playing cards at a nearby table, put down their hands to listen.

"You paying for information?" the barber asked.

"As a matter of fact, we are – if the information leads us to one of the top twenty contenders."

The baker drained his grappa and deposited his glass on the bar with a crack. "How much?"

"Three thousand euros."

"Cash? Under the table?"

"If that is the winner's wish."

"I'll go get my wife."

The butcher let out a booming laugh. "Your wife! Sure, Lorenzo. How're they gonna fit her on one page? Listen, *amico*, don't waste your time with this buffoon. I'll bring you a real woman – my daughter."

"Yeah, right," hooted the barber. "You otta see her. She's fifteen, and already I gotta trim her mustache."

"So who you gonna bring, wise guy?" the butcher said. "Your mother?"

"What's wrong with my mother?" spat the barber, turning red in the face.

"Signori, please," Luigi said. "Let us not quarrel. As long as there have been women, we men have disagreed over their merits. Fortunately, it is not our job to decide who is the most beautiful. That difficult task falls to the magazine editors in Milan. And, Signori, don't forget: your candidate need only be in the top twenty, and you will receive your commission.

"So bring me your beautiful women – your wives, daughters, mothers, cousins, it does not matter who they are. You may enter as many candidates as you wish. And should there be some fair maiden who is not available for our cameras, do not overlook her. Give us her name and address, and we'll place her on your list of candidates."

The three pillars of Noale – the baker, the barber and the butcher – grumbled their assent. Friends again, they marched out into the storm, laughing and slapping each other on the back.

Soon, an army of large cheerful peasant women clumped into the cafe, bumping each other with sow-like rears to get closer to the camera.

Kiyo, hidden beneath a cloth as black and shapeless as her subjects' dresses, snapped their pictures to squeals of delight.

When the noisy herd finally trudged out, leaving the floor awash in mud and manure, Kiyo shook her head. "Well, Luigi, from now on we'd better limit ourselves to the larger towns."

"I suppose you're right."

"Signora, Signore!" The sharp whisper came from the bartender, who hadn't said a word during the entire photography session. "You must not leave Noale yet. There is someone here you should take the trouble to find. We never see her in town, but I've heard about her from the dog trainer who works at Signor Puzzo's villa. He tells me she is the most beautiful woman on earth. Very young, very black hair, satin skin, legs to die for, breasts like . . . "

He glanced at Kiyo and cut his description short.

"Signor Puzzo?" Luigi asked.

"Yes, Signor Giorgio Puzzo. The oil man who lives outside of town. He is very rich. He owns the refinery in Malcontenta. You've heard of him, no?"

"I've heard of him," Kiyo said.

"This girl must be his daughter. Go have a look at her. And don't forget my reward."

* * *

Dante drove north at 190 miles an hour, splitting the darkness with 300 watt projector headlights.

His confidence in his Franco-charged Lamborghini had never been higher. The custom-built German starter was in place – no chance he would be stranded again – and the finish, so badly mauled by Graziella Calvino, had been restored to its original luster.

He was approaching the outskirts of Fiesole, home of his bell tower, when he received Luigi's call on his car telephone.

"You held a *what*?" he said, trying to hide his irritation.

"A beauty contest, Signore. In the village of Noale, near Venice. I know it sounds silly, but before you waste your energy berating me, I should tell you that it worked. Signore, we have done it! We have found your uncle's killer!"

Dante downshifted into fifth, and his mighty engine let out a howl.

"I'm sorry, Luigi, but there must be some mistake. It is unthinkable that this girl would appear in a public contest so soon after Vittorio's death. After all, there *were* people who saw the two of them together."

"You haven't let me finish, Signore. She did not appear in person at our beauty contest. I knew she wouldn't show up herself, so I allowed the village men to include all the women they thought were beautiful on their list of candidates – even those unable to attend to photographing session. It was the bartender who supplied us with the winning entry. She lives on the estate of a man named Giorgio Puzzo, an entrepreneur who owns a refinery in Malcontenta. No one ever sees her in town, but a dog trainer works with her at the estate. He told the bartender about her."

"Luigi, I agree this sounds worth checking out, but for now you have a lead, nothing more. Figure out a way to get a look at her."

"But, Signore! I have spent the entire day in the clouds, hovering in the helicopter well out of sound range, my eye glued to the infrared scope. She came out at ten o'clock this evening with five enormous dogs. It's her, Signore! The telescopic lens does not lie."

"Are you positive?"

"She is not to be confused with any other living female."

Dante hit the gas and blasted by his exit. "Then, Luigi, I

congratulate you on a fine job."

"Thank you, Signore. What's next?"

"I'll join you at once. I want you and Kiyo to meet me at Grandfather Giuseppe's farmhouse. Remember where it is?"

"Of course, Signore. We went on a mushroom hunt there last fall. But will Giuseppe remember us? He must be ninety years old."

"Ninety-three. He's visiting a girlfriend in Rio. I don't expect him back before Christmas. Break in – if he remembered to lock the door."

"*D'accordo*, Signore."

"And, Luigi, I know you're tired but it would be very helpful if you could investigate Puzzo's security system while I'm on the road. If possible, I want to enter the estate grounds before dawn."

"Consider it done, Signore."

* * *

Dante arrived at Grandfather Giuseppe's farmhouse just after four o'clock in the morning. Kiyo was waiting for him, tending a fire in the old stone hearth. She greeted him warmly and gestured to an immense wormwood table.

"Antipasti, Dante. I know you function better on a full stomach."

"Most thoughtful." He poured himself a glass of the local red wine – not Chianti but it would do in a pinch – and sampled Kiyo's imaginative Italo-Japanese spread of *crostini* and cheeses. "Where's Luigi?"

"Still at the estate wall searching for a place where you can get in. He's radioed back several times. He'll be along shortly. He has bad news. It seems the entire wall is wired with shock detectors."

"Hmmm. And Puzzo? What do we know about him?"

"He was born in Naples in 1952. He spent a decade in Yemen as a young man, then worked his way up the corporate ladder with AGIP. Five years ago, he left his firm and acquired the refinery he now owns and operates in Malcontenta. I uncovered no evidence of criminal ties. However, there was something that struck me as odd. He was in serious financial trouble eighteen months ago, but last December he paid off a billion-dollar note. He now owns the refinery outright."

"Interesting. What about the girl? Who is she?"

"According to the public record, Puzzo was never married and has no children. I don't know who she is."

"I'll ask her in the morning."

"Dante, I think you should wait until we're better prepared. We don't have the slightest idea what we're up against."

"Neither do they."

* * *

"Good evening, Signore," said Luigi, stomping into the room in a pair of Grandfather Giuseppe's muddy hunting boots. "Kiyo's mentioned the sensors in the wall?"

"She has."

"Well, that's not the only problem. Those dogs I told you about run loose at night. They didn't like me on the *outside* of the wall."

"Dogs will not be a problem, Luigi." Dante took a slender device that looked like a TV channel changer from his breast pocket. "Know what this is?"

"A sonic oscillator?" Kiyo said.

"Correct. I had it manufactured by the German branch of CRC to activate my new starter – in the likely event that the Italian ignition switch fails. The oscillator emits high-frequency sound waves inaudible to the human ear. But to our canine listeners, this thing will sound like a hyberbolic horn. Are there trees on both sides of the wall, Luigi?"

"Yes, Signore. Big oaks."

"Good. We'll make a rope bridge over the top."

"But, Signore, they've taken measures against a squirrel-style entry. The trees have been trimmed back. Their branches are at least thirty feet apart."

"Do you recall, Luigi, the instrument my grandfather uses for plucking hard-to-reach mushrooms?"

"You mean that retractable titanium rod?"

"Precisely. It extends up to forty feet and has pincers on the end. If we can find it, the rest will be easy."

* * *

An hour later, Dante entered the estate on a high wire of nylon mountaineering rope. He rappelled silently down the tree trunk on Puzzo's side of the wall and started across the soggy, leaf-strewn earth toward the villa.

Yesterday's storm had blown out to sea. Dawn broke steel gray to the east. The light of the new day absorbed the stars and drained the color from the crescent moon, leaving it as lifeless as an X-ray.

Dante had Kiyo's pistol with him. The gun fired hard rubber bullets with great accuracy. He could immobilize an assailant without killing him, important when one was trying to unravel a complicated crime. He had plenty of rope; he could tie up anyone he needed to restrain. And Luigi was on standby alert in his helicopter, ready to swoop down if Dante needed help.

The dawn closed in around him, its damp silence magnified by the sound of his footsteps. He tried to make less noise, but the loamy earth sucked in his boots and protested with a slurp each time he lifted them.

He abandoned his beeline approach and moved to higher ground, keeping to the rises in the gently undulating terrain.

Better. The blanket of leaves remained thick and wet, but the earth relaxed its grip on his feet. He picked up his pace. Through a gap in the trees, he could see Puzzo's villa.

Without warning, a vine hidden beneath the leaves snared

him around the ankles. He went down on all fours, cursing furiously under his breath. When he looked up, five wolfhounds were coming at him, their bared teeth glinting with dawn-lit saliva.

He was ready. He reached calmly into his breast pocket for the oscillator and pressed the button.

The dogs skidded to a stop, cowered and turned to run.

In Grandfather Giuseppe's barn, the Lamborghini awoke with a roar.

Dante drew his pistol and fired five rubber bullets before the dogs could flee, five perfect hits. Working quickly he bound the stunned beasts' snouts and legs with rope. Then he continued on toward his destination, propelled by a fresh surge of adrenalin. When he was 50 yards from the villa, he crouched in a dense hedge.

The place had new money written all over it. White stucco walls, an immaculate red tile roof, wrought-iron balconies that shone like polished ebony.

He hadn't gotten comfortable yet when the garage door went up. A black Mercedes limousine with blackened windows pulled into the drive and stopped. The uniformed driver got out, stretched and waited.

Minutes later, the front door of the villa opened. Dante watched through his binoculars as a gaunt middle-aged man stepped into the cool morning. The man wore a business suit and held a steaming mug. His breath rose in short, nervous puffs.

Puzzo, no doubt.

The man called for the dogs. His alert dark eyes combed the grounds. A look of disgust spread over his face.

"Gina," he shouted, turning toward the villa. "Gina, the damned dogs aren't back yet. Fire the trainer when he shows up."

He slammed the villa door and got into the limousine, which departed at once.

* * *

It was hate at first sight, but Dante understood his uncle's fatal folly when the girl Puzzo had called Gina came outside.

She was beautiful. Her cheekbones were high and prominent, and her glossy, shoulder-length hair was so black it looked nearly blue.

He refocused the binoculars and tried to find fault with her appearance.

Her nose was straight and handsome, with those slightly flared nostrils all perfect female noses have.

Her lips were full, her teeth – the pitfall of many farm girls – were white and straight.

Her eyes, he thought, would be her undoing. The eyes of this monstrous criminal would be a window to a bitter and hardened soul.

She looked toward him, calling her dogs, and he saw that they were black and lovely, and bore no hint of malice. There was even innocence in them, and the mist of some profound sadness.

Her face had passed his critical review, but what about her body? He couldn't see much because of her clothes: leather boots, gray wool pants, a black wool jacket with an upturned collar. In fact, he couldn't see anything. A good thing, he decided.

She took a few steps toward the edge of the woods, calling the name "Bruno" in a sweet lilting voice. He crouched lower and held his breath. She was silent for a moment. He could hear the great barren oaks rustling in the breeze and fog horns moaning on the Lagoon.

She stood still, as if something had suddenly made her wary. She kicked the gravel with her toes. When she looked down, her hair spilled forward. She brushed it back and called "Bruno" again.

Amid the noises of the morning, Dante heard a distant whining. One of the muzzled wolfhounds was trying to answer her!

He saw a flash of concern on her face. She listened for a few more seconds, then ran into the woods. He gave chase, using tree trunks for cover.

When she reached the writhing dogs, she covered her mouth with a hand. "Oh, poor dears, poor dears."

He spun from behind a tree and grabbed her arm.

"Don't worry about your dogs," he said coolly. "They'll be all right as soon as they are untied." He gave a yank. "Relax, dammit. I'm not going to harm you."

Her beautiful black eyes darted from Dante to the dogs and back to Dante. She was startled, frightened, confused. He held her more tightly, fearing she would try to run away.

"Let me go!" she cried.

He did.

She knelt and petted the largest dog. "Bruno, poor Bruno." She tried to untie the knot in the rope, but it was pulled too tightly.

"How could you do this?" she said, twisting her torso to look at him. "How could you be so cruel?"

He moved behind her and put his hands on her shoulders.

"Signorina, you can see that your dogs are not hurt. We had a minor disagreement over my right to visit you, nothing more. I am a dog lover, I was careful not to injure them. When you lured my uncle to your hotel room in Orte, I wish you had shown him the same consideration."

"What are you talking about?" She quickly averted her eyes.

"What am I talking about? Vittorio Passoni, your victim, as you well know. My name is Dante Passoni. Don't lie to me, Gina. I'm not in a benevolent mood." He removed her hand from Bruno's long, pointed snout.

She was staring at him now, the mist of profound sadness still in her eyes. "But . . . how did you know my name?"

"That's not important. This is." He took his uncle's fine gold medallion of Venice from his pocket and dangled it in front of her. She winced.

"Stand up, now. You are going to tell me *exactly* what happened after the gala."

"I . . . what gala?"

"Don't play games. You'll regret it." He jerked her roughly to her feet.

"I . . . I . . . Really, Signor Passoni, I have no idea what you're talking about."

He returned the medallion to his pocket. "You met Vittorio Passoni on top of Monte Mario. You took him to his death bed in Orte. There are witnesses. Either you tell me what happened or we're going to the police right now."

She shivered and turned away. He took her chin in his hand and twisted her head until she could not avoid his eyes. "What happened?"

She was silent for a long time, lips quivering. Finally she broke down. "I did not kill him," she sobbed. "I swear I did not kill him. They told me I was bringing him to Orte so they could talk to him about refinery business. You must believe me."

"I'll believe you if you help me find his murderers."

"But . . ."

She seemed in a daze. He felt like slapping her. "Wake up! You have a decision to make. Make it. Are you going to help me, or are you going to jail?"

"I . . . I . . . cannot help you. It's not possible. I can't, Signor Passoni."

"Dante, please. Why not?"

"Because they'll kill me just as they killed your uncle."

"You're wrong."

"You don't know them."

"They won't kill you because I am going to protect you. If you help me, you will not be in danger. When it's time for you to flee, I'll make sure you have a way out of here. I'll arrange accommodations on the outside. You'll have a safe place to stay until I bring these criminals to justice."

"But . . . how can I help?"

"By telling me what happened the night of the gala. By telling me who 'they' are – and what they are doing in the refinery. You must trust me, Gina. If you don't want to spend the rest of your life locked up on the Island of Sighs, your only hope is to cooperate with me. What can I do to make you trust me?"

"I . . . I don't know . . . the dogs . . . release the dogs."

"Release them?"

"Yes."

"All right. But if they turn on me, I won't be as gentle as I was the last time."

"They won't harm you. Not if they think you're a friend."

"Am I?"

"Yes," she whispered. "Yes."

"Then free them." He handed her his knife and crouched beside her while she cut the dogs loose. He petted the great killer beasts as they came out of their ropes, apologizing to them for his excesses.

One by one, the dogs clambered shakily to their feet. When Gina stood, they formed a well-behaved circle around her, waiting turns for affection. After a good rub from his mistress, Bruno staggered over to Dante and sniffed his hand.

Gina handed him back his knife. "I can tell you about the gala," she said. "I can tell you who 'they' are. I know who strangled your uncle and who hired him to do it. But I don't know what's going on inside the refinery. Giorgio used to make me clean the central control bunker twice a week. Now, since the engineers have come from Pakistan, I'm not allowed near it."

She started to sit down on a log, but Dante caught her by the arm. "We have a lot to talk about, Gina. I think we'd best go inside. I haven't had my morning coffee yet, and I want to take a look at Puzzo's affairs."

"We should stay out here. It's safer. Besides, you won't find any records in the villa. Giorgio keeps everything in the refinery."

"Then you and I are going to put our heads together and figure out how to smuggle me into the refinery."

"No! That's impossible! You'll die! Please, no!"

"Calm down. You're upsetting the dogs."

"Listen to me! There are guards everywhere. They have machine guns and Tasers and antiaircraft rockets. There are land mines and electric fences and new security systems."

"Come along now, Gina. You can tell me more about them over breakfast."

CHAPTER NINE

When the Philanthropist was not dispensing crumbs of his great wealth he could be found up north, tending his far-flung empire of gold and diamond mines. His work was mostly administrative: he was, after all, C.E.O. and sole owner of Godessohn Resource Management, Ltd., one of the world's 50 largest corporations.

But he was no ordinary chairman of the board. On cooler days, he often labored behind the controls of a bright orange 1200 horse bulldozer, his shirt sleeves rolled up past his elbows and his bald dome tilted as if he were listening to a whispered word.

Nor did he shy away from the lowliest jobs. Once a month he joined his 20,000 Bantu miners underground, where he attacked the stubborn rock walls with a diamond-tipped air hammer.

The Bantu miners liked Godessohn but thought he was crazy. Why, they wondered, would anyone worth billions bust his ass in a mine?

Which was exactly what one of them asked him today at lunch.

Godessohn looked up from his bobotie sandwich. "You really want to know why, do you?" He nodded at the dozen dirty miners with whom he had sat down to eat. "Very well, then, I'll tell you. I believe a boss who never puts himself in the place of his workers cannot understand their hardships, needs and gripes. A boss who doesn't understand his workers cannot run an efficient enterprise.

"I'm in business to make money, men, lots of it. I also want to provide a better life for *you*. Never mind what the leftists say. There is no conflict. I prosper, you prosper."

He washed down the last of his sandwich with a swallow of beer.

"Take a moment to look at the facts. I have extended to all of my employees the six-hour day – at triple the average South African worker's wage; I have granted you free medical and free day care, subsidized housing, a generous pension plan, job security and ten weeks paid vacation a year.

"And consider this: even though unions are prohibited at Godessohn Resource Management, I have six hundred thousand active job applications in my files – during a national labor shortage."

A chortle of gratitude rose from the throats of the Bantu miners. The whistle blew, ending lunch. Wiry black men scrambled to their feet, put away their pails and shook his hand. Pulleys whirred on well-greased hubs. Dormant conveyor belts stretched and shuddered and started to crawl. Ore carts resumed their clangorous trek down narrow rails, and jack hammers awoke in loud brittle bursts.

Godessohn excused himself. Sorry he wouldn't be able to finish the shift, but urgent duties called him to the central administration building 200 miles away.

Above ground, Vihari Hivali was waiting in a GRM jeep. The two men drove to the company airstrip and flew in the corporate jet to the city of Graskop, where the firm's mining division was headquartered.

* * *

Vihari that afternoon sat at his desk, waiting for Godessohn to finish his workout and come upstairs from his private gym. He surveyed the hordes of technicians and managers working in the cubicles that lined the plate-glass walls. Which of these miserable fellows, he wondered, had been scheming to take away his job?

There had been someone; this he knew from the Philanthropist himself. Humorous, actually. Who among these donkeys thought he had the brains to translate Godessohn's wishes into the precise language of the computer? Who among them knew that Vihari was the boss's sole heir and beloved surrogate son?

Godessohn stepped out of his office, smelling of talc and men's cologne. Beads of sweat still glistened on his forehead.

"Sorry I'm late, Vihari. My sparring partner insisted on going another three rounds. I shouldn't have let him. Joachim quite exhausted himself. Let's greet the employees. We haven't been to the Graskop branch for nearly a month."

"Good idea, sir."

Vihari could not help but be impressed by his boss's energy. A morning in the mines, an hour in the jet, an hour in the gym, and he seemed as fresh as he had at breakfast.

Godessohn, with Vihari close behind, moved from cubicle to cubicle, warmly shaking hands. He addressed his employees by name and inquired about the tiniest details of their personal lives – about a child's recovery from the flu, or the outcome of a dispute over a traffic ticket, or a drainage problem slowing the construction of a new home.

For such a folksy, unscientific man, thought Vihari, Godessohn had an incredible memory, a veritable computer. A trifle strange, actually. The memory didn't seem to fit with the rest of Godessohn's brain – a brain Vihari found wise and practical but weak on the technical side.

Well, this Philanthropist was one of a kind. No use dwelling on his idiosyncrasies. The important thing was that he had become Vihari's ticket into the South African social and financial elite. Not that Vihari was ambitious. Really, he wasn't – or hadn't been until now.

* * *

Godessohn's Graskop office was identical to his office in Johannesburg – a windowless cube located smack in the center of a modern skyscraper's eighth floor.

Inside the office were several deep leather armchairs, two mahogany desks with computer terminals, and a small bar. One of the windowless walls was dominated by the stainless steel double doors of the elevator that ran to the basement gym. Another wall belonged to the great electronic screen. The remaining two walls were adorned with photographs of distinguished South Africans.

Upon entering and locking the door behind him, Godessohn deviated from his normal routine. Instead of taking a seat in his armchair, he went directly to the second mahogany desk and switched on the computer.

Vihari had always believed the second desk and second computer were strictly for show. But today Godessohn began hammering away at the keyboard as if he knew what he was doing.

"Have a seat, Vihari," he said, glancing up from his typing. "No, no, not at your desk, over there where you are closer to the screen."

Perplexed, Vihari let himself down in one of the armchairs. "What are you up to, sir? I didn't realize you could type."

"There are a lot of things you do not realize, Vihari. Watch the screen."

An electronic map faded in. Simultaneously, the office lights dimmed. Vihari watched a stark black outline of Europe and Northern Africa come into focus.

More hammering at the keyboard, and the oceans sprouted colored contour lines.

"Depth," Godessohn said. "These lines represent depth."

"But, sir, excuse me sir, what is this? I did not make you a map of the oceans. Is that competitor of mine already doing my work?"

"Don't be ridiculous, Vihari. You don't think I'd need help with something this trivial, do you?"

"Trivial? But, sir – "

"Shhh."

Godessohn's typing grew more violent, shaking the legs of the heavy desk and sending ripples across the carpeting. A snaky red line crept out of Le Havre, turned west in the Channel, crossed a dark blue contour line and entered the deep water of the Atlantic.

The line looped around the Cape of Brittany, followed the

coasts of France and Spain to the south and west, turned abruptly east and slithered through the Straits of Gibraltar.

It traversed the shallow Mediterranean, glided between Sicily and North Africa, rounded the heel of the Italian boot and moved up the Adriatic coast.

Near Venice, it turned west, entered the Lagoon through the deep Chioggio Inlet and stopped.

Godessohn slapped the desk with his palm. "Quite a journey, eh?"

"Sir, in all honesty, I'm afraid I don't understand. What is this? A new computer game I do not know about?"

Silence.

Ah, yes, that would be it, Vihari thought. A new computer game! In his spare time, Godessohn had learned how to type and mastered some obscure computer game.

Come to think of it, that's what he must have been doing in the evening when he stayed on after work!

Now, in his warm and touching way, Godessohn wanted to show off his accomplishment.

Godessohn's voice, when he finally spoke, did not sound warm and touching.

"That's right, Vihari, this is a new computer game. The red line represents the course covered last week by a steel fish with a load capacity of two tons, an ability to dive seven miles, a sonar guidance system that allows it to hug the ocean floor like a Cruise missile and a memory that steers it to within a meter of its preprogrammed target – after a nuclear-powered swim of fifteen thousand miles."

Don't offend him, thought Vihari. A clumsy word could cost you your inheritance. He straightened his turban and cleared his throat.

"Yes, yes . . . I see. Well, sir, I must say, it sounds like quite a good game, demanding much high technology. Perhaps I'm being a bit dense, sir, but let me make sure I've properly grasped the game's objective. Do you try to maneuver the fish somewhere specific?"

Godessohn did not answer.

More hammering at the keyboard.

The map faded into another, this one covering the Near East and India as well as Europe. The names and locations of eleven nuclear power plants appeared in mauve. Saffron lines of varying thickness crept out from these power plants, crept warily over broad plains, crossed rivers and mountain ranges, passed through large coastal cities and embarked on familiar marine transport routes. Finally, the lines converged on an offshore tanker port in the Persian Gulf.

Still more hammering, which rattled the inside of Vihari's head like his three-year-old son spilling marbles on their tile floor.

Now, little gold lines, dozens of them, departed the tanker port and moved like spring sap through leaf veins, moved along many different paths, converging on the same Chioggia Inlet of the Venice Lagoon through which the steel fish had swum.

The single remaining gold line, thicker than the others, crawled across a narrow finger of land outside the village of Malcontenta and stopped.

"Weapons grade plutonium," Godessohn said. "Enough for the construction of a fifty-eight megaton warhead. The warhead has been built, Vihari. In Malcontenta, in a refinery I rescued from corporate bankruptcy."

"But, sir . . . do you not think the game at this point is somewhat unrealistic? Where would one find a technical staff capable of building such a device in a refinery?"

"The staff was supplied by the Pakistani engineering firm, Girta, and three Russian nuclear scientists I bought for a song after the breakup of the Soviet Union. I trust you Indians have come to appreciate the good work of these Pakistani technical people."

Godessohn, thought Vihari, was beginning to sound a little bit crazy, so carried away with his game one could nearly take him for a lunatic.

Vihari knew from personal experience how obsessed an otherwise sane person could become with computer games. He'd had his own bout with the Sickness. One night he came out of the den so glassy eyed his own son was afraid of him! That's when his wife, Tamina, had convinced him to look reality in the face.

He was playing less now – and feeling a lot better. He must help his boss, a severely addicted novice, find *his* way back to reality.

He said, "Yes indeed, sir, it is of course true that the Pakistanis produce a few decent engineers. They would be capable of assisting the ex-Soviet experts. More importantly, I believe I now understand the objective of your game."

"Good, Vihari. Why don't you describe it to me? I shall be interested in observing how your mind works."

"Yes . . . yes, I shall. Some terrorists, you see, are trying to do something very evil. You, the Friend of Mankind, must stop them and teach them a lesson. You must give them what I shall call a 'philanthrobash.'"

Vihari laughed nervously. For some reason his boss did not find his terminology amusing. No smile, no comment – nothing but bone-chilling silence.

"Sir," stuttered Vihari, desperate to demonstrate his good will, "I have an idea. I could stand in for the bad guys whenever you wish to refine your impressive new computer skills."

"I don't think so, Vihari. The game does not accommodate two players. A single player, working alone, tries to deliver the bomb where *he* wants it. Then he detonates the bomb and the game is over."

Godessohn typed some more.

The map faded, and the screen became a live underwater

television picture of something that looked like the mouth of a sewer pipe.

"Sorry the water's so dirty, Vihari. Very soon you and I are going to devote a little thought and money to the pollution problem plaguing Venice. Fortunately, my fish doesn't mind the filth. It will swim wherever I send it – even through that muck. Pay attention. When my cargo is ready for transport, the fish will enter the refinery through the pipe you see. Then it will swim back out through the Lagoon and into the Adriatic.

"It will swim fast for a while, sixty knots, until it's beyond the Straits of Gibraltar. Once in the Atlantic, it will dive too deep to be detected by any existing anti-submarine equipment. It will slowly feel its way along the ocean floor to its preprogrammed destination."

Poor Godessohn! thought Vihari. He really was going mad. Right here in his sealed bunker of an office. Maybe it wasn't the temporary insanity of a computer-game addict. Maybe it was the real thing!

Vihari felt he had better do something quickly. But what? Nurse him back to sanity with words?

Yes, yes, that was his only option. The boss had been under stress lately, too much stress. He'd cracked. I must coax him out of his delusions right away. If I do that, perhaps there will be no lasting damage. Flatter him without being obsequious; interest him in my point of view.

"Yes, yes, I understand," Vihari stammered. "Intriguing, very intriguing. It's just that I still don't quite grasp the game's objective. My fault, no doubt. My thick headedness is most certainly to blame. But, sir, let me try to explain myself. With the computer games I play, there are difficulties and obstacles to overcome. In fact, overcoming these obstacles *is* the point of the game. But here, all you seem to do is say that certain lines represent certain things and then . . . and then, well then that's it."

Vihari felt a wave of despair. It was no use. He shifted and fidgeted. What should he do now? He couldn't rush out and get help. The office door was always locked, and Godessohn had the remote control opener.

At last the sick man spoke. "Perhaps, Vihari, given your intellectual limitations, I should have mentioned that there *were* obstacles at the beginning of the game. Perhaps I should also have mentioned that I've already *won* this game. Perhaps that is what confused you, Vihari – and I must say, you do look confused."

"My fault for not seeing this, sir. Yes, of course, clearly you have already won the game. Quite clearly, you have won."

"Be quiet. Don't blather. As I said, there was a game and there were obstacles."

"Obstacles. Yes, yes, obstacles. That's what I was asking you before, sir. What . . . what were these obstacles?"

Godessohn's tone grew icier. "Why don't you tell me, Vihari? Let's assume it is *you* who wishes to build a nuclear-powered fish with a two ton payload that will swim wherever you send it. Let's assume it is *you* who wishes to construct a thermonuclear device capable of warming by one point eight degrees Celsius a square of the South Pacific a hundred miles on a side. And let's assume that you must do all of this without the knowledge of a single person other than yourself.

"Speak up, Vihari. This will tell me whether your 180 I.Q. and your Harvard doctorate equip you to face the challenges that interest me. Address your first obstacle. How do you begin?"

Remain rational, thought Vihari, show him there are things to grab on to, hard facts and logical conclusions; show him the difference between reality and the shifting sands of delusion. Show him these things, or he will turn on you and your inheritance will be gone forever.

"With all due respect, sir, my opinion is that the construction of such a fish could not be accomplished by one man without the knowledge of others. Hence there is no first step. Science by definition is teamwork, sir. A project of this complexity and magnitude would require the close cooperation of many thousands of people."

"Well, my dear Vihari, your opinion must be wrong. The project has already been completed. By one man. By me. Others do not know about it – or did not know until I informed you."

Godessohn stood.

Vihari had forgotten how big he was, 230 pounds of muscle with a head like a wrecking ball and the neck of a rhinoceros. He straightened the lapels of his ill-fitting jacket and fixed Vihari with a withering stare.

Those eyes! They were like his memory. They didn't fit the rest of the man. They should have belonged to someone else.

Worse, Vihari could feel them feasting on his confusion, delighting in it.

He was beginning to get scared. He fought to think clearly. This huge man on whom his future depended was turning into someone else right in front of him. What was Vihari supposed to do? He needed to help Godessohn; he also needed to help himself.

He felt paralyzed, he could not breathe. Godessohn was sucking up all the oxygen in the room and replacing it with a vile mixture of carbon dioxide and disease. He looked at his hands. His nut-brown skin had turned sickly green, and his fingers trembled like reeds in a gale.

Could he be in real danger? No, no, certainly not. This man loved him enough to will him billions of dollars, loved him like a son.

Then what *was* going on? Was it *Vihari*'s mind playing the tricks? Was he having some sort of a waking nightmare or anxiety attack? Or coming down with a fever? His little boy had had a fever earlier in the week . . .

He watched, wide-eyed, as Godessohn came toward him.

When the huge man veered to his right and sat softly in his armchair, Vihari experienced a wave of relief.

Godessohn shifted his weight without taking his eyes off his assistant. "Why is it, Vihari, that men born with superb brains, men such as yourself, turn out to be such timid souls? If you can answer that one question, I will be eternally grateful, for you will have explained to me why fools run the world.

"You disgust me, Vihari, you and the rest of your timorous colleagues. You men of science have forgotten how to be men. You have forgotten how to have fun. You have forgotten how to *destroy*. You've let yourselves become the sycophants and court jesters of those who should be serving your drinks. I'm happy to say that I haven't allowed myself to sink to your pathetic level.

"Now, back to my game. Step One, obviously, was to create a communications system that would allow me to work incognito with whomever I chose anywhere in the world. What did you think I was doing on my bulldozer, Vihari, when I dug five hundred and fourteen miles of trenches through the middle of Bantu country?"

Just answer, don't think. Answer and pray that something snaps, that Godessohn turns back into himself . . .

"I, well, sir, I believed exactly what you told the world. I believed you wished to bury the power cables to your mines so that . . . the environment would remain unspoiled."

Godessohn erupted in a mighty laugh. "Wrong again, Vihari. There's a transmitter five hundred fourteen miles long buried with those power lines. It emits ultra-low-frequency electrical waves. They travel through the earth and water, and enter any nation's power grid undetected. They hum like silent ghosts through phone lines, unlock military computers and feed me their secrets. They send my orders, transfer others' funds, GET THINGS DONE.

"So that, Vihari, was Step One, difficult but obvious. It took me nine years to make my communications system operational. The rest has been trivial.

"Take the fish, for instance. I needed to know only a few details to have it built. Such as how the French Department of Defense goes about ordering its top-secret prototypes. Such as which shipyards and which aerospace industries were capable of constructing it. Such as how payment for secret prototype orders is made. Trivial, Vihari. I ordered my fish and let the French pay for it.

"Plutonium from the power plants came to me in a similar fashion. I employ a Sheik who knows me only as a telephone presence, an *untraceable* telephone presence, you will understand. A trace on our conversations would lead to the outer extremities of his nation's power grid – and then to nowhere.

"This Sheik has been instrumental in helping with certain logistical aspects of my game, such as the transport of plutonium and the procurement of the spot where I actually built the bomb.

"As you little men the world over like to repeat ad nauseam, we need better communication. I couldn't agree more.

"Toward the end of the next severe El Niño, Vihari, thanks to all of this *communication*, the average high temperatures over the Central United States will rise by twenty-seven degrees, turning the world's greatest bread basket into the world's greatest desert."

"But you, sir, you . . . you are not a scientist. You should not be thinking about such awful things. You cannot have done this. If you were a great scientist – "

"And who, Vihari, do you believe I am?"

"What?"

"Who am I?"

He has forgotten who he is! thought Vihari. Reinforce his sense of self. Bring him back to reality! "Why, Mr. Godessohn, sir – you are the most honorable Pieter Godessohn."

"I am not Pieter Godessohn. Pieter Godessohn wasted his life with a nomadic tribe in Zimbabwe. You will remember C.P.

Wittersand, the source of my fortune. I fraudulently inherited his estate."

Vihari was about to say something when a long-buried memory flashed through his awareness. It was a memory of his father, a quiet, learned South African correspondent for the *New Delhi Times*, who had covered the Wittersand inheritance trial for his newspaper.

The Hivali family had been at the dinner table when news of the court's decision came over the radio. Vihari saw it all as if it were yesterday, saw the gentle man with the frizzy white hair leap to his feet and bang the table so hard he knocked over his water glass.

"Bullshit" roared old Hivali, "bloody damned bullshit. That man is an impostor, and I am going to prove it if it takes me the rest of my life."

Hivali Senior hadn't had a chance to prove anything. His life had ended the next day with a massive stroke.

Could his father possibly have been right? Could the man who this very second was breathing up all of Vihari's air be someone else? He forced his gaze up from his hands and looked into his boss's face.

Those eyes! Where had he seen them before?

Godessohn must have read his mind. He smiled pleasantly and pointed to a large photograph on the wall. "Third from your left," he said.

Vihari looked at the photograph. The eyes, there they were! But to whom did the face in the picture belong? It was a unique face, one he had seen many times before. Prominent cheekbones, thin taut lips, a beak like an eagle's, long blond hair parted in the center. And the eyes, Godessohn's eyes, boring into him like an augur.

Textbooks. . . physics . . .

And then he remembered. Physics, 1989, the Nobel Prize!

The mind, the memory! Holy Jesus Christ, it could not be.

Could not be . . . and yet, if it was, how neatly certain pieces of today's puzzle fit together.

"Say my name," boomed Godessohn. "NOW! Who am I?"

"I . . . I don't – "

"SAY IT!"

"Laar?" sputtered Vihari. "Nils Laar?"

"Good, Vihari. Tell me, are you frightened of me?"

"No, no, I . . . shocked, sir, well, a little shocked, yes, as you can – "

"Because if you are not frightened, you are an even greater fool than I believed. I have killed my own sons. If I decided to kill yours, what earthly reason would deter me? I have slaughtered men and women for whom I had no particular dislike – scorn but not dislike. Is your wife safe from me? I should think not. And Vihari, what about *you*? I have given you a place all your own, a lofty, forbidding and *dangerous* place, a place very near the sun. You and you alone know my secret."

Godessohn's voice sounded like distant thunder. Vihari was becoming disoriented. His ears rang, his vision blurred, he scarcely knew where he was. "But . . . but . . sir, I did not ask to know. It is not my fault that I know. Why did . . . you tell me?"

"Because I *wanted* you to know, Vihari. You are someone who can appreciate the work and intelligence behind my achievements. I have labored for seventeen years without recognition. I feel much better now. But what am I to do with *you*? I can't let you out of here with your knowledge. You're going to have to commit suicide."

"Sir, really. That's hardly necessary. I – "

"Shhh." Godessohn leaned close and patted him on the back. "Chin up, now, Vihari. It won't be nearly as bad as you think. Everyone has to die sooner or later. You'll get through it with less pain than most. Just walk to the elevator. When the doors open, step inside. The elevator will not be there. The eight stories of free fall won't take long. I'll provide your wife and son with a generous stipend."

Vihari felt a chill run down his spine. The smartest man in the world seemed to want him dead. How was he to save himself?

Beg for mercy, that's what he must do.

"Sir, please, you must believe me. Our relationship does not have to end with my death. I will never betray you. Never! Why can't we go on as before? I will be your friend and your assistant. I will listen to your accounts of fabulous secret triumphs. I will help you with new and even grander exploits. I will – "

"That's enough, Vihari. A man as desperate as you are to avoid death can always be made to talk. Should you be taken into custody and tortured, you could not remain silent."

"Yes, yes! Just that. I could! I would never talk. I promise you, sir. I would never ever betray you!"

"And it does not disturb you, after working ten years for the good of humanity, that if you stayed on with me, you would be helping to stage natural disasters that would kill millions?"

Vihari felt a warm tug of hope. He was being given a chance! "Mr. Godessohn, sir . . . I took an oath of allegiance to you. You remember? It was the day you named me sole beneficiary of your will. I was serious when I took that oath. Oh, yes, so very serious I put my loyalty to you above all else. Whatever you command, I shall do with single-minded devotion."

"I'm glad to hear that, Vihari. It makes matters much more simple. I command you to commit suicide. We'll see whether your single-minded devotion is to me – or to yourself."

Vihari's head began to spin. Nausea filled his gut. He heard himself gag. He couldn't throw up here, not in Godessohn's office. "Sir . . . that makes no sense! If I die, I will be of no use to you."

"Wrong, Vihari. You will be of great use. You are forgetting the entertainment value your suicide will afford me. Life for an intelligent man is a struggle against boredom. Your death will divert me for a few seconds."

Vihari tried to speak, but his vocal chords had turned to mush. He watched in horror as Godessohn took a micro-syringe out of his desk.

"Cyanide, Vihari, a small dose. What I am asking of you is evidently causing you some difficulties – even though you have sworn and reaffirmed your absolute obedience to me. Therefore, I want to help you carry out your obligations.

"Cyanide is an old drug, but a good one. As I'm sure you know, Vihari, it acts on the central nervous system. With this dose, which I have calculated with great care, you'll be able to breathe just enough to stay conscious for eight hours. During those hours, you'll feel as though you're trapped under water sucking air through a clogged tube. Your lungs will begin to burn. The pain will eventually become unbearable. In the end, you will panic. This will increase your body's need for oxygen – and result in your suffocation.

"But . . . but – "

"Be quiet."

Godessohn sat and typed a command on his keyboard. The gleaming stainless steel elevator doors opened without a sound. The elevator was not there.

Vihari heard a whirring noise. A huge triple-pronged iron meat hook came down the dark shaft, spinning slowly on a cable. The hook had been heated: it glowed reddish orange and gave off the odor of a smelter. The hook stopped its descent just inside the doors.

Vihari threw up on the front of his tan suit.

Godessohn typed another code. The hook ascended, the elevator doors closed.

"Well, Vihari, let's get this over with before you render my office uninhabitable. I'll summarize your options. You may obey me, as you solemnly promised to do, and jump. The result will be a painless and honorable death. Or you may refuse to jump, thus demonstrating that your oath of allegiance was nothing but a ploy to inherit my empire. If you choose the second option the result will be death without honor – and with excruciating pain. You've seen the syringe, you've seen the hook. You know what I have in mind for you."

"If you decide to jump, please note that you'll have only three seconds from the moment the doors open until they close again. If you're still standing in my office at the end of those three seconds, you have selected the second option by default. And now, Vihari, look at your watch. You have two minutes to make your decision – or have it made for you.

Vihari gulped down another eruption of vomit. He began to shake more violently; he could no longer control his body. "But, sir . . . you . . . you must explain to me – "

"No more questions, please. You'd best concentrate on your choice."

Vihari staggered like a newborn deer toward the elevator. He would jump, his tormentor meant what he said, there was no way out.

Across an ocean of blue-gray industrial carpet, he saw the stainless steel doors shimmering like tin cans under murky water.

He wobbled ahead, gasping for breath. He inhaled the smells of vomit and overheated metal, of Godessohn's talc and his own sour sweat.

"Twenty-six seconds, Vihari."

He saw his father teaching him to read one summer night on the flagstone terrace. Oil lamps were lit against the darkness, and great beasts howled in the veld. He had been afraid of the night. But when he slid under his father's arm, he felt warm and secure.

The elevator doors swam up in front of him. He had made it across the carpet sea. He talked to himself, talked aloud, heard his words but did not understand them.

The smell of the hot iron meat hook was stronger here, and more pungent, seeping like a noxious gas from between the doors.

He did not know what had happened, what had gone wrong. A few hours ago his future had never looked brighter.

His future! He would not jump! He could not!

No?

He felt Godessohn lifting him in the air while he kicked and shrieked helplessly; felt Godessohn pitching him into the empty elevator shaft; felt barbed, red-hot meat hooks tearing into his flesh like crucifixion spikes; felt the cyanide paralyzing his lungs.

Don't be a fool!

You must jump!

Steady yourself before you faint. You are going to die, so die painlessly. Take the little bit of happiness you have known during your life to the grave with you; don't let eight hours of torture cancel it out.

Jump!

He leaned against the wall and squinted. How much longer, how much longer?

He had been afraid of his wedding, afraid of their first night, afraid of Harvard, afraid of the birth of his son. Why should he not be afraid of death? Yes, afraid. Christ, he was afraid. He couldn't go through with it.

He had to.

He couldn't.

He thought he heard footsteps behind him.

Three seconds, the doors would stay open three seconds. He would make his decision then.

The doors moved.

He wasn't crazy!

He would jump!

Wait. WAIT! The opening was too small. Time had

stopped. The doors parted inch by black inch, parted so slowly it seemed he would have to wait forever.

Would he fall this slowly? Would he hurtle through a dark chamber for days while the cables in the shaft hummed an indifferent dirge?

Suddenly the doors shot open. Before he could move, they began to close.

Now! He could not wait another instant.

He hurled himself through the opening with a scream on his lips – and crashed spread-eagle on to a carpeted platform.

He flipped on his back and saw a thick hand coming through the sliver of light between the doors.

Godessohn switched on the elevator's interior lights. He said, "The old Vihari has died, my son, just as Nils Laar died seventeen years ago. The new Vihari will soon be born. It will be interesting indeed to see how he turns out. I want you to go down to the gym now and clean up. We are leaving for Venice in an hour."

"Ve . . . Ve . . . Venice?"

"Yes, Vihari. The city needs my philanthropy, and I need a pretext for being there. We're going to watch history in the making. We're going to watch the departure of my fish."

"But . . . my wife . . . my clothes . . ."

"Don't worry about such trivial matters. Your wife has been informed of your journey. Your wardrobe has been brought up from Johannesburg. You'll find your bags in the gym. All you have to do is shower and dress – and enjoy your rebirth."

Godessohn stepped back into his office. The doors closed and the elevator descended smoothly. Vihari still lay trembling on the carpeted floor when the elevator came to a soft stop in the basement.

PART II

CHAPTER TEN

Luigi, alone at the controls of his helicopter, broke through the clouds that had engulfed him since his departure from Grandfather Giuseppe's meadow. A half moon shone brightly on the rim of the star-filled night and the overcast, below him now, stretched like a gray cotton sea to the horizons.

Reaching his prearranged coordinates 12,000 feet above the Lagoon of Venice, he put the helicopter on automatic hover and pointed his infrared telescope in the direction of the refinery. A few seconds later he located the ghastly place, its byproduct stacks flaming like torches in the scope lens.

Luigi shook his head. He had to agree with Kiyo. Dante was taking on too much this time. The murder of his uncle had made him crazy. To think that Dante was putting his trust in the murderess herself! It was a sad commentary on the Signore's mental state.

Why wouldn't Dante listen to reason? Why did he insist on rushing headlong into a trap – alone? This was a disaster! Once he got inside the refinery, neither Luigi nor anyone else would be able to help him. He would be gone, shot down, tortured, fed to the petroleum rats.

How did Luigi know? Well, it didn't take a genius to figure it out. Kiyo had done a weapons trace and discovered that Puzzo had an arsenal in there which included 40 Stinger antiaircraft missiles.

Madonna! Dante was normally such a rock of rational good sense. Why hadn't he at least assembled a well-armed support team? Or better yet, just gone to the police?

Luigi checked his radar screen. Good, good. Heavy squalls were approaching from the southwest, growing more violent as they neared the sea. Maybe his thickheaded Signore would listen to the Voice of Nature.

He flicked on his mike. "Kiyo, are you picking me up?"

"Loud and clear, Luigi."

"This is important. Tell Dante he doesn't have a choice: he *must* postpone the mission. The weather has turned bad, really nasty. There are squalls moving in from the southwest, purple on the radar – lightning, hail . . . not possible to fly an ultralight in that stuff."

"I'm afraid, Luigi, that he's already airborne."

"What? He was supposed to wait until I radioed."

"He said you were too slow. You'd better contact him directly."

"Give me his frequency. He wouldn't give it to me."

"Nor to me, Luigi. It doesn't matter. Just talk. You can be sure he's listening in on us."

"You're a fool, Dante! Turn around! You'll never get out of there alive. You won't even *get* there alive."

"Luigi," said Dante, his voice deep and calm in the helicopter speaker, "you are supposed to be guiding me to the refinery, not speculating on my prospects for success. Forget about the squalls. This craft is designed to handle any weather. Find *me* on your radar. Hurry. I can't see a thing."

"Madonna, Signore! I beg you as a friend. Please turn around!"

"Luigi, please."

* * *

Dante checked his gauges. Altitude: 900 feet. Airspeed: 30 miles an hour. The refinery fence was about ten miles away.

He switched on his landing lights for a look at the night. Heavy mist swirled in the backwash of the silent, electrically driven prop. He couldn't have asked for better weather. His ultralight would remain hidden in a blanket of cloud until he was nearly ready to touch down.

He turned off the lights and went through his mental checklist again, marveling at his good fortune. Giorgio Puzzo, last year when he had secured his facility, had made the mistake of purchasing CRC equipment. Using company records, Kiyo had been able to penetrate the refinery's computerized security system. Dante had the codes he needed to go wherever he wanted to go.

He also had a disguise in the rucksack behind his seat. He would be impersonating Dr. Giovanni Gotti, a high-ranking Italian employee of the Pakistani engineering firm, Girta, sent to the refinery to check on his company's operations. Thanks to Kiyo's ingenious computer snooping, Dante had the real Dr. Gotti's ID numbers and pass names.

Dante had considered carrying a gun but decided against it. If he were searched, he wanted his disguise to hold up. No gun, just a bit of simple Taser-proofing to prepare him for the blond giant Gina had warned him about.

No reason to worry – as long as Gina didn't betray him.

Well, he'd know soon whether she was trustworthy.

If they opened up with antiaircraft missiles the instant he came out of the clouds, she was not; if they were waiting for him on the roof of the administration building when he touched down, she was not; if Puzzo's office windows hadn't been unlocked, she was not; and if, by dawn, she hadn't checked into the room he had reserved for her at the Zitti Palace, she was not.

But she *was* trustworthy. She was also his friend. During the six hours he spent with her, he'd felt her affection for him growing steadily.

And if he still had doubts, he needed only to think about the information she had given him on the refinery. All of it was accurate, as Kiyo's exhaustive investigation had shown. If Gina intended to betray him, she would not have divulged so much.

He thought about her life story, the one she had told him in the kitchen of Puzzo's villa. She was a Saudi girl who had been passed around like a piece of chattel. She had been resigned to her fate until Vittorio's murder shocked her out of her passivity. Now she wanted nothing more than to escape the evil men who controlled her. She wanted a life she could call her own, a life Dante had promised to help her find. She had switched sides to help herself. This was his ultimate guarantee, infinitely more reliable than friendship.

No, she would not let him down.

He glanced at his watch. Almost midnight. In a few minutes she would be leaving the villa on the rope bridge he had built over Puzzo's wall, her exit scheduled to coincide with his entry into the refinery.

He could see her now, standing in the rain amid the great dripping oaks saying good-bye to her dogs.

When she arrived at the Zitti Palace, she would need a long, hot bath.

He could see that, too.

Bursts of cold rain splattered against his body suit. Turbulence jolted him around like a stretch of bad road. The bones of his ultralight emitted agonizing squeaks.

Lightning flickered nearby, illuminating the craft's water swept wings. Dante shivered. He was glad the Dutch and not the Italian division of CRC had built his electric motor. It wasn't as powerful as he had hoped, but at least he could depend on it.

"Signore, excuse the delay," blared Luigi's voice through the speaker. "I've got you on my radar screen now."

Dante turned down the volume. "Good, Luigi. Where am I?"

"Drifting a little north. Looks like you've got a southwest wind of seven knots shoving you off course. You need to come around ten degrees."

"Thank you, Luigi. How far to the refinery fence?"

"Not far enough. Five miles. You're going to be in there in no time, Signore. Are you sure you don't want to reconsider your foolish method of entry?"

"I'm sure, Luigi. Stick to what you're doing. How's my course now?"

"Better, Signore. Worse, I mean. You're on a beeline to your grave."

"Thank you, Luigi." Dante adjusted the trim to compensate for the cross wind and began a gradual descent. When he reached 400 feet, he no longer needed Luigi's directions: the lights and fires from the refinery burned up through the clouds, providing landmarks.

Still in the overcast, he leveled off, flew straight until the lights dimmed, then pitched the ultralight into a 180 degree turn for an upwind landing.

Lights again, growing brighter. Tatters of mist whipping by his rain-splotched goggles.

At 300 feet, he came out beneath the clouds. Flames shot up at him from tall stacks; their reflections lapped down at him from the sagging night sky.

He spotted the main administration building a mile ahead and settled into a flat glide toward its tar and gravel roof.

He noticed a streaked gray-white wall of rain coming at him head-on. A squall. He'd have to beat it to the roof. He *would* beat it.

Down, down.

He drifted between towering stacks and passed over a tangle of giant aluminum-clad pipes. He glided near a generating plant whose transformers and grids filled the night with a high-voltage hum he could feel in his bone marrow. He floated over a mud swamp whose rain-dimpled surface foamed with petroleum wastes.

Down, down. He would approach just below roof level, pull up and stall at the last second. A shorter roll. A safer landing.

LINES ACROSS THE NIGHT!

Slender support cables were connecting the stacks in front of him! They hadn't been visible from the helicopter during his surveillance flights!

He cursed out loud. His path to the roof was barred.

Nowhere to go, no time to think. He veered right and dove steeply, just missing a ladder which ran like a raised seam up the side of a distillation column.

He caught a glimpse of the administration building roof out of the corner of his eye. His drastic maneuver had cost him more altitude than he realized. He would have to recoup it before he could land; he would have to circle back the way he'd come.

Now he had plenty of time to think. He was being forced to fly a semicircle with a 3000 foot radius to gain the needed 100 feet, a semicircle that would take him halfway to the refinery border and the Lagoon.

Holy Mother, he was going to lose his race with the squall!

He gave full throttle. The alloy prop slapped feebly at the rain; the tiny Dutch engine whined and moaned. God, how he hated wimpy engines. He should have gone Italian.

Still coming round, still climbing.

He gained the 100 feet and zeroed in on the roof again. The cables joining the stacks slid harmlessly beneath his wheels.

He focused on his next problem, the weather wall, which was already bearing down on the administration building.

The wind, at his face now, rose in blustery gusts.

The administration building disappeared in the storm. A few seconds later, a barrage of hailstones slammed into him, pinging in the prop, battering man and machine.

He battled the controls to keep the ultralight from flipping. A downdraft shoved him earthward. Before he had dropped very far, a hot updraft stopped his plunge, its harsh chemical components scorching his nostrils and searing his lungs.

He looked down through the swirling hail. The wind had suspended him motionless over an open storage tank half the size of a soccer field! Rust marks oozed down the tank's internal walls, disappearing in some vile chemical brew whipped to a dirty lather by the hail.

Lightning flashed, thunder cracked. The odoriferous tank came alive, a great sparkling bubble bath.

He was riding his stationary bull, ripping through his non-existent options, when the leading edge of the squall passed and the administration building emerged from the soup.

The wind died, his ground speed rose from zero to something he could live with. The hail turned back to rain as he flew away from the tank, flew over mud swamps and elevated concrete service roads and more pipe jungles.

The ledge around the top of the administration building rushed toward him. He hauled back on the controls, cleared it, stalled and nosed the ultralight forward. His wheels touched the roof with scarcely a bump.

Quickly he climbed out and secured the craft to several vents. Reaching into the luggage area behind his seat, he pushed his parachute aside and took out the rucksack holding his disguise. Then he hooked his climbing rope on to the roof ledge and lowered himself toward Puzzo's office windows.

* * *

Vihari sat by a window in Godessohn's corporate jet, watching the storm. Rain and hail pounded the Plexiglas, and lightning silhouetted the ragged night sky.

They were low now, skimming the black water of the Lagoon. He caught a glimpse of a fishing boat, its lanterns heaving in the waves.

Wing flaps trembled, wheels came down with a clunk. Vihari listened to the changing tones of the engines, thankful for the firm seat beneath him.

Down, down, almost into the water. The runway, lined with yellow lights, appeared out of nowhere. Wheels touched, reverse thrust came on with a roar.

Vihari glanced at his watch: midnight, a half hour ahead of schedule in spite of the weather.

They taxied toward the terminal. He saw an unruly crowd of reporters swarming on the tarmac behind a heavy police cordon. He had expected a press conference, not a riot.

Vihari followed his boss to the door, which swung up as soon as the stairway was in place. Godessohn stopped on the top ramp, filling the open doorway like a painting too big for its frame.

Vihari was surprised: not only did Godessohn not seem to mind the chaos outside; he even raised his arms in a friendly salute, as if he approved of it!

The cheering rose to a crescendo. Godessohn, apparently caught up in the enthusiasm, thundered down the stairs and past his makeshift podium. He pushed the narrow-hipped cops who were supposed to be protecting him aside, ducked the cordon, and plunged into the crowd.

Vihari went after him with the umbrella but the police stopped *him*! Chattering like monkeys, they guided him to the podium. Vihari watched helplessly as hailstones the size of grapes pelted his boss's dome.

Finally, Godessohn returned and mounted the podium. Vihari planted himself at the great man's side and held the umbrella over him.

The press conference began.

"No, ladies and gentlemen," said Godessohn, very cool, very composed in response to the first question, "I never met Senator Vittorio Passoni. Be quiet, please. I am talking. I'll get to you in a moment. No, it was not Passoni's murder which moved me to come to Venice. It was rather the unconscionable behavior of the corporations that had promised to support his International Commission."

"Sir! Mister! Would you – "

"*Per favore*! The people of Venice, of Italy, indeed of all the civilized world, have received a rotten deal. Are we to believe what the corporations tell us: that Vittorio Passoni and no one else in this fine and spirited country can efficiently manage an effort to save Venice? Nonsense, I say!"

Lightning, wind gusts, wild applause as Nature tried to rip the umbrella from Vihari's grasp. Godessohn had already done what the police could not do: he had taken control of the crowd.

The reporters fell silent, waiting like well-behaved school children for him to continue.

"My friends," he boomed, "you must understand the corporate mentality to understand what happened after Senator Passoni's murder. The corporations agreed to put up money for the salvation of Venice *not* out of love for the city but because they believed they would *look bad* if they did not. Once they had made their pledges, however, once they had demonstrated their social responsibility to the buying public, Venice became nothing more than a drain on their profits. So they withdrew their pledges, using as an excuse the murder of Senator Passoni."

A great uproar. "Sir! Signore! Mister Godessohn! Are you implying that the Senator's corporate sponsors had a motive for eliminating him?"

"Look, I'm not a detective. You'll have to draw your own conclusions on that one. I'm trying to explain why the corporations withdrew their support after the Senator's murder; and what I intend to do to offset the effects of their reprehensible decision. Ladies and gentlemen, I am personally going to donate the funds needed to save Venice."

"Sixty billion dollars?"

"Sixty-*five* billion."

Silence. Stunned incredulity. Then a grateful stirring, a rising chorus of shocked voices.

"And you sir! You, Mister Godessohn! Are you going to head up a new commission?"

"Of course not. Venice is an Italian city. The head of the new commission should be Italian."

"But who, sir? Who?"

"That is up to the Italian people. My own preference would be a man I'm sure you're all familiar with."

"Are you prepared to give names, sir?"

"I'm speaking of Vittorio Passoni's nephew, the C. E. O. of a corporation which, unlike most, has managed to give efficiency a human face."

"CRC?"

"Dante Passoni?"

"That's correct. And now, ladies and gentlemen, if you'll excuse me. It's been a long flight."

"Sir! Mister! Where are you spending the night?"

"That bit of information, my friends, your government does not wish you to know. I told them I wouldn't mind a little attention from the press, but they would hear nothing of it. I'm afraid you are going to be taken into custody by members of your Secret Service until I am ensconced in my room. Good night."

Laughter, as if Godessohn were joking; short-lived laughter.

Vihari gaped in disbelief as 200 antiterrorist police came surging out of the terminal, night sticks drawn and assault rifles in attack position.

Outraged hoots of protest echoed across the tarmac.

Godessohn laughed pleasantly. He leaned over and whispered in Vihari's ear. "What you see is the work of my communications system. Those men, Vihari, believe that they have received their orders from the President of the Republic."

"But . . . but, why, sir? Why did you go to all this trouble to have some friendly journalists arrested."

"Friendly? They are rodents, Vihari. I didn't want them disturbing our sleep." Godessohn took his arm. "Come along now. An official car is waiting to drive us to the gondola docks."

"Gondola docks?"

"Yes, Vihari. The hotel's gondola will take us from there."

CHAPTER ELEVEN

One of the windows was unlocked.

Dante, still in his body suit, raised his goggles and looked around Puzzo's dimly lit office. Nothing to impress the interior decorators here . . . white walls, their monotony broken only by an occasional photograph of the refinery; brown tile floors; marble statues of wolfhounds; a huge steel elevator door with CRC retinal and thumb print scanners mounted on the wall beside it; a slate inlay desk with model tankers plying its rock sea; a computer; and a marble bar which rose like a breakwater around a gleaming restaurant-sized espresso machine.

He hurried to the toilet, where Gina had promised him he would find a shower, leaving an uncomely slick of roof gravel and muddy water on Puzzo's immaculate floor.

The shower was large, clean and of the same ugly brown tile as the floor. Puzzo, he could see, was one of those men who prided themselves in putting function ahead of beauty, as though there were a conflict between the two.

When Dante had showered, he opened his rucksack and laid out his clothes. They had survived the rainy, open-cockpit flight in good shape, thanks to Kiyo's computer-designed "roll fold."

He checked his reddish-brown bench made shoes, giving special attention to the right one. The copper heel plate was firmly in place, and the insulated wire that ran from the plate through the sole had been properly secured. The wire, coiled loosely in the bottom of the shoe, was several inches long, and had a tiny plug-style connector on the end.

He slipped into his underwear, his socks, white silk shirt and heavy gold filigree vest, an antique his cousin had rented for him from a medieval clothing store in Venice. He examined the well-insulated wire dangling from the bottom of the vest, which was identical to the wire in the shoe. Everything seemed to be intact.

Keep up the pace.

He tied his magenta and yellow silk tie – a garish splash of color he knew any Pakistanis he might encounter would appreciate – and took a long look at his trousers. Another wire had been sewn inside the lining. It ran down the crease at the back of the right leg. The female plugs for the wires attached to his vest and shoe were artfully hidden, one inside the waist band, the other behind the cuff. If someone wanted to search him, he wouldn't object too strongly.

Trousers on, shoes on, shoe and vest wires plugged into the trouser wire, establishing an electrical connection between the grid of current-bearing gold thread in his filigree vest and the copper plate in his heel. As long as he stood on a grounded surface, he would be Taser proof; he could now worry about more interesting things.

He put on his navy pinstripe suit jacket, straightened his official Girta identification badge and combed his hair. To complete his disguise, he donned his yellow hard hat, which matched the yellow in his tie.

At the elevator, he subjected his eye and thumb to the CRC scanners' careful scrutiny. Nothing to worry about here: Kiyo, working through CRC's central computer, had programmed the scanner to recognize him. When he had passed this test, a sign lit up overhead, announcing that the elevator had begun its two and a half mile journey from the refinery's central control bunker to Puzzo's office.

Dante frowned and stared at one of the black marble dogs, trying to remember a specific scrap of conversation. Hadn't Gina told him the elevator would be waiting in Puzzo's office, not at the other end of the shaft?

Yes, she had, he was sure of it. What did this discrepancy mean? Was Puzzo working late tonight? If so, it could mean trouble.

The elevator reached Puzzo's office and stopped soundlessly. The door opened, Dante stepped inside, the door closed and he was on his way.

An LED display above the door read 5:41. It was ticking off the seconds backwards, spooling toward :00 – arrival time in the central control bunker, he surmised.

Gina had told him about the elevator trip. First a vertical descent deep into the earth, then a long horizontal underground passage to the sunken control bunker over two miles away. Dante had time to kill and nothing to do. The prospect of spending five minutes idle in the midst of so critical an operation made him nervous. He'd fix himself an espresso, he decided. That should consume a good three minutes.

He stepped up to the bar stretching across the back wall of the elevator compartment. The espresso machine here looked like a cafe-sized version of the restaurant behemoth Puzzo kept in his office. Dante punched the ON button. A red light lit up. While he waited for it to turn green, he noticed small cameras mounted on the ceiling, swiveling like snake heads. So much for the hope that he might reach Room 12 undetected.

The light flashed green. He twisted out one of the oversized filters. It was already packed with freshly ground coffee, enough for at least five cups. After twisting it back in, he put a mug – he couldn't find a demitasse – under the nozzle and slowly pulled the handle. A dense black stream trickled out. While he waited, he watched the numbers on the backwards-whirling digital clock slip under three minutes.

The sugar bowl was a ceramic dog's head. He lifted the lid. The contents looked like powdered sugar.

He took a taste: cocaine.

Not tonight, Puzzo. After a mug of your coffee it would be redundant.

He drank his espresso straight. His pulse quickened, his mind grew sharp. The numbers on the clock dial spun down toward zero. He straightened his tie. He had passed the time well. He felt ready to face whatever awaited him.

*　*　*

Dante stepped into an alien world. Transformers hummed like a field of summer crickets. Subtly tinted rose and green auras glowed above a dozen control centers. The air was full of static electricity, and it smelled of chemical compounds he couldn't identify.

On the high wall opposite him loomed a massive electronic flow diagram. Black and red lines writhed like eels on its pulsing face.

Manfred, the blond giant Gina had warned him about, looked up from his desk 20 feet away. "Stay where you are," he ordered, rising slowly and deliberately to his feet. "Did you have permission to use the coffee machine in the elevator? You probably didn't know I watched your entire trip here." He smiled, tapped the monitor on his desk with a gnarled knuckle. "Please answer my question."

"I was told by Mr. Puzzo to make myself at home."

"That so? Well I never heard of Puzzo letting anyone use his espresso machines."

"Mr. Puzzo and I go way back."

"Yeah?"

"Yes."

Manfred wore jeans, a sleeveless "Save Venice" T-shirt and a name tag which read M. Strasser, Plant Security. His tattooed arms bulged at his sides like stamped prosciutto hams. He came round the desk and stopped in front of Dante, towering over him, a superior smile creasing his pockmarked face. "So what are you doing here?"

"You, if anyone, should know," Dante said. "Mr. Puzzo told me I'd find you here doing your duty. He was to fill you in on the reason for my visit. Perhaps it's slipped your mind. I'm Dr. Giovanni Gotti, a systems analyst with Girta. I am going to carry out some evaluations of my staff's performance here in the refinery. I shouldn't need more than a couple of hours."

"You're too late, *ragazzo*," Manfred said. "Your people left for Pakistan about four hours ago. Them, the Sheik, the whole crew. You Girta guys are the biggest screwups I've ever met in my life – and believe me, I've met quite a few."

Too late! The Pakistanis had left! What was Dante to make of this startling bit of information. He tried to slow down the tempo of the conversation, to stall so that he could think.

He said, "You seem rather quick with your assumptions, Mr. Strasser. The evaluations I've been sent to conduct *require* that the staff people be absent. They are not called 'post-completion performance evaluations' for nothing. Arrangements have been made to admit me to Room Twelve, the overview room. If you'll excuse me, I'd like to get on with my assignment now."

"Hey, I like your tie. Goes real nice with that shiny vest. Turn around, hands on the tile, palms flat. We'll talk some more about where you're going after I've frisked you."

"This is ridiculous."

"I said, turn around. Hurry up."

Dante obeyed, shaking his head.

Beefy hands came probing up the inside of his legs. Manfred slapped his penis, which drooped lower than most. "Sorry, pal, you didn't tell me you were hung like a bull."

Dante turned to face the huge Aryan. "Enough nonsense, Strasser. Either you let me do the work I was brought here to do or I'm going to lodge a formal complaint with Mr. Puzzo. You know damn well I'm authorized to be here. You were informed."

"I was *not* informed."

"Well, if that's true – if you didn't simply forget – someone must have overlooked telling you. Think about it, Strasser. How would I have gotten in if my visit hadn't been authorized?"

"I don't know. All I know is, I got certain rules I follow.

Which means you're not going anywhere until I have permission from the man himself. I can't call him now because he's in Room Nineteen, and when he's in Room Nineteen, nobody bothers him except in the most dire emergency. You wanting to get home early so you can take that wurst of yours on a walk is not what I call an emergency. You'll wait with me until Puzzo comes out. It might be an hour. It might be a day. It might be a month. Here, look at these."

Manfred opened his desk drawer and pulled out an official Girta folder and a bottle of plum schnapps. He took a drink of schnapps and handed the folder to Dante, who opened it and shoved it back at him.

"I didn't come to look at pornography, Strasser. I thought I had made myself clear. I have work to do. Now, either you let me pass or I'm going to move you."

The giant stuck his nose in Dante's face, nearly suffocating him with a humid blast of schnapps fumes. "How you gonna move me, *ragazzo*? You're not armed and you don't weigh an ounce over one seventy. Subtract the schwanz and you're down to one sixty. I'm not in the habit of letting runts tell me what to do."

"I'm sorry to take advantage of you, Strasser, but you leave me no choice."

The giant let out a belly laugh that echoed off the bunker's tile walls. "Take advantage? Take *advantage*? How you got that figured?"

"You'd have to be a little brighter to understand."

Dante hit him with several short stiff rights to the solar plexus. It was like hammering on a side of beef.

Manfred backed up with measured steps, put the pornography folder and schnapps bottle carefully on the desk, and raised his hands. "Don't, mosquito fist."

Dante attacked, jabbing and ducking, jabbing and ducking, jabbing and backing off. He drew blood from Manfred's nose and split his lip.

"That's enough, *ragazzo*," Manfred growled. "I don't want to bang you up – just in case you're supposed to be here. But you keep on like this, what am I supposed to do?"

Dante hit him four more times. Manfred walked through his punches, grabbed him by the jacket and hurled him with tremendous force against the elevator door. Dante slumped to his knees. As he struggled to his feet, he saw Manfred draw the Taser and aim it at his heart.

Dante froze, careful to keep his copper heel pressed against the steel door jamb.

"You know what you're lookin at?" Manfred said, a hint of a smile blossoming on his ugly face.

Dante feigned a shudder of trepidation. "I don't know anything about guns, Strasser, but I do know this: if you shoot the man your boss brought here for a post-performance evaluation, *you* are going to receive a lot worse than a gunshot."

"Wrong again, *ragazzo*. Cause this is an electric gun." The giant patted it like a pet. "Electric, understand? No bullets, no scars, no permanent damage. That's why the cops like 'em. I pull the trigger, you get struck by lightning. You're down and out for a while, and real submissive when you come around."

"I don't think your gun is going to have any effect on me, Strasser. I enjoy being struck by lightning. The experience leaves me reinvigorated."

Manfred laughed. "Yeah, right. I've heard bullshit before, but that takes the torta." He laughed some more, held his breath and pulled the trigger.

A 100,000 volt dagger of lightning hit Dante in the chest. In his mind's eye, Dante watched the current whiz along the tributaries of his filigree vest, shoot down the wire in his pants and leave his body through the copper plate in the heel of his shoe, passing harmlessly into the well-grounded door jamb.

Manfred's mouth dropped open. He fired again, and Dante's vest glowed like molten ore. "A very pleasant tingle, Strasser."

The flustered giant pulled the trigger a third time, but the Taser was out of juice. He hurled it to the floor and lunged at Dante with balled fists.

The first left hook came in wide and slow, like a wrecking ball that hadn't yet picked up speed. Dante jerked his head to the side and Manfred's knuckles shattered on the door jamb, still hot from the current.

Dante could hear breaking bones over the howl of the big man's scream, and he could smell burning flesh. He easily dodged a haymaker right, which after years of tunnel driving at 200 miles an hour looked like a balloon drifting lazily toward him on a spring breeze.

Spinning away from the door, Dante fired off a six punch combination, flattening Manfred's nose and widening the split in his lip.

A tooth struck the floor with a tiny click.

The giant was mad now, and in hot pursuit. Dante raced behind the desk and threw the folder of pornographic photos into his face, careful not to hit the big red alarm button beside the monitor. While Manfred battled fluttering silicon breasts and neatly trimmed triangles of pubic hair, Dante got a heavy desk drawer unstuck and brought it down squarely on his head. The giant staggered backwards, howling and cursing.

"This is beginning to bore me," Dante said. He took off his Girta ID badge and straightened the needle. "It's a syringe, Strasser, polar bear tranquilizer. I hope it agrees with you."

Manfred charged, looking more like a rhino than a bear. Dante stepped to the side, tripping him and injecting him in the buttocks as he sprawled face down.

Manfred rolled around, got to his feet and lurched with an

outstretched arm toward the alarm button.

Dante cracked his broken fingers with a fat marble ashtray, then delivered another combination. The first punch glanced off the giant's right cheekbone, the second lacerated the cartilage in his nose, the third and fourth trampolined off his windpipe.

Hold him at bay! The stuff should begin working soon.

What was going on? Manfred was still fighting back, making strident sounds as he gulped air through his flattened larynx!

A thunderous right whistled past Dante's ear; a left hook grazed his chin. Again Manfred lunged for the alarm button. Dante stopped him with a knee to the groin.

Manfred groaned and sank to all fours. When he started to get up, the tranquilizer finally kicked in. His arms and legs collapsed outward, his belly slapped the floor, his mouth flopped open and he immediately began to snore.

Dante shoved a few sheets of porn closer to him, removed the lid from the schnapps bottle and placed it beside his head. Then he straightened his tie and headed for Room 12, hoping that Puzzo would stay put for a while.

* * *

The submarine-gray steel door guarding the room closed behind him with a clunk. Fluorescent lights came on, illuminating vast expanses of white tile.

With a bed in the center, thought Dante, this place would look like an operating room. But there was no bed, only a bank of white desks. On each desk were keyboards, TV screens and monitors.

The smell of strong disinfectants hung in the air, here and there more saccharine from the lingering fragrance of Pakistani cologne.

The engineers must have worked right up to their departure. Dante felt the beginnings of despair. Had he gotten here too late?

He sat at the center keyboard and typed the command Kiyo had designed to get him inside the elaborate closed-circuit TV system linking all of the secured rooms in the bunker. A menu came up on the monitor, prompting him for the room he wanted to "visit." Wishing to proceed systematically, Dante resisted the temptation to drop in on Puzzo. He selected Room 1.

The color TV screen in front of him came into focus. An electric cart, squat and stout, stood motionless on narrow-gauge rails. On the cart was a gold petroleum pump the size of a man. Various diameter nozzles ringed the cylinder, a standard tanker pump but for its color. The top had been removed. Dante played with his keyboard until he got the camera to move and give him a glimpse of the inside.

Interesting, he thought. There were no passages to the nozzles. In fact, the interior walls of the pump were as smoothly polished as Lamborghini cylinders. No, this was not a pump. It was a massive gold container made to look like a pump.

But why gold? He could think of only one reason, a reason he hoped was wrong. Containers built to transport radioactive materials were usually made of lead. Gold had a higher specific density than lead and would work just as well. Gold was not used because it was too expensive. But for Gina's stepfather, the Sheik, gold might have been more readily available than lead, and cost might not have been an issue.

If the pump *had* been used to bring radioactive materials into the refinery, it had probably been covered with oil and grease. Thus disguised, it could have been taken inside from a docked tanker, ostensibly for repairs. No one would have noticed anything unusual.

Was it really possible that Puzzo's masters were using this wretched place to do the work of the Devil? If so, it would certainly explain why these men had feared inspections by Uncle Vittorio's International Commission.

To hell with the systematic approach. He'd better check on what Puzzo was doing.

He called up the menu for the closed-circuit TV system, and selected Room 19.

The screen went blank, then lit up with a snapshot-clear image of a room that resembled the inside of Puzzo's elevator: dark pile carpeting, leather armchairs, a long bar on which sat two bowls with ceramic wolfhound heads for tops and a brass twin-handled espresso maker.

Puzzo, a shine-hard little man in a tightly fitting black suit stood at the bar, simultaneously pumping both handles of the espresso machine. His face was drawn, and his small beady eyes blazed with wild intensity.

As Puzzo worked the handles, Dante watched the thick black liquid ooze like clotting crude into the cups beneath each nozzle. As soon as the stream dwindled to a string of drops, Puzzo emptied both cups into a large mug, which he drank in one long swallow. He wiped his mouth with the back of his hand. His darting eyes settled on one of the ceramic bowls. He lifted the dog head top by the snout. White on black: the bowl, like the one in the elevator, was filled with cocaine.

Puzzo held a silver spoonful of the powder to his nose and snorted. He jerked the top from the second bowl: it was filled with syringes. The benzedrine Gina had mentioned.

"Disgusting," murmured Dante, watching Puzzo pull back his sleeve and shoot up. He expected the tense little man to become even more frenetic, but the drugs actually seemed to calm him. He sat in his armchair, settled comfortably, placed a small keyboard from the coffee table on his lap and began typing.

The wall he was facing rose like a theater curtain, exposing a plate glass window rimmed with coordinates and a large green pool beyond. A miniature narrow-gauge railroad bridge spanned the pool a few feet above the water. On the far side of the bridge, resting on a cart similar to the one that carried the fake pump, was a large polished steel cylinder. Leads sprouted by the hundreds from its shiny skin.

It was unmistakably a bomb – but was it nuclear? And if so, how big was it and where was it going? These were the questions Dante had to answer before he left the refinery.

He left the picture of Room 19 on the screen and moved to another desk. He visited the remaining rooms of the bunker one by one, picking up little scraps of data left on tables and chalkboards, none of which told him anything.

Using a fresh set of codes, he called up a directory of the information stored in the main computer.

Nothing! No information at all! The disks had been erased! He had no way to find out how big the bomb was – or where, if anywhere, it was going.

He thought about confronting Puzzo, but dismissed the idea. He doubted Puzzo knew a whole lot more than he did. Based on what Gina had told him and what he had observed himself, Puzzo was a bit player in somebody else's grand scheme, a man valuable to the criminals only because he had a facility in which certain operations could be carried out.

No, no, he mustn't confront Puzzo. He would blow his cover without learning anything, and the big fish, thus alerted, would get away.

He returned to the television image of Room 19. Puzzo was still in his armchair. He was watching through the plate glass window now, no longer typing.

A crane swung out over the pool. The cart bearing the bomb rolled out on the rail bridge, moving very slowly. The glow of the water lent the bomb a soft green hue.

For a moment, when the bomb reached the midpoint of the bridge, all motion stopped. Then the crane started up again, swinging farther over the water and hooking the bomb through the stout steel manufacturing handle built into its skin.

The crane lifted the bomb so smoothly off the cart that the bomb did not even pivot. Slowly, the crane lowered its charge into the water.

Five feet down the bomb came to rest on a stand, shimmering brightly through the tiny waves its submersion had left on the pool's surface. The crane, its work complete, swung out of view. The ruffled water settled to a dead calm.

At the far end of the pool, Dante spotted a large round portal. The facility had obviously been designed to smuggle its produce into the Lagoon, but where was it going from there? Was it meant for Venice or some destination thousands of miles away?

Puzzo got up and made himself another espresso. He snorted coke, shot benzedrine and, looking relaxed, sat at his keyboard. Dante could just make out the words appearing on Puzzo's monitor . . .

> Dear Mr. Puzzo:
> Thank you for the use of your facility. Until now you have been most cooperative. I asked you to erase beyond recovery all computer files relating to the project. By "all" I am including any backups in your office. If you have not destroyed these yet, do so IMMEDIATELY.

Puzzo's expression darkened. He gave the monitor a two-pronged Italian bird, settled more deeply into his armchair and closed his eyes.

Holy Madonna, he was taking a nap! If Dante was lucky, he could search Puzzo's office, find the information he needed and get out of the refinery without blowing his cover.

He rushed to the elevator, his head spinning with

unthinkable hypotheses.

CHAPTER TWELVE

Signor Heller, a dour, bony man of 75, had been the Zitti Palace's dead-watch receptionist as long as anyone could remember. From one o'clock in the morning until dawn, he ruled his domain like a divine-right monarch, protecting the venerable old institution from the rising tide of the masses.

In his half century of night service, Heller had developed an odd quirk: he was able to sleep standing up. During these naps, his right eye did not close but kept an unblinking watch over the great glass doors that opened on to the gondola dock, the hotel's main entrance.

Heller had always been able maintain a clear line of demarcation between the portion of his brain that held vigil and the portion that slumbered and dreamed. But recently the barrier between his two states of awareness had sprung a leak. Now it was not uncommon for him to awaken to the ghostly silence of the lobby, wipe the sleep from his left eye and think about the guest he had placed in Room 211 or the Senatorial Suite – a guest who had entered the hotel only through his dreams; or, conversely, to awaken with a start and find himself face-to-face with a guest his right eye had tracked all the way to the reception desk but his brain had dismissed as a figure in a dream.

Apart from these small lapses, Heller was still very much in control of the Zitti's nights. Immaculate in a dark suit, with a starched collar as stiff as a leg iron around his wrinkled neck, he would straighten his wire glasses and carefully size up the hotel's late arrivals. On the basis of his first impression, which was rarely mistaken, he made important decisions regarding the rooms to be assigned and the proper level of respect or rudeness to be shown the newcomer by the staff.

When an unacceptable party came to the desk, Signor Heller was quick with his ejection. This he accomplished by placing his antique brass and walnut COMPLETO sign firmly on the counter and announcing with a single word – "completo" – that the establishment was full. The sound of that heavy sign coming down conveyed pure authority, like the crack of a judge's mallet. Even on occasions when the hotel was obviously *not* full, the unwanted arrivals usually left without protest.

Tonight, a little after two a.m., Signor Heller's right eye registered the arrival of a big bald man, who burst like an intruder through the glass doors into the elegant lobby. Heller wiped the sleep from his left eye with his linen handkerchief, hoping he had awakened from a dream.

No such luck. This arrival was real, and he was carrying his own bags! What, Heller wondered, did the *stronzo* think he was doing, carrying his own bags into the Zitti? Couldn't he see that there were two bellhops at his beck and whim? And couldn't he hear Ugo, the hotel's night gondolier since the days of Mussolini, running along behind him *begging* to be of assistance?

The glass doors opened again, and Heller's spine stiffened in disbelief. The newcomer's servant, a maroon-turbaned foreigner obviously born and bred to carry bags, had both hands free! Didn't anyone in this disintegrating world know his role anymore? These barbarians were as out of place at the Zitti as the American woman who had used her bidet for a bowel movement, then complained to management about the plumbing.

Heller glanced at his huge leather-bound reservation book. Two parties holding rooms hadn't arrived yet. They were Signora Passoni, for whom the honorable Dante Passoni had booked the Senatorial Suite, and Signor Godessohn, who had booked the even more luxurious Presidential Suite next door.

This newcomer clearly wasn't Signora Passoni, a young woman who rarely looked the same two visits in a row but always looked very beautiful. And the newcomer wasn't Godessohn, either. For Godessohn, whoever he was, was a man of class and breeding. He had reserved the most expensive suite in the hotel, and his name in the reservation book was marked with a blue star, indicating that he should receive special treatment.

No, no, this was not Godessohn. It was unthinkable that this *disgraziato* thundering across the lobby carrying his own bags would qualify for the Zitti's coveted special treatment.

"I'm Godessohn," announced the big man, tossing his passport on to the fine old cherry wood counter. "This is my assistant. Vihari, give the man your passport."

Frowning, Heller watched the servant tear his awestruck commoner's gaze from the spun-glass chandeliers and pat his cheap double-breasted jacket with a hand that should have been dusting, scrubbing or carrying. "Here it is, right here, right here," he muttered, putting his passport on the counter. He gave a quick little bow, as if guests were the ones who were supposed to do the scraping and bowing.

It was only because of the blue star that Heller bothered to open the documents at all. What he saw further substantiated what he already knew. South Africa! A breeding ground for the undiscriminating masses second only to the United States! Something was terribly wrong. How had this man gotten the blue star beside his name?

The answer came to Heller in a flash. The star was obviously a mistake. Signor Marrone, the day shift monarch, had been sleeping on the job with *both* eyes shut. That star was meant for Signora Passoni. Marrone had put it on the wrong line. Easy enough to do when you were asleep.

Nonetheless, Heller wanted to be absolutely certain before he threw the barbarians out. He was getting old. He sometimes made errors in judgment. He could not help remember the painful episode last summer when he sent the crown prince of Thailand to a flophouse in Mestre. Rather than take chances, he decided to subject this hulking, ill-behaved man to the most infallible of all tests – the shoe test.

Heller bent his long neck against the strangle hold of his collar, adjusted his rimless glasses and peered over the counter.

Ah, there it was, the confirmation. The man's shoes were thick-soled, misshapen and – God forbid – unpolished! They made his feet look like the hooves of a plow horse planted on the Zitti's priceless oriental carpets! This man and his assistant were unreconstructed plebes.

Heller reached under the counter for his COMPLETO sign and put it down with a crack that made the man with the head bandage jump. "I am sorry," he said in stiff school English. "The hotel is full."

The big man's face remained impassive, but his muscled arm came round with the ferocity of a bear paw. He snatched the reservation book from under Heller's nose, glanced at it and slammed it down so hard the binding split.

"Look here, I'm in the Presidential Suite." He hammered at the name with his index finger.

"Up here, old man, up here. G-O-D-E-S-S-O-H-N. See it? You'd better get yourself some new glasses, HELLER, or you could irritate the wrong person."

Heller! Hearing his name on the lips of an ill-bred loony sent a chill down his spine. No late arrival had called him by name since he had stopped wearing his nameplate more than three decades ago. He had learned way back then that the cold stare of anonymity defused a commoner's wrath better than the most carefully chosen words. But this commoner had already pierced the anonymity barrier – and was still coming. What did he want?

The old man, suddenly a trifle nervous, glanced around for his bellhops. He spotted them through the rain-streaked glass doors. They were under the canvas awning that stretched over the gondola dock, smoking cigarettes and chatting with the ancient gondolier, Ugo. If there was trouble, they would be of no help at all.

Heller fondled the COMPLETO sign, his symbol of power

over people like this. The walnut seemed to have grown mysteriously light, like balsa. Well, he wasn't going to let fear get the best of him. It was his moral duty to get these swine out of the hotel, even if it required a little white lie.

He said, "*That* Godessohn, sir, the Godessohn you see in the book, is another. The reservation is for Count Federico Giovanni *di* Godessohn, a long-time patron of this establishment."

Godessohn caught the old man off-guard with a warm smile. "Tell me something, Heller. Are you acquainted with the rules of American baseball?"

"Excuse me?"

"I said, do you know the rules of American baseball? Speak up before I lose patience with you."

Heller's bony fingers tightened around the COMPLETO sign. He imagined it turning to rot, like the inside of a fallen tree. To hell with the sign. He hockey-pucked it down the counter. No sooner had it skidded to a stop than he wished he had hung on to it. For now he felt totally stripped of his armor, like a knight called upon to joust naked.

How did this commoner know his name? It was the use of his name that had peeled off his breastplate. He must find out! If he found out, perhaps he would not feel so defenseless.

"American baseball?" Heller mumbled. "No, sir, I do not know the rules. It is not one of the games we follow here in Italy. Now, sir, I would like to ask *you* a question. How is it that you know my name?"

Godessohn yawned. "I was here for a short uneventful stay in nineteen fifty-nine. You wore a nameplate back then. On your nameplate was written F. V. Heller. I'm glad to see you've gotten rid of the nameplate. You looked rather like an employee of the State Railways. Now, Heller, back to baseball. Since you don't know the rules, I'm going to explain them to you. Three strikes and you're out. That's it, Heller."

"Three . . . strikes? I don't believe I understand, sir."

Godessohn gave an exasperated sigh. "Come closer, Vihari. I want you to hear what I am going to tell Signor Heller."

"Yes, sir."

Godessohn said, "What I'm doing, Heller, is playing a game of American baseball with your city. It's me against Venice. The winner will receive sixty-five billion U.S. dollars. The money is in a special account in Johannesburg.

"Now, Heller, Venice is at bat and you are representing your city. If I am treated by you in a manner distasteful to me three times before I am shown to my suite, Venice strikes out and the game is over. You already have two strikes against you, Heller. One more makes three. One more strike and I go to the press with the story of how you cost Venice sixty-five billion U.S. dollars. If that happens, Heller, you'll go down in infamy. You'll be remembered as the most hated Italian in the history of the Republic. I wouldn't be surprised if angry crowds stoned you in the Piazza San Marco."

A lunatic, thought Heller. Worse. This character might be dangerous. He tried to catch the eye of his bellhops, but they still had their backs to him. What should he do? Reach for the phone? Excuse himself to go to the toilet?

He began to fidget. He had better stall until the bellhops came in. "I'm afraid . . . terribly afraid, sir, that none of this makes much sense to me."

"Vihari," said Godessohn, "perhaps you would like to try your luck with Signor Heller. He seems rather dense."

"Gladly, sir, most gladly."

The idle servant puffed up his chest and rubbed his smooth brown hands together. He fixed Heller with the smile that seemed to be a permanent part of his physiognomy.

"Signore," he said, "I have just figured out what's wrong with you. You are behaving stupidly because you don't know who this great man is. Well, let me introduce you. You have the honor of welcoming the world-famous South African philanthropist, Pieter Godessohn, the new Savior of Venice. He has come bearing a gift of sixty-five billion U.S. dollars – a gift, not a loan.

"But, Signore, the money hasn't yet changed hands. Imagine now, Signore, that *you* wished to make a large gift to someone and that someone treated you rudely. Imagine your dismay! Would you not reconsider? Yes, yes, of course you would. The great Mr. Godessohn is merely doing the same thing. He has been treated rudely by a representative of the city he came to save. He is telling you that he has almost had enough. If you do one more thing which displeases him, the Venice money will go to another cause."

"Thank you, Vihari," Godessohn said. "I hope everything now makes sense to you, Heller. Give me the key to my suite."

The telephone rang. Godessohn swiped the receiver from its cradle and passed it to the old man. He picked up a second telephone, punched into Heller's line and held the receiver between himself and his servant.

An excited voice boomed through the earpiece. "Hello, this is the mayor. Who's on the line?"

"Heller, Signor Mayor."

"Ah, yes. Tell me, Heller. Do you have a guest over there by the name of Godessohn?"

"Yes . . . yes, Signor Mayor, we do indeed."

"Good. I thought that's where he'd go. Listen, he's just held a press conference at the airport – caught us all a little by surprise. He's reviving the Passoni commission to save Venice. He's tossing a lot of money our way. *A lot* of money. I want him taken care of properly, understand? I want him treated better than visiting royalty. I want no expense spared. You're in a public capacity now, *capisc*? The city will reimburse the hotel for whatever expenses it incurs. The city will be able to *afford* to reimburse the hotel. Do I explain myself?"

"Yes, Signor Mayor," said Heller, thoroughly baffled. "I'll see that he gets very special treatment. You'll be happy to know we were planning on it as it was. He has a blue star beside his name in my reservation book."

"One more thing, Heller. Keep the press off his posterior. Tell them he's not at your hotel, and make them believe you. We don't need those bastards irritating him – not until we've got his money in the bank." The mayor chuckled gleefully and hung up.

Heller handed Godessohn the key and began to warble a chorus of servile apologies.

Godessohn told him to be quiet. He picked up both bags himself, brushed aside a returning bellhop and, with his servant in close pursuit, marched up the marble staircase to his suite.

Heller shook his head. Had he almost committed the faux pas of the century or was this some kind of a grandiose hoax? He did not know.

He was suddenly too tired to think. He walked to the end of the counter to fetch his COMPLETO sign, straightened up the pages of his damaged reservation book and stood facing the great glass doors of the entryway. Soon his left eye closed, and he drifted into a world of bittersweet dreams.

*   *   *

Heller dreamed that he was young again, handsome and full of hope. It was his first night on duty at the Zitti, and he stood watching the gondole disgorge their prestigious guests.

Ah, how important he felt, an orphan from the provinces who had risen to this high post! They streamed toward his desk, the cream of Europe, barons and counts, generals and statesmen, rich entrepreneurs with their mistresses and maids and rosy-cheeked children.

Heller opened his heart to this glittering procession of upper-class humanity. He wanted to be part of it or, if they wouldn't have him, at least to be noticed and appreciated. But when they came to his desk to register, they treated him no better than an insect to be crushed underfoot.

He heard a haughty baroness with high cheekbones and a tiny waist whisper to a decorated general that the receptionist was an orphan – yes, yes, she had it on good account. He must never be trusted with jewels or secrets. As you know, General, orphans are worse than Gypsies . . .

They went to their rooms, the noblemen and military heroes and rich entrepreneurs, leaving Heller, the despised orphan, to defend their castle and their values.

He was alone in the lobby, just as he had been alone in his childhood, alone as only an orphan can be, surrounded by elegant chandeliers and priceless oriental carpets and marble as cold as the inside of a tomb.

Heller stared sadly through the great glass doors. A misty, melancholy rain was falling, and fog sifted in amber halos around the gas lamps on the gondola dock.

He was a young man. His whole life lay ahead of him. What was he to do with it? Spend it defending those who thought him unworthy even of politeness? Or return to the country, where the people were poor but kind?

Ah, how the prospect of simple pleasures and honest emotions pulled at his heartstrings!

But tonight he was too tired to make a decision.

His right eye tracked the approach of a sleek black gondola slicing through the fog. When the boat came closer he recognized Ugo, a half century too old, standing on the stern, poling with a sleepy, rhythmic motion.

Ugo brought the boat to dock and extended his hand to the passenger. When she emerged from the shadows, she took Heller's breath away.

She was a young girl of the laboring classes, that much was clear. Beneath her raincoat, which was soaking wet, rumpled and much too short, hung the last few inches of a denim smock.

The girl had no luggage. She passed through the great glass doors, which Ugo held open for her, and came toward him.

Yes, come, angel. Come closer! She was an orphan, he knew it! Though she was beautiful beyond words, he could see that unmistakable confusion in her big dark eyes. And the sadness! How well he knew those feelings. She must not stay in the city! He must warn her! She must not squander her life serving a vain and corrupt upper crust.

They would go away together, she and he. They would return to the land, where life was simple and happy.

She came to the counter. When he tried to say something, he awoke with a jerk of his head. He had been dreaming again! He was not young. He looked at his hands. They were shriveled and flecked with liver spots. Something was wrong. He blinked and wiped the sleep from his left eye.

Yes, something was very wrong. The girl still stood before him.

"Are you all right, Signore?" she asked.

The voice pierced his heart. It was as sweet as birdsong, full of the motherly concern he had never known.

"Yes," sputtered old Heller, pulling himself erect. "Yes, I am quite all right.

Now the bad memories flooded over him. He had not gone back to the country as he should have. He had stayed on at the Zitti for a lifetime, defending those who despised him. The girl in his dream must have turned around and gone back. She had found the source of eternal youth, and now she had returned.

"My room has been reserved in the name of Signora Passoni," she said. "I was told that you would have a suitcase for me – Signor Passoni said he would send a suitcase."

Heller reached under the counter for his COMPLETO sign. What could he do? He could not allow a person dressed like a cleaning woman to check into the Senatorial Suite, even if the honorable Dante Passoni had made her reservation.

The wood when he touched it seemed to burn his fingers. He looked into Gina's eyes; tears came to his. He could not say no to her.

"Yes, Signora, everything is in order. Your suite is ready, and I've had your luggage sent up. My name is Heller, if you need anything. A moment of patience, please, and I'll buzz a bellhop to accompany you."

* * *

In his suite, Godessohn said, "Don't get too comfortable, Vihari. I would like you to return to the lobby as an observer."

"Observer, sir? Observer of what?"

"My latest invention. Go now. I have my communications system on the line."

"Certainly, sir. But aren't you going to tell me what this invention is supposed to do?"

"I don't think that will be necessary, Vihari."

* * *

While Gina was waiting for her bellhop, a man in a tan suit and maroon turban strolled into the lobby. He took a seat in one of the antique chairs, rubbed his slender brown hands together and smiled. He gave her the creeps.

* * *

From a 500-mile-long transmitter buried in the veld north of Johannesburg, low frequency electronic waves hummed undetected through the earth. They passed under the seas and entered the Italian power grid at Bari.

* * *

The telephone at the reception desk rang. Gina watched old Heller pick up the receiver.

The foreigner in the turban squirmed in his chair.

She heard Heller say, "Struck out? But why . . . why have

". . . I . . struck . . . "

The receiver fell from his shoulder and cracked on the marble floor. Heller grabbed his head as if he were trying to tear it off. He took a few tottering steps and collapsed face down.

Gina cried out for help.

"I'll get someone!" stammered the foreigner.

Gina ran behind the reception desk, kneeled and loosened the old man's collar. She put a hand on his forehead, but withdrew it instantly: his skull was as hot as a frying pan.

She looked at the telephone receiver lying on the floor beside him. A murder weapon? She made herself pick it up. It seemed to be a normal receiver, normal temperature.

The foreigner returned with the two bellhops.

"Touch his head," Gina cried. "Touch it! He's cooking!"

One of the bellhops started to reach out, then stopped. "It might be contagious," he said. "Stand back, please. I'll call the doctor."

"Poor old guy," the other bellhop said. "He never had a life outside of the hotel. No wife, no kids, no nothing."

"Well," said the foreigner, rubbing his hands together, "if he had to die, perhaps it is a very good thing that he died here. At least he wasn't alone."

"He was alone," whispered Gina, who had seen the orphan in him that he had seen in her.

CHAPTER THIRTEEN

Puzzo awoke with a start and stared at the message on his computer screen. All right, he thought, all right, I'll go do it now. There wasn't any need to hurry, but that message in front of him made him feel as though the Presence were looking over his shoulder, a feeling he could do without.

He snorted half a gram of coke, injected a syringe of benzedrine and pumped the long arms of his espresso maker. While he waited for the most potent of his three drugs to trickle out, he watched the green pool through his glass window.

It was calm and surgically clean, the way he liked things. That would change, he thought irritably, when the portal to the Lagoon opened. He imagined filthy brown water surging in ahead of the mechanical fish, a cascade of sewage and wine bottles and mutant crustaceans. Why couldn't the Presence have designed the delivery system so that the cargo would be picked up *outside* the refinery? He was going to have his hands full getting the pool cleaned up.

He drank his espresso and started toward the elevator. As he was walking past the first work station, his three drugs came on in a dizzying rush. He tottered, reached out for something to grab on to and knocked a monitor off a desk. It landed with a sharp crack on the tile floor.

Puzzo dropped into a chair and closed his eyes. The whirling dervish inside his head scooped up scenes from 30 years past and paraded them behind his pulsing lids.

He was a kid again in the slums of Naples. Narrow houses rose shimmering from the street, joined together like pastel segments of a windowed wall. He saw peeling paint and ramshackle shutters closed against the sun; he saw garbage on the ancient cobblestones and balconies all askew, like scaffolding about to collapse. He heard laundry flapping in the sea breeze – and remembered the night when old Nonno next door had jumped.

Why had he jumped, the kindly, white-haired grandfather who used to bring Puzzo hard caramels from the market? No idea, not then, not now. Puzzo, back from a clandestine mission, was slinking along the deserted street, hidden in the oily shadows of a Neapolitan night. The old man came out on his balcony, looked around to make sure he was alone . . . and jumped. When he hit, the crack of his head on the cobblestones reverberated endlessly, an echo trapped in the labyrinth of crumbling stone buildings, reverberated still, some 40 years later.

Puzzo realized with a surge of self-disgust that he was listening to the crack of the monitor he had knocked on to the tile floor. He heaved himself to his feet.

He was feeling better when he reached the elevator. But when he discovered that the elevator was at the other end of its shaft, his good mood vanished. What was going on? That South Tirolean yokel, Manfred, must have gone for an unauthorized ride.

Well, the Presence had made it clear what the punishment for that kind of irresponsible behavior was. Puzzo patted the 9 mm. automatic pistol in the shoulder holster beneath his tightly fitting jacket. He detested Manfred. He wouldn't mind a pretext to do away with him.

He pressed the "Return" button and watched the display above the door. The elevator was moving now, but it would take forever to arrive.

He strode over to Manfred's desk. Something hard and small crunched under the sole of his loafer. He reached down and picked up a tooth.

He glanced beyond the desk and felt his jaw drop: the bunker's spotless tile floor resembled an early morning Naples street scene. Pornographic photos were strewn about in great disorder, and a man lay unconscious, a capsized bottle in a puddle near his mouth.

Puzzo kicked Manfred in the side. The strong smell of plum

schnapps nearly made him retch. Disgusting how this Kraut abused alcohol. He kicked him again, harder. Manfred's head and feet jerked, but neither his torso nor his brain responded. What had he done? Drunk himself to death?

Puzzo rolled him over, breathing hard from the effort, and leaped back in shock when he saw the giant's face. Badly bruised eyes, split lips, nose broken and shoved to the side . . .

Porca Madonna, someone had gotten in here! Yes, of course, what had he been thinking? The tooth, the elevator. Jesus God in Heaven, he hadn't erased the computer records in his office yet!

Calm down, CALM DOWN! No one could break the codes needed to get into those files. He was all right. Something had gone wrong, but the consequences weren't disastrous. The intruders were probably in his office right now, trying to figure out the information security system. He'd catch them, dispose of them, conceal this minor bit of news from the Presence.

He shook Manfred again, screamed at him to get up and help. When Manfred did not move, Puzzo yanked out his pistol and emptied the magazine into his chest.

Feeling cleansed, he pressed the alarm button on Manfred's desk. His chief security guard, a man they called the Sicilian, answered. "You got trouble down there, Manfredo?"

"This is Puzzo. We've been hit. Seal the refinery, activate the antiaircraft units and issue Red Alert. Then get over to my office with half a dozen men. Be prepared to fight. The intruders might still be in there."

* * *

Dante couldn't believe it. With each file he searched, a piece in the puzzle fell into place – and what a puzzle it was!

He glanced at his watch. He had been working at the computer in Puzzo's office for 40 minutes; it felt like 40 seconds. He knew he should begin thinking about his departure, but he couldn't tear himself away, not when so much more remained to be learned.

The bomb in the green pool *was* thermonuclear. It had been built here in the refinery from scraps of plutonium collected all around the world. At 58 megatons, it was among the most powerful warheads ever constructed, powerful enough to destroy a lot more than just Venice. And it was being picked up by some sort of a mini-submarine at nine o'clock the next morning, the hour of peak boat traffic on the Lagoon.

That was what he knew. What he didn't know kept him at the keyboard, oblivious to the passing of time. What did they intend to do with the thing? Who *were* they? Most important, was there an emergency command hidden in this morass of technical data that would allow him to disarm the bomb from where he sat? If so, he would do just that. Then he would assemble a team of top CRC professionals to wait for the bomb to be picked up. They would follow the castrated monster until it led them to its makers – and to Uncle Vittorio's murderers . . .

He opened a file named UNFORESEEN CONTINGENCIES, but an ominous purr interrupted him before he could delve into it.

Madonna, the elevator was approaching! He hadn't heard it leave, must have been too engrossed in what he was doing. Now, already, it was returning.

The purple "in transit" light above the door went out, the green "arrival" light came on. The elevator door began to open.

No choice, there wasn't time to turn off the computer.

He ran to the window through which he had entered and climbed out on to the ledge. As he reached back in to close the blinds, he caught a glimpse of Puzzo stepping into his office.

Outside, the situation was no better. Two high-performance jeeps filled with guards were careening down the raised concrete road toward the administration building. He shrank back in the shadows and watched.

Some of the guards toted large-caliber machine guns, their ammunition belts glistening in the rain. Others carried RPGs or Stinger antiaircraft missiles, those ancient but still deadly heatseeking darts that could shoot down a jet fighter.

As soon as the jeeps stopped, their hood-mounted searchlights went to work. It wasn't long until the dazzling white beams congregated on the administration building, crisscrossing nervously as they lapped at the concrete walls.

Up, up, a floor at a time, pausing at every window.

When they reached him, his gold vest would sparkle like a chest of spilled treasure.

He parted the blinds and peeked inside. Puzzo stood at the computer screen, an automatic pistol drawn.

The lights came closer . . . third story, forth story.

At last Puzzo turned away. Dante slipped back inside the office and ducked behind an armchair. Puzzo was distracted by something; he didn't hear, didn't notice.

The lights flickered through the blinds, casting eerie shadows across black marble dog statues.

Puzzo bent over to examine the mud and gravel on his floor. The searchlights moved elsewhere.

Now!

Dante slipped soundlessly out the window and started up the rope he had left. As he climbed to the roof, he saw the guards running from their jeeps toward the building entrance.

A lucky break! If he managed to get his ultralight airborne before they spotted him, he might have enough of a head start to escape.

* * *

Okay, okay, thought Puzzo, shaking uncontrollably. Things were starting to make a little more sense. That filthy slick of mud and gravel pointed in two directions: toward the shower and toward the window. They had apparently entered through the window. Must've descended from the roof and gone into the shower to clean up.

He thought he heard something and spun around, tightly gripping his gun. His heart pounded, his ears screeched, but there was no one. The office was empty.

This was bad, a lot worse than he'd thought. The intruders had somehow gotten hold of the security codes. This was clear from what they had left up on the computer screen; and from the fact that they'd been able to ride the elevator to the bunker.

Jesus Holy Madonna, why hadn't he come up here the instant he'd gotten the message from the Presence? And who had betrayed him, who had given the intruders the security codes? There was only one person he ever allowed in his office alone. That person was Gina.

Yes, she had to be the one. They must have schooled her in exactly what to look for. Come to think of it, she'd been acting strange these last few days . . . nervous, suspicious. If he got out of this thing intact, he was going to punish her in a way that would make Manfred's death seem almost gentle . . .

What now? If they were still here, the Sicilian and his men would take care of them when they arrived. Nothing to do but wait and think – and hope that the intruders had not yet left the refinery.

He followed the slick to the window and pulled up the Venetian blinds. The glass was open, the ledge was damp. He stuck his head and pistol out into the rainy night.

No one to the sides, no one above or below. He noted with relief that the Sicilian's jeeps were parked beside his Mercedes in the lot five stories down.

He decapitated the marble wolfhound statue on his desk and took a double snort of cocaine.

Better, much better. He had himself under control.

At the window again, he watched orange flames from a by-products stack flicker on the sagging overcast.

And then he saw it: a great black bird swooping down toward the parking lot, passing so close to the side of the building its wheels almost touched him. Puzzo leaped back in terror, the wind from the prop whipping his face.

The intruders! This was their escape! They were diving from the roof to get up enough speed to fly! Well, they weren't going to fly very far.

Recovering quickly from his shock, he opened fire with his automatic pistol.

The craft was still diving toward the parking lot, still gathering speed. It pulled up directly over his limousine and climbed steeply as it flew toward the windowless building where the Pakistanis had stayed.

The shots from his gun rang in Puzzo's ears, amplified by the screaming rush of cocaine. His hand was shaking violently again, he'd already peppered everything but the plane. Didn't matter, didn't matter, his men would bring it down.

As the black ultralight disappeared around the corner of the building, Puzzo got a good view of its pilot, who was momentarily illuminated by the glow of a distant stack fire. He was a man wearing a gold vest that looked like it belonged at a knights' ball. He did not stand a chance.

The Sicilian and his men burst into the office. "Check the shower," Puzzo hollered, his voice breaking.

Two men kicked open the door and came out with a black body suit, a shaving kit and a couple of nylon bags.

"So there's just one!" Puzzo shouted. "Just one intruder! He flew off the roof in an ultralight about ten seconds ago!"

"Sure you're not seeing things, boss?" the Sicilian said.

Puzzo wiped his nose with his sleeve, leaving a chalk line of cocaine on the dark material of his suit. He stared at it for a split second. "Don't look at me like that," he said. "I know what I saw.

The fool will be an easy target. He's wearing his own spotlight – a gold vest."

"A gold vest?" the Sicilian grumbled. "You sure you're all right, Mr. Puzzo?"

"I'm sure. Let's go." They started down the stairs. "Are your men equipped with their antiaircraft weapons?"

"Stingers, machine guns, canon, RPGs. Don't worry, boss. This guy isn't going anywhere."

Fourth floor, third floor, shoes scuffing on tile, big men rasping for breath, shoulder-slung weapons clattering on walls.

"How fast will your vehicles go?" Puzzo snapped.

"They're Alfa Romeo four-wheel drives, boss. One forty, easy."

Second floor, first floor, out into the night.

"Good," said Puzzo, running toward the Sicilian's jeep. "That plane I saw can't possibly do more than thirty knots. I want it shot down before it reaches the perimeter."

* * *

Night closed around Dante as he flew away from the stack flames and light-ringed distillation columns. Not wanting to make himself an easy target – a black crow silhouetted against an orange sky – he stayed low.

So far, so good. He was now approaching the swampy northeast quadrant of the refinery, where huge unlit byproduct tanks loomed like shipwrecks in the murky darkness. If his luck held, he would soon be beyond the electric fence and out over the Lagoon.

A concrete service road slipped beneath his wings. He flew over slimy rain lakes topped with splotches of crude; over mud flats, smooth and barren as a seal skin; around the rusted shells of abandoned storage tanks, some still simmering with noxious chemical residues.

The Dutch engine droned steadily, no highs, no lows, nothing Italian about it.

He flicked on his radio mike. "Luigi, come in."

"Signore! Holy Madonna! Where are you?"

"What do you mean, where am I? Haven't you been watching me through the infrared scope?"

"No, Signore, no! I had to go back to Giuseppe's for fuel. When I returned, your ultralight had left the roof of the administration building. I couldn't find you on radar, so I was forced to assume . . ."

"No assumptions, please, Luigi. You'll find me somewhere in the northeast corner of the refinery, flying rather low. I'll be approaching the fence shortly."

"Signore . . . I'm so . . . relieved. There, there, I see you. Signore! What are those vehicles chasing you?"

Dante heard them before he saw them, big Alfa engines revving near the red line. "*Merda.*"

"I'm coming down to divert them, Signore! I'll blast them with the hyperbolic horn!"

"You'll stay exactly where you are. They've got missiles, Luigi. You'll be a fireball within seconds."

"What about you, Signore? WHAT ABOUT YOU?"

"Keep your voice down, please. I'm trying to figure that out."

Bright lights brushed the tank to his left. He banked to the right and flew behind another, larger tank. The jeep motors stopped. The night was silent but for the drone of his engine, and the patter of rain on his wings, and the rustle of Luigi's breathing in the speaker.

Lights stroked the clouds above him, and stroked the sealskin mud of the swamp beyond. He cut his speed to near stalling velocity, hoping to use the protection of the tank as long as possible. From the compartment beside him, he pulled out his three magnesium emergency flares.

The searchlights extinguished just as he flew into the open.

Motors roared to life, and the jeeps sped off toward the fence at the refinery border.

They had passed beneath him without seeing him! They were in front of him!

The briny smell of the nearby Lagoon strengthened his determination. He was close, so close.

He watched his pursuers pull up to the fence and turn their jeeps around. Dammit, they were setting up another search post. He couldn't head back toward the center of the refinery complex: other teams would be out looking for him by now.

What should he do? Land and go it on foot? He glanced at the oily muck beneath him. Bad idea.

The searchlights began their crisscrossing hunt. He drifted behind an enormous tank . . . and smelled ethylene!

"Luigi!"

"What, Signore? WHAT?"

"Do you see me?"

"Like a black dog squashed on the road."

"The tank I'm approaching – is it covered?"

"Yes, Signore, but one of the roof panels is off. Looks like it's undergoing repairs."

"I am saved."

"No, Signore, you are doomed. You just flew out of the shadows."

Dante gave full throttle and took on altitude, the steepest climb angle he could maintain without stalling. A searchlight beam skittered over his wing, then leaped back and stuck to him. He heard excited shouts. Another beam nailed him in the vest. He grabbed the first of his flares and waited.

When he saw a twin flash near one of the jeeps, he yanked the ring off the flare and fired it into space.

Two Stingers came hissing at him, chose the hot anus of the flare over his ultralight's cool electric engine and arched up in a graceful curve. They collided as they intercepted the flare, filling the sky with fireworks.

Two more Stingers came after him, spewing corkscrew trails of smoke. With his second flare he sent them in a wild boomerang back toward the jeeps. The guards dove for cover. He reached behind his seat for his parafoil.

He focused on the tank as he struggled into the shoulder harnesses. He was high enough now to see the opening on the roof.

Steady . . . steady, this was a shot he couldn't afford to miss.

He fired the final flare. It disappeared into the opening. He grasped the controls tightly.

The ethylene tank exploded with a deafening roar. Burning debris showered his wings and set them on fire. Smoke from the violent explosion billowed skyward. The firestorm sucked him irresistibly toward its center, pulling him into a maelstrom of blistering heat and gagging vapors.

* * *

Dead! Dante was dead!

Luigi doubled over with grief as he saw the ultralight flutter like a burning toy out of the smoke.

The guards opened up with their machine guns, and soon the plane was pirouetting earthward, raining pieces as it fell.

It hit on the road, did a somersault and came to rest with its surviving wheel pointed at the sky. As they approached in their jeeps, the guards kept a thick stream of tracers whistling into the wreckage.

Poor Dante. Luigi was glad his mother had passed away last year and wouldn't have to hear the news.

"Kiyo," he said. "Kiyo, can you hear me?"

"Yes, Luigi."

"Dante didn't make it. He's . . . Kiyo, he's gone!"

CHAPTER FOURTEEN

Holding his last breath of fresh air, Dante clutched his parafoil rip cord ring and guided his ultralight into the angry, up-rushing column of smoke. When he reached its turbulent center, he jumped out and pulled the cord.

With his arms wrapped tightly around his head, he plummeted feet first toward the savage blaze in the ethylene tank. Before he had fallen very far, the parafoil opened with a yank. Soon he was no longer falling but soaring skyward, his chute riding the inferno's mighty updraft, rising like a runaway balloon inside the billowing column of smoke.

The searing heat gradually decreased, and it wasn't long until Dante heard rain drops sizzling on his gold vest. Cautiously he sniffed the early morning air. His nostrils were singed, but not so badly he couldn't smell the briny breath of the Lagoon.

He opened his eyes and breathed deeply of the fresh air. He was out of the smoke and in the clouds now, still invisible to his assailants as he drifted slowly through the cool gray mist. The wind blew from the southwest. He would come down over the Lagoon where Luigi, loyal Luigi, would be hovering to pick him up.

He started to descend. When he broke through the overcast, he could see the refinery behind him. Sirens screamed and firefighting equipment lumbered toward the tank he had torched.

Below stretched the placid water, its blackness broken only by the lights of distant fishing boats.

Lower, lower.

He listened for the comforting sound of the helicopter, but heard only the sirens from the refinery and the plaintive caws of the gulls.

Had Luigi lost sight of him in the smoke? Had he let pessimism cloud his vision? Whatever had happened, it was beginning to look as though Dante would have to make his own arrangements for getting to shore.

Squinting into the penumbra, he spotted an unlit fishing boat near the point where he would come down. If he maneuvered just right, he might be able to land on its deck and spare himself a cold bath. He altered his course, curved a few degrees to the right and smiled: he was on target for a perfect landing.

The boat, he could see, had a makeshift cabin of plywood. On the roof, beside a blackened chimney, was a radio antenna. Excellent. He would contact Luigi and have him back here in no time.

Fifty feet . . . 40 . . . 30.

A grizzled old fisherman hobbled out of the cabin, hooking up his suspenders as he surveyed the water.

"Buongiorno," Dante said, touching down softly behind him. The codger must have been hard of hearing. Dante unstrapped his shoulder harnesses and let the parafoil crumple in the water. He straightened the lapels of his suit jacket and tapped the fisherman on the shoulder.

When the old man saw the gold vest, he screamed and went for his knife. Dante relieved him of it as gently as possible. "I'm not going to hurt you," he said. "I just need to use your radio. RADIO, understand?"

Evidently not. When Dante turned toward the cabin, the old man hurled himself overboard.

"Very well," said Dante, shaking his head. "As you wish." He tossed a rubber dinghy in after him and went to find the radio. It had been removed. The antenna wire now served as a clothesline, and was hung with socks and underwear.

Not to worry, he told himself. At least he had a boat.

He started the engine, which coughed and sputtered feebly, and set out toward shore. No matter where he placed the throttle, no matter what he did with the mixture, he couldn't get his speed above three knots.

Another wimpy motor: he was beginning to sorely miss the

Lamborghini.

He hadn't gone far when he remembered that Graziella Calvino had come to Venice for a big convention of women scientists she had organized. In yesterday's paper, he had seen a photograph of her 100-meter yacht docking amid a male protest on the other side of the Giudecca Canal.

Graziella spent at least four months a year on board that behemoth yacht, running her company from sea. The vessel, he had learned from Kiyo's artful spying, was technically better equipped than her central offices in Milan.

Graziella would be staying at the Cipriani Hotel, she always did when she came to Venice. When she learned how urgent the situation was, she wouldn't mind that he had borrowed her yacht for a few hours . . .

He turned back the other way. Passing the old fisherman, now safely in his dinghy, Dante offered him a lift. But the man paddled frantically in the other direction.

Well, he'd survive – if the bomb didn't go off. And if it did, he would be no worse off than anyone else within 50 miles.

* * *

It was getting on eight o'clock when the ramshackle little boat chugged up to the great white yacht. Dante climbed the side ladder, hoisted himself aboard and walked along the gleaming teak deck toward the cabin entrance. Before he reached the door, Graziella Calvino came out in a pink bathrobe that showed the usual slice of cleavage. She was carrying breakfast on a tray.

"Bull Balls! How thoughtful of you to pay me a visit. Did they tell you at the Cipriani I had decided to overnight here?"

"Graziella . . . ugh, yes. Listen, darling, we're in the midst of a terrible crisis. I need to borrow your yacht."

She put down her tray and looked at him suspiciously. "What have you been up to, Dante. What is the meaning of your costume? I must say, it's not very attractive on you. And all that filthy face paint! You look more like a chimney sweep than a medieval baron."

He rubbed a hand to his cheek and stared at the black soot on his fingers. "So that's what he was afraid of."

"Excuse me?"

"The fisherman whose boat I borrowed. I couldn't understand what frightened him into jumping overboard. Graziella, I don't have time for a lot of explaining, so I'll get directly to the point. There's a fifty-eight megaton warhead in the refinery across the Lagoon. It was built there by ex-Soviet scientists and a Pakistani engineering firm.

"In a little over an hour, it's being picked up by a mini-submarine. This is all the work of the men who killed my uncle. They must have feared his Commission would conduct inspections that would reveal their secret . . . so they murdered him. I started out just looking for the killers. But, Graziella, it seems I've stumbled on to a whole lot more.

"I don't know where that warhead is going or what they plan to do with it. All I know is that we must locate and follow the minisub coming to pick it up. With your yacht – and my butler's helicopter – I can do that. Otherwise, I'm helpless."

"You, helpless?" Graziella shrugged her shoulders, sipped her cappuccino and licked the foam from her full red lips. "So where's your loyal butler right now? It would appear you've wasted a lot of time putting around in that primitive sloop."

"My plane was destroyed over the refinery. Luigi must have seen it go down and drawn some premature conclusions. I'll radio him right now and get him out over the Lagoon. We can continue our negotiations for my use of your yacht as soon as I've spoken with him."

Graziella took a bite of her croissant. "Aren't you forgetting a little something? Last time we spoke was in a restaurant in Genoa. I came to ask you for my fair share of the Russian deal, and you fled in a most cowardly fashion. Before we turn to *your* requests, we're going to have to reach an accord on mine."

"Graziella, for God's sake! How can you pick this hour to discuss a personal matter between the two of us!"

"You stole the Russian deal from me, Passoni, and you know it. That's why you ran away. You didn't want to discuss equity and fairness with a woman! You're a male pig like the rest of them."

"That is *not* why I ran. I had just received the news of my uncle's murder. You saw Kiyo come to me with a message. And *you* had no right to do what you did to my car. I should have billed you for the repair. It wasn't cheap, you know."

"Well, Dante, I was prepared for an amicable chat over cappuccino, and perhaps even a trip to the bedroom if you managed to behave yourself. But it seems your swollen male ego once more intrudes. I am speaking this afternoon in front of professional women from all over Italy. They will enjoy hearing about your puerile antics. Please leave now. I have some important business to attend to."

He took her arm. She jerked free, but he grabbed it again, more forcefully this time. "Madonna, haven't you heard anything I've said? This is a crisis. I need your yacht to prevent what could easily become the greatest human disaster since the War."

"My dear Dante, do you wish to hear my analysis of the situation?"

"No."

"There is no danger to Venice. Even if the warhead exists, it is being transported elsewhere. We Italians can't worry about the world's problems; we have enough of our own. What's driving you is not your concern for humanity but your ego. As male head of the Passoni clan, your honor depends on avenging your uncle's death. I liked your uncle. I'm sorry he's gone. But I don't care to be a player in your little male game."

Dante glanced at his watch: three minutes after eight. He was going to have to subdue her and take the yacht by force if this nonsense continued.

She must have read his mind. He grimaced in frustration when she took a gold Beretta from her nightgown pocket and aimed it just below his belt. "Don't even think about it, Passoni."

"Okay, Graziella, okay. I'm desperate. I admit it. What can I do to secure your cooperation?"

"Give the Russian deal to Altel."

"But that's forty billion dollars."

"What's your answer?"

"All right, for God's sake, it's yours. Now I'm going to call Luigi."

"Not until I draw up the papers and you sign them. And there's something else, Dante, something very important."

"Yes . . ."

"Tell me how you plan to proceed with this operation."

"I'm going to put Luigi up above the Lagoon with his infrared and ultraviolet scopes. He'll be able to find and track the minisub. You've got diving gear on board, don't you?"

"Of course."

"Good. How long is the yacht's towing cable?"

"A half nautical mile."

"All right, listen. I'm going to devise a way to get that cable attached to the minisub before it leaves the Lagoon. I'll follow it unobtrusively with your yacht. When we reach the open seas, I'll winch the sub on board and have my experts disarm the warhead."

"Sorry, Passoni. If the bomb is for real, the publicity you'll get by disarming it will more than offset my earnings from the Russian deal. If you want my help, it'll have to be on my terms. Want to hear them?"

Dante looked at his watch. "Hurry up."

"I shall, Dante. You hook this bomb-bearing fish and then

you bow out. I and the women of Altel will take it from there. We have the expertise and courage to disarm the warhead. We will make the women of Italy proud to be women. And it will give me a stunning announcement to make at the convention. Don't look so defensive, Dante. I know what you're thinking, and you're wrong. I'll share any information with you that will help you capture your uncle's killers."

"Graziella, in the name of the Holy Mother, I've been working on this mystery day and night. You don't know the first thing about it."

"I'm a fast learner – or have you forgotten? Now make up your mind. There's nothing as annoying as a well-endowed male who can't make decisions."

"All right, Graziella, I accept – with one condition. You allow a CRC representative to be on board the yacht with you at all times, to be privy to all information and to report freely to me on all developments."

"I will allow one *nontechnical* CRC representative. I don't want you coming back later saying your one token male was responsible for the heroic feat of my women."

"Would Luigi be acceptable?"

She threw back her head and laughed. "That atavism? He'll do just fine, Dante. During the slow moments, I'll make sure his archaic attitude toward women receives a thorough adjustment. Go on, now. Radio him. I'll draw up our agreement transferring the Russian deal to Altel."

* * *

"Signore! I thought you were – "

"I'm fine, Luigi."

"But . . . but how – "

"If you had had enough faith in me to stick around, you'd know. As it is, you nearly caused me a very unpleasant early morning bath. Now, I want you to get yourself back up over the

Lagoon, same altitude, same coordinates. Some sort of a mini-submarine I'm not yet able to describe is going to approach the refinery around nine o'clock. That's in less three quarters of an hour, Luigi. I'm counting on you to locate the sub through your ultraviolet scope. When you spot it, radio me *subito* on the usual frequency."

"But . . . Signore, where are you now?"

"I am having breakfast with Graziella Calvino aboard her yacht. She's very generously volunteered to help me snare and capture the sub."

"No, Signore! Not Graziella Calvino! Why couldn't you have chosen someone else? She's nothing but trouble."

"I think, Luigi, that it would be wise for you to change your opinion of her. If the snaring goes well, you'll be going to sea with her. I would like you to take off at once."

"What? WHAT? You're going to throw your trusted friend and servant to the dogs? I should have guessed it, Signore. You've come back from the dead only to torture those who loved you."

"Luigi, please."

CHAPTER FIFTEEN

VENICE SAVED: that's what this morning's newspaper had announced in three-inch-high headlines. Vihari stood on the balcony of the Zitti Palace's Presidential Suite, high above the water, wondering if his boss was really going to spend 65 billion dollars on this dump of a city. He hoped not.

It was just after sunrise. The storm had passed. The air, though it stank, was pleasantly warm, and the sky was pale blue.

This was a big improvement over the weather last night, thought Vihari, but how could he enjoy it with all these nerve-jangling noises rising from the Grand Canal? A never-ending procession of boats sloshed beneath his balcony, their engines gurgling and roaring. On the hotel's gondola dock, a group of ill-bred boatmen shouted and sang like drunk opera performers.

Noise, so much noise, and at such an early hour! His three-year-old son, he thought, would feel right at home here.

He squinted into the golden light. Spires and red tile roofs stretched from one hazy horizon to the other. Across the Lagoon he could see the high stacks of the refinery. It was inconceivable to him that his boss had manufactured a warhead in there that was going to change the climate of the United States.

But he had; and in a few hours, Godessohn's gift to the Land of the Brave would be on its way.

Vihari imagined amber waves of grain turning to grain dust in the red heat of the drought. He imagined verdant Ohio, which he had visited while he was a student, baking mercilessly beneath a killer sun.

Ah, yes, this was a very evil thing for the Philanthropist to do. But Vihari had to admit that the perverse experiment excited him.

In the short time since he had learned Godessohn's true identity, Vihari's life had been full of mental and emotional upheavals. At first, it had seemed like the end of the world. No longer. His boss had tortured him, had *forced* him to become his assistant. Vihari had lost his freedom of choice. But in its place, he had gained something he had never known: freedom from responsibility. It wasn't as bad a trade as he might have imagined.

What would he do? The only thing he *could* do. Follow his orders and try not to make any dumb mistakes that would irritate his boss.

If he proceeded wisely, things would continue to improve. When Godessohn died, Vihari would use his massive inheritance to undo some of the damage to humanity his boss had done. Or maybe he would just go live in peace somewhere – with a lot of servants he could order around.

He puffed up his chest, crossed his arms in front of him and gazed out over the water. In school he had read how the Doges, Venice's medieval rulers, stood on balconies like this one watching the republic's merchant ships return home laden with goods from Northern Europe, Africa and Asia. The goods, the wealth of Venice, would be unloaded, and with them the Doges' enemies, who would be led across the Bridge of Sighs to their dungeons.

Those Doges had been impressive men, he thought, but they had not been as powerful, nor as intelligent, as his boss. For a brief moment, in spite of the suffering and humiliation Godessohn had put him through, Vihari felt privileged to be associated with such an awesome human being – even if Godessohn's professional objectives were not exactly above reproach.

The fragrance of some exotic perfume wafted by. Vihari glanced at the neighboring balcony and recognized the girl who had been at the reception desk late last night when the old clerk had struck out. She had been dressed very badly then, but now, in an elegant pink robe, she reminded him of a beautiful young countess.

He wondered idly whether his second incarnation would provide him with the opportunity to sample beautiful women such as this one. He had always wanted to, but had always lacked the nerve to approach them. That, he supposed, was why he had ended up with plump, homely Tamina.

He turned toward her and smiled, placing his hands behind him on the balcony railing in what he hoped was an urbane pose. His fingers closed around a wet, warm, snail-like substance. He recoiled in disgust, his smile wilting, when he saw what it was: fresh pigeon shit! He wiped it on his handkerchief and glanced toward the beautiful girl again, smiling sheepishly. But she had already gone inside.

* * *

"Vihari," called Godessohn, "come here, please."

"Yes, sir."

Vihari stopped beside the breakfast table, where his boss sat picking a scrap of prosciutto from between his teeth. "You wish, sir?"

Godessohn pushed his coffee cup aside. "Vihari, it's almost eight o'clock. There are a few loose ends to tie up before we go sightseeing. I thought you might want to watch."

"Absolutely, sir."

"Then bring me the telephone."

Godessohn picked up the receiver. On the touch tone dial, he hammered out a 78-digit number.

"What are you doing, sir?"

"Establishing a link with my communications system. Turn on the TV, channel one, no sound."

"Yes, sir."

The screen was snow.

Godessohn hammered away at the telephone in staccato bursts, using it as a computer keyboard. Soon, the interior of a large office materialized on the TV screen. Vihari wanted to inquire after the meaning of all the black marble dog statues. But fearing the question would reveal his ignorance, he remained silent.

Godessohn sat back and nodded toward the balcony. "This

live television image is coming to us from the refinery across the Lagoon. You may have seen the refinery when you were on the balcony."

"Yes, sir, as a matter of fact, I did."

"You are presently looking at the work place of the refinery owner, Mr. Puzzo. Your explanation please, Vihari, of how I was able to bring this image to our television screen."

"Yes, sir. Very ingenious, sir. You instructed your communications system beneath the South African veld to tap into a camera already in place in Mr. Puzzo's office – perhaps a security camera. Using some procedure I am not familiar with, you then modified the camera's signals so that we may receive them here."

"That is correct, Vihari. It was a trivial exercise, unlike the intercontinental transmission of microwaves over telephone lines."

"Microwaves, sir? Is *that* how you struck out the old clerk last night?"

"Yes, Vihari."

"But how – "

"We'll discuss the technical details later. Right now our time is short. There's Puzzo – see him at the coffee machine? I've gathered his medical records, always a wise idea when you enlist someone into your service. He was involved in a motor scooter crash when he was a young man. He came away with a severe skull fracture. His cranium was repaired with a stainless steel plate, standard surgical procedure back then. Let's give him a call."

"A microwave call?"

Godessohn smiled and pounded on the buttons. "Watch closely now. When he answers his phone, he'll hear a recorded message from South Africa – untraceable, of course. Simultaneously he'll receive what Heller got last night – a dense stream of microwaves through the ear. With Puzzo the effect should be even more rapid than it was with Heller: in approximately four seconds, the steel plate in his head will become hot enough to boil his brain."

Puzzo, who had been pulling on the twin handles of his espresso machine, heard the telephone and jerked upright. He hurried to the desk, his face drawn and tense. He reached for the receiver, but drew back his hand before he touched it.

Godessohn frowned. "The man looks sick. He's nervous about something. Go on, Puzzo, answer. We don't have all morning."

Vihari stared wide-eyed as Puzzo finally lifted the receiver to his ear. His lips formed the two syllables of the Italian hello. His brow furrowed as he listened impatiently to the message.

And then, without warning, his eyes crossed. He staggered toward his desk with his feet tangled in the phone line and the receiver still clutched in his hand. Terrible convulsions racked his body, like the onslaught of an epileptic fit.

Vihari's jaw dropped when he saw a brown ring appear above Puzzo's eyebrows. Puzzo tottered crazily for another grotesque instant as the ring went from brown to black. Then he pitched forward and fell. His limp head struck one of the marble dogs.

CRACK!

Vihari stiffened: this was a silent movie, but he was sure he had heard the sound that went with the image.

Godessohn resumed his telephone typing.

Vihari, whose breakfast rumbled in his stomach as if it were about to come up, bit the inside of his lip.

A bunker with a great, multicolored flow diagram appeared on the screen.

Godessohn activated first one and then another of the many security cameras, examining the bunker from different angles. His final angle, from above the elevator, seemed to give him pause.

Vihari could see why. Sprawled on the floor was a big blond man, his chest shot full of holes.

"Sir, who is – "

"Just a moment. This was not part of the plan." Godessohn typed furiously. The camera zoomed in for a close-up, revealing an overturned schnapps bottle and a heap of pornographic photos.

"That, Vihari, was Puzzo's top security man at the refinery. Puzzo must have shot him for drinking on the job. Let me show you one more thing."

The green pool housing the bomb came into focus. "Soon, Vihari, my fish will enter that pool through the portal you see at the bottom left of the screen. The warhead will be picked up and taken to its destination. Now let's move to another spot."

Furious typing.

The TV screen divided into four squares – four scenes unfolding simultaneously.

In the lower left corner Vihari saw an enormous Sheik, reclining half-naked on a bed of pillows.

In the upper left corner he saw a tanker's bridge, where an Arab captain was holding watch over the Adriatic.

In the upper right corner he saw the bridge of a great battleship. It was populated with clean-cut American sailors – the kind of young men, he thought, whose families would fry in next summer's Great American Drought. Beyond the bridge, Vihari could see the foredeck, with its reconnaissance plane and enormous 16-inch gun turrets.

In the lower right corner was a radar screen, its circulating line sweeping over multiple blips.

"You'll enjoy this little piece of entertainment," Godessohn said. "The scale is one inch to twenty miles. That yellow blip you see on radar is the American battleship New Jersey, back in service for a third – and perhaps final – time. The red blip is the tanker Donatello. It is carrying the Sheik who assisted me in my operations, the Russian nuclear scientists whom I employed when their country opted for the free market, and each and every one of the Pakistani engineers who worked in the refinery. When the Donatello was last in dry dock, I had her hull packed with plastique explosives.

"You will notice that the ships will pass within roughly fifteen miles of one another; or would if I allowed them to continue on their present courses. But, Vihari, I shall not allow that. I am going to take over both helms."

"You . . . are . . . excuse me, sir?"

"Old technology. The device with which I shall steer the ships is a modification of a little unit called 'the Mongoose' that sent NTR Flight 31 into Mont Blanc seventeen years ago – and set me free. In tandem with my communications system, the Mongoose is capable of producing a lot of interesting 'deviant' behavior. Perhaps we'll fly the next American space shuttle, Vihari, or have some fun with test launches of America's next generation of anti-ballistic missiles. Imagine a multi-billion dollar projectile that insists on coming down in midtown Manhattan regardless of where it takes off or where it's aimed."

"Incredible . . . incredible."

"Hardly. Your attention please. I'm going to lock the tanker on a ram course with the New Jersey. Let's see how the Americans react."

Godessohn returned to his typing. Soon, the tanker captain was spinning the wheel in one direction while the Donatello veered in the other.

"Look here now, Vihari." Godessohn tapped the screen with a thick finger.

In the upper right quadrant, the American sailors noticed the approaching blip of the Donatello on their radar screen. A circle of officers gathered, there was a brief conference and a decision was reached. The battleship launched its reconnaissance plane, which started out in the direction of the tanker and suddenly turned toward Turkey.

Godessohn laughed. "The two ships are now eight miles from one another and closing. The battleship has opted for evasive action."

Chaos broke out on the bridge as the New Jersey defied its captain's input and continued on a ram path with the tanker.

In quadrant number one, the Sheik had gotten an alert. He arrived on the bridge of the tanker, his bell shaped jowls shaking with each word he spoke. He wrestled the wheel away from the captain.

Godessohn laughed again. "Five miles and closing, Vihari. Our players can probably see each other now. It appears that the Americans are going to use force."

Vihari watched the New Jersey's great 16-inch guns pivot and fire. The shells dropped into the water and exploded so near the battleship's hull that towering geysers were visible on the screen.

Godessohn roared with laughter, slapping his thighs. "Dead powder, Vihari. I ordered it for them." He pointed again. "This blip is the aircraft carrier Vincennes. It appears that the New Jersey has asked it to hit the tanker from the air. I have, of course, prepared for this contingency."

Vihari gaped at the screen. Twelve smaller, swifter blips, obviously jet aircraft, moved away from the carrier and turned toward the tanker.

The blips suddenly curved away to the southwest.

Godessohn laughed so hard tears came to his eyes.

"Baghdad!" he shouted, and slapped his thighs again. "The sorry bastards are locked on a one-way course to Baghdad! They will be ejected over the city! Welcome to Iraq, boys. Let's see how well you get on with the insurgents. Now, Vihari, look over here or you'll miss something."

Open mouths and terrified eyes populated the bridge of the Donatello. It was evident that some of the crew were preparing to jump.

"They'll escape!" cried Vihari, caught up in the emotion of the moment. "Sir, they'll escape, and your crime will not be perfect!"

Godessohn wiped away tears of laughter. "Have you no faith in me, Vihari? A special device I had built into the tanker's hull is presently electrifying the surrounding water."

Everything; he had thought of everything!

Vihari struggled to watch all four screens at once. "What's going to happen? Are they going to ram?"

"I don't know, Vihari. It depends on whether the Americans have shells from an older batch. If not, we'll have to involve the Vincennes. That would be no less entertaining."

Massive laughter. "Look here at the radar. They're only two miles apart – and closing."

Vihari watched the New Jersey's guns, almost horizontal now, belch smoke. They had evidently found good ammunition. In the upper left quadrant of the TV screen, a violent impact shook the Donatello's bridge. An instant later, the entire quadrant went blank.

"That's all," Godessohn said, his laughter slowly winding down. "The show's over. The explosives in the tanker's hull went off. The ship and all its parts, including my cameras, have been destroyed."

He daubed his forehead with his handkerchief and glanced at his watch. "Now, Vihari, we'll make one more microwave call and be on our way."

"To whom, sir?"

"A woman who works for Puzzo. It's possible she knows too much."

A bedroom appeared on the screen in response to Godessohn's typing. The bed was made with a simple white eiderdown, and the shutters were open.

"Where is this, sir?"

"The girl's room inside Puzzo's villa. It appears she's

already up. That's good: we won't have to waste time rousing her."

He switched to another of the villa's security cameras, this one in the drawing room. A telephone on an oval-shaped marble-top table came into focus.

Godessohn said, "She might take longer to die than the others, Vihari. Not everyone has a steel plate in his head, like Puzzo, or is as decrepit as old Heller."

"How much longer, sir?"

"Why don't you time her? It would be interesting to know."

"Very well, sir."

Vihari held up his watch without taking his eyes from the screen. As the camera zoomed in for a closer shot, he noticed a silver-framed photograph of a very attractive young woman on the table beside the phone. She stood in gray slacks and a red windbreaker next to a waist-high dog that looked like the same breed of dog depicted by the statues in Puzzo's office.

The camera moved closer.

"Sir!" sputtered Vihari, "Mr. Godessohn, sir! Is *that* the girl you wish to microwave?"

"Yes, Vihari. Unless you would like me to spare her for your entertainment."

"No . . . no . . . sir . . . you don't understand. She will not answer the phone. She will not! I promise you!"

"You could be right, Vihari. It has rung ten times now. Tell me, on what factual data do you base your prediction?"

"Sir, she's in the suite next door!"

"Excuse me?"

"Yes! I saw her check in last night. She was there when you cooked the clerk. I saw her again this morning when I went out on the balcony!"

"That's very interesting, Vihari." Godessohn hung up, and the television screen went blank.

"Are we . . . are you . . . sir, are you going to call up next door and do the job?"

"Perhaps. First let's see if this is anything other than pure coincidence." He dialed the reception desk.

"Good morning. This is Godessohn in the Presidential Suite . . . yes, thank you, everything is fine. I'm sorry I don't have time to chat – I'm late for an appointment – but I wanted to ask your assistance in a small matter. There is a party in the suite beside mine, the Senatorial, I believe, which I would like to honor with a gift. If you would be so kind as to give me the name under which this party is registered . . . yes, I'll hold . . . Signora G. Passoni? Would you know off-hand if she is any relation to the industrialist, Dante Passoni? . . . I see. I didn't realize Mr. Passoni was married. . . . Of course. I shall be very discreet. Thank you."

Vihari expected a frightful display of rage, but received a broad smile instead.

"Well, my son, it would seem that Vittorio Passoni's nephew has gotten lucky with his hunches. *He* is apparently the reason Puzzo's girl is here."

"But . . . but . . . "

"Get hold of yourself, Vihari. Don't forget why we play our games. We play for amusement. A game with neither obstacles nor difficulties is of no interest. *This* game was becoming boring. If Dante Passoni is everything he's cracked up to be, perhaps he can make it interesting again.

"Come, now, Vihari. I'm going to show you one of the most delightful aspects of this hotel – its secret medieval passages. The Passage of Presidential Mistresses runs from beneath our bar to an obscure garden near the Ca' Rezzonico. When we emerge, an especially outfitted boat will be waiting for us."

"But . . . but . . . the girl. What about the girl? You must take care of the girl before we leave. What if she goes to the police? Sir, what if – "

"Relax, Vihari. Hysteria is unbecoming to a man of your

intellect. The girl will not go to the police. She is working for Dante Passoni, and he obviously has something else in mind. The last thing we want to do is kill her. She's too valuable to us, Vihari. She will lead Dante Passoni to me, though not in the way Passoni plans. Let's go watch history being made. We'll discuss how best to use the girl on our return trip."

CHAPTER SIXTEEN

"Signore! Signore! Can you hear me? I've spotted it!"

Dante sat on the aft deck of the yacht. He turned down the volume on the Altel Mini-Spy transmitter/transceiver Graziella had placed on his breakfast table, then answered his butler, who was again hovering in his helicopter two miles above the Lagoon.

"Good work, Luigi. Tell me what you see."

"Well, Signore, I don't quite know how to describe it. When I first picked it up on radar, it was nothing but a motionless cylinder on the bottom of the Lagoon. I dismissed it as debris from a sunken ship. But just now it started to slither."

"Slither?"

"Yes, Signore, it's hugging the bottom and moving in sneaky curves, like your competitor from Altel."

"Watch yourself, Shrimp Schlong," hissed Graziella Calvino.

Dante said, "Both of you, stop it. Luigi, I thought I told you that Director Calvino and I will be collaborating on this delicate operation. You will speak of her with respect now. Continue your description, please."

Dante and Graziella had brought the yacht to within a mile of the refinery and dropped anchor. The fishing boat Dante had commandeered earlier that morning was tethered to starboard, hidden from anyone who might be watching from shore.

While Graziella's starched and subservient male crew scurried about assembling diving gear and loading it into the smaller boat, Dante devoured prodigious quantities of breakfast pastries, hoping they would give him strength for the snagging maneuver.

"Well, Signore," said Luigi, "it's about fifty feet long and six feet in diameter. From up here, it looks like some sort of a bizarre fish."

"And exactly where is the fish at this moment?"

"Near the tanker port in front of the refinery, slithering along very slowly. The water's not real clean, but I can see it clearly through the ultraviolet scope. It looks unfriendly."

"I'm sure it does. Put your scope on full power. I need to know if there's anything to which I can fasten a towing cable."

"Just a minute, Signore, just a moment of patience . . . there, I'm focused. Looks like you're in luck. She's as smooth as an eel. She's got steeply back raked side fins, a split tail and a vertical stabilizer, nothing else on the sides or top. But in back, right where the tail splits and just above the screw, there's a fat eye hook. They must have hung the thing up during construction."

"Luigi . . ."

"Yes, Signore."

"Can you see the spot where it will enter the refinery complex?"

"I believe so. There's a big pipe that looks like a sewer drain, and there's some kind of a concrete channel leading up to it."

"Get me a sonar reading on the water depth at the mouth of the pipe."

"I've already done that, Signore. It's shallow, just over thirty feet."

"Good. How long until the fish goes inside?"

"Not long, Signore. If it continues at this speed, I'd say less than ten minutes. You'll have to hurry."

"There's time, Luigi. It's going to be in there for a while picking up its cargo. I'll accost it on its way out."

"Not if it's hell-bent for its destination, you won't."

"I've seen the cargo, Luigi, as well as the pool beneath the refinery where it will be picked up. Once the fish swims into the pipe, there's no place for it to turn around. It will have to come out backwards and turn around in the Lagoon. That's when it will be most vulnerable."

"Most vulnerable doesn't mean vulnerable. That eye hook

is right near the screw. So what's the fish picking up, Signore? Why is it necessary to hook the thing and risk getting yourself hacked into spiral strips? Why can't I just follow it from up here?"

"It might be going too far and too deep, Luigi."

"Then let's blow it up."

"We can't destroy it without risking disaster. Our only option is to keep a physical grasp on it. We must get both the fish and its load on deck, where we can carry out a proper disarming. We're going to have to proceed very gingerly."

"Why, Signore? I still don't get it?"

"Luigi, the cargo is a fifty-eight megaton thermonuclear warhead."

"Holy Madonna! Christ in a Knocking Shop! That's what Signora Altel and I are going to have on the end of the line?"

"Yes, Luigi, if I succeed in hooking it."

"Holy Mother of – "

"Luigi, please. I'm going to take the fishing boat and wait above the pipe. I want you to help me position myself for the snag. Graziella, is the diving equipment ready?"

She called down to her crew and got a thumbs-up. "Everything's ready but you, Dante. Take my radio and hop to. Let's get this little job done." She clapped her hands, and her gold bracelets jangled. *"Come on, come on. You're moving like someone who drinks tea!"*

* * *

"Just a little farther to your left," Luigi said. "Good, good. You're two hundred feet from the mouth of the sewer pipe and right over the concrete channel the fish swam up."

"Thank you, Luigi." Dante was sitting in the dilapidated fishing boat, observing the refinery as he bobbed on choppy little waves in the tanker port. Idle cranes towered above him, and seagulls scoured the oily concrete docks. The place had the feel of an abandoned factory. In the distance, the ethylene tank that had been his salvation still burned brightly.

He wore a beret and fisherman's clothes, compliments of the old man who had jumped overboard. Graziella's state-of-the-art communications and diving equipment lay hidden beneath a tattered wool blanket.

A few feet behind him, a large orange buoy – one of many in the port area – bobbed in time with his boat. This buoy, though it looked identical to the others, had a different function: it marked the end of the long, submerged towing cable that Dante had ferried from the yacht and let sink to the floor of the Lagoon.

As the final element of his cover, Dante picked up one of the fishing poles on board and cast his bait toward the nearest pier. To his boundless irritation, the cork went under, and he found himself engaged in a tug of war with a stubborn, bottom-sucking fish.

He reeled lackadaisically, aware of how exhausted the events of the previous night had left him. Perhaps it was a good thing Graziella had insisted on taking over with Altel people. He was bone-weary. He might have made a tragic mistake.

He looked at the smoky silhouette of the refinery and shuddered. He had just come from there. In a bunker beneath those ugly stacks and tanks was a facility devoted to the dissemination of death.

His eyelids grew heavy. His mind, delirious with fatigue, conjured up an image of a musty medieval cellar teeming with infected rats. The rats, huddled around an open sewer, were holding a conference on how best to spread the plague from one end of Europe to the other.

Bunkers were bad places.

He was falling asleep.

He wondered how effective he was going to be under water.

He swung the fish he hadn't wanted to catch into the boat.

It was bearded, scaly and repulsive, like some prehistoric creature, half living, half stone. If Puzzo's oil hadn't killed it, he doubted his knife would do the job. He unhooked the grotesque, gawking thing and heaved it as far out in the Lagoon as he could. Then he lay his head back and drifted off.

Luigi's voice blasted him out of his strange dreams.

"Signore, it's coming! Tail first like you predicted, nice and slow!"

Dante leaped to his feet. In seconds, he had stripped down to his wet suit and prepared for the dive.

A final check: oxygen tank on and secured; knife on; fins and goggles in place; halogen diving lamp firmly attached to his head.

He addressed the Altel radio. "Graziella, Luigi, I'm going in."

"Good luck, Signore."

"Careful, Bull Balls. Keep away from the screw or I'll have to rename you."

He dove into the chilly water and swam to the buoy. He followed the rope attached to the buoy 30 feet down to the bottom of the harbor. He dug the end of the towing cable from the muck and slipped his arm through the latch. It was heavy, it weighted him down like an anchor.

He was ready, and none too soon. He could feel the submarine approaching. It sent low-pitched vibrations humming through his bones.

He switched his diving light on. Its beam disappeared in the murky water. His feet sank deeper into muck. Orienting himself by the sound of the sub, he walked to his left in search of the channel.

He was close now. A shadowy form oozed into view, led by a swirl of silt and harbor debris. He moved toward it as it inched backwards, clutching the cable and dragging it.

He reached the channel, felt it with his toes, and glided carefully down its steep concrete side. The fish was bearing down on him. Good, good, he could see it clearly now. It was high in the channel. If he lay on his stomach, it would skim over him. He would grab a side fin as it passed and ride with it while he made his way to the tail.

He tried to lay down, but as soon as his chest touched the bottom, his body started irresistibly up the side of the channel, borne by a powerful underwater current. Before he knew what had happened, he was coming down the other side of the channel, then swishing along the bottom, then rising again.

He was spinning in a slow circle! Nothing to grab on to, no way to stop himself!

Cold panic seized him when he realized he was caught in the vortex of the sub's screw. Not only caught: he was being sucked toward the blades as he twirled!

Leaving the latch at the cable's end around his arm, he took hold of his diving light with both hands. No use resisting this monster physically: its power was too overwhelming. He must use his mind! He struggled to relax his body and break the stranglehold of his panic. He succeeded, but his mind told him that he was lost.

The whirlpool tightened its grip on his torso, spinning him faster and faster, dizzying him and preparing him for the kill; the cable got looped around his chest, wrapping him up like a boa constrictor and pressing the air from his lungs.

The end. He was totally helpless.

Damn her anyway! Graziella Calvino had jinxed him with her remark.

No . . . no . . . mustn't blame her. He had made the fatal mistake. In his exhausted state, he had failed to analyze the currents he would encounter behind the sub.

He closed his eyes and watched the sickening smear of colors whirl behind his lids. This was no way for a distinguished Florentine, a man of learning, culture and style, to check out. He was going to be reduced to fish bait in a filthy Lagoon! Never, never had he considered the possibility of such an ignominious death.

    His dizziness went to nausea. His ribs felt as if they would snap as the cable tightened around him still more. He cried out with his last breath and waited for the guillotine to finish him off.

    And then, as if he had awakened from a horrible nightmare, the noise of the great engine stopped. His limp body twirled in silence. Soon the vortex fizzled completely, and the cable around his rib cage loosened its terrible grip.

    He was disoriented. His head spun, he was still nauseous. His mind had shut down. There was only the cold, the depth and the darkness, pierced by a band of foggy light.

    He sank like a stone to the bottom of the channel, weighted by coils of cable around him. Hitting with a bump, he opened his eyes. The sleek gray beast was still coming at him, its screw feathered but spinning.

    Move!

    He couldn't, nowhere to go, so he pressed himself flat on the channel bed. The fish passed over him, and he could almost feel its weight. Its tail whacked his heel, and his oxygen tank clattered along its belly.

    Running on willpower, he swam out of the loops of loose cable, rolled on his back, grabbed the horizontal stabilizer fin as it whisked over him and climbed aboard. He checked his right arm. The cable latch was still around it.

    He got to his knees, careful not to lose his balance on the fin's smooth, polished surface.

    He straightened his diving light, which had been pointing off his left ear.

    The fish was rising out of the channel now, drifting backwards in a wide curve. He would have to keep up a good pace. When she came around a full 180 degrees, the pitch on the screw would be reversed, and the engine restarted.

    He draped his torso over the fish's body, trying to ignore the pain in his ribs. He waited an instant to let his strength return, then threw a leg over her and, straddling her, shimmied to the vertical stabilizer.

He could see the big eye hook clearly but couldn't quite reach it. Carefully, without letting go of the vertical stabilizer, he slid down the fish's side until his feet were touching one of the horizontal tail fins. The surface was slick as black ice; it had obviously been coated with some high-tech compound to keep barnacles from sticking. He might have been able to balance on it if he hadn't been strapped with the cable. The water would have buoyed him up, making him nearly weightless. But because of the cable, he had gravity to contend with. No way he could stand on that surface, not even for an instant.

He hauled himself up on the fish's back and contemplated the eye hook some more.

The screw! It had stopped spinning! It was a four-bladed clover. Even if it was coated with the slippery material, he should be able to balance on it. He would rest his feet on the two horizontally opposed blades while pressing his knees and thighs against a vertical blade for support. He would have his hands free for latching the cable to the eye hook.

He sucked in a deep breath and tried not to dwell on the dangers of this intimate embrace. It was his only chance. He hadn't come this far to let it pass him by.

He pushed himself downward off the fish's back, catching the screw with his four limbs as he brushed past it and hanging on like a primate.

The screw, which was about his height, had absolutely no resistance in its shaft: it moved back and forth like a frictionless seesaw, threatening to tip him on his head the instant he stood up.

Well, he would just have to take it slow, not letting anything upset his concentration or balance.

Still hanging off the back of the screw, he worked his feet

into the crevices between the blades, waited for it to stop seesawing, then hauled himself upright with his arms wrapped tightly around the vertical blade.

The screw started rotating slowly clockwise. To counteract this motion, Dante slid his left foot out along the blade. Too far! The screw swung in the other direction. Soon he was tottering back and forth like a tight rope walker in trouble.

As he struggled to still the movements of his unstable platform, he could see the eye hook sweeping past in front of him, not three feet away.

He realized with freshly surging fear that the fish had come all the way around. She was lying as still and silent as a submerged log.

Moving his feet and shifting his weight the tiniest amounts, he gradually brought the screw into equilibrium. Good, he was getting the feel of this diabolical device.

He took his arms from the vertical blade around which they had been wrapped, holding himself with his knees and thighs. The screw seesawed a few times and was still. Little by little, balancing precariously, he managed to slide the cable latch off his arm.

He squeezed the latch open with both hands to get a feeling for how difficult it was. Difficult. One hand would not do the job.

He focused his concentration on the eye hook and inhaled deeply.

Now!

He reached both hands forward, holding the latch open. He instantly lost his balance. The eye hook seemed to dart away as the screw seesawed wildly.

He fought not to tip on his head, regained his equilibrium little by little. He had moved too fast. He'd have to approach the eye hook like a cat sneaking up on a bird.

He felt dull vibrations in his feet.

This he did not need.

The vibrations were already rising to a hum, setting his bone marrow in motion.

Easy, take it easy. Nuclear engines need time to come on.

No trembling. No jerky motions. No *breathing*. He let go of the screw and moved the latch a quarter inch at a time toward the eye hook.

The vibrations pulsed through his body like an electric current. The hum was rising to a whine.

Slowly, slowly. A quarter of an inch at a time.

He was close now, the length of a hand. He fought back the temptation to lunge.

The whine became a wailing siren.

An inch to go now . . . a half inch . . . The siren rose in pitch until it sounded like an air-raid alert.

He felt resistance in the shaft!

No choice, the cat had to pounce.

Whack! A bull's eye.

He slammed the latch shut and threw himself off the screw. The siren became a roar as 18,000 impatient horses started to run. The screw twisted with the torque of a hundred turbocharged Lamborghinis, and the hooked fish pulled away.

* * *

"Passoni! Answer me! Are you all right?" Graziella shouted for the tenth time.

It had taken Dante all his strength to heave himself over the side of the fishing boat. Now he was finally able to speak. "Yes, yes, I'm fine."

"You made your butler hysterical," she said.

"Well, I'm sorry. What about the fish? Do you still have her on the line?"

"Yes, Dante, but it's a him – big and stupid. I'm following unobtrusively at three knots. We're going to pass through the Chioggia Inlet and enter the Adriatic shortly. I'll continue to follow very discretely, no tension on the cable, and I won't land him until we're at least fifty miles out."

"Thank you, Graziella. Have you put together a disarming team yet?"

"Of course. Its members, and my division directors, will be joining me on board in an hour. Right now, Luigi is preparing to land on deck. I'll make sure he keeps you informed."

"That's right, Signore, I'll keep you informed. Just tell me where I can you reach you."

"At the Zitti Palace," Dante said. "Senatorial Suite. Use Director Calvino's boat phone. She has assured me it is in good working order."

"No, Signore! You're utterly exhausted. You must go where you can sleep! I know you, Signore. Listen to reason. You will not be able to resist the – "

"Luigi, please."

Dante turned off his radio and headed across the Lagoon to Venice, wondering if Gina would be at the hotel when he arrived.

CHAPTER SEVENTEEN

An hour before Dante snagged the fish, Godessohn and Vihari left the Zitti Palace through the Passage for Presidential Mistresses. They moved quickly, hunched over because the secret tunnel would not permit even Vihari to walk erect. When they reached the end, Godessohn unlocked the medieval iron portal and they stepped into a secluded courtyard overhung with vines.

Vihari breathed in the cool morning air, more pleasing than the air over the canal. Dappled sunlight made fine patterns on pastel walls, and birds chirped and fluttered all around him – no pigeons, he hoped.

After a brief pause, Godessohn surged forward, his bald head leading the way like a battering ram. Vihari hurried to keep up: this wouldn't be a good day to fall behind. They passed beneath a crumbling arch and followed an ancient cobbled path through a garden to a busy pedestrian thoroughfare.

Godessohn took Vihari by the elbow. "Have a look to your left. Our transportation is waiting in the canal."

Vihari stared down the crowded street. Beneath an ornate stone bridge, moored to a gondola dock, he saw a luxurious cabin cruiser, its engines idling and throaty.

"Very nice, sir, very nice." Vihari knew a lot about boats. He was about to praise the craft's elegant lines when he noticed that no one was at the helm. "But, sir, where is your captain? You don't suppose he's slipped into one of these bars around here, do you?"

Godessohn laughed: he seemed to be laughing a lot today. He pulled Vihari closer. "There is no captain. My communications system delivered the craft."

"But . . . will the system drive us, too?"

"I enjoy doing some things myself, Vihari. Come."

"But, sir, you're not a boatman, not that I'm aware. Will you be able to navigate in all this crazy traffic."

"I should think so, Vihari."

Inside the cruiser, Godessohn opened a closet and pulled out two bulky life vests. He offered one to Vihari, but Vihari waved him off. "No thank you, sir. I can swim a hundred miles if need be. And you, sir? Don't you swim?"

Godessohn glared at him. "What kind of a question is that? We're going to sea. Before we leave, Vihari, I would like to have a word with you about our relationship. I have placed you in my last testament as the sole heir to the Wittersand fortune, which under my stewardship has grown one hundred fold. I have made you my only confidant. I have provided you with the opportunity to escape the doldrums of your timid bourgeois life, to observe and participate in the most exciting scientific ventures of our time. That's quite a lot, isn't it, Vihari?"

"Yes, sir. It certainly is, sir. I want you to know how appreciative I am."

"It isn't your appreciation that interests me, Vihari; it's your competence, your faith in me and your absolute loyalty to me. These are the qualities I expect of you in return for my gift. And to make sure I'm getting them, Vihari, I'm going to subject you to little tests from time to time. You have a good scientific mind. These tests will be well within your ability – provided you are thinking clearly. However, if you let fear get the best of you, your thinking might suffer and you might fail.

"Do not let that happen, Vihari. Have faith in me and in *my* ability to protect us both from harm. Finally, Vihari, there is your loyalty to me, which I shall test only in the most critical situations. You won't want to fail here, for the consequences of failure will be most unpleasant."

"I understand, sir. I am loyal, so I will not fail this type of test. But, sir, what about the others? In the realm of problem solving, it is possible for everyone to have a bad day. What happens if I fail one of these tests of my competence, as you put it?"

"It will be preferable, Vihari, not to have a bad day."

"But . . . if I do?"

"We will return to the elevator in my office."

"I . . . see. Well, sir, I'd better not fail."

"Precisely."

Vihari watched Godessohn put on his life vest. In it he looked even larger, even more menacing. He made a few minor adjustments to the straps, then sat in the captain's seat and wrapped his thick fingers around the wheel.

"Ready?"

"Yes, sir."

Godessohn gave full throttle. The cruiser accelerated with a thunderous roar, its wake swamping a group of tourists who had gathered to admire the boat.

Vihari grabbed his seat rails and held them so tightly he squeezed the color from his fingers. Did Godessohn have any idea what he was doing? A powerful boat on crowded waters was as dangerous as a powerful car on a race track, all the more so when the other drivers were Italian. He must have faith! He must not let his fear get the best of him! Otherwise Godessohn might use the moment to surprise him with a problem he could not solve, a test he could not pass.

To Vihari's dismay, Godessohn became even more reckless. He flung the speedboat into a sharp turn, barely missing the rusty metal bow of a garbage barge, and took aim at the mouth of a canal so narrow it looked like a crack in a solid block of buildings.

Ancient walls draped in shadow hurtled by to either side. Vihari's world dissolved into a blur of crumbling facades, flapping laundry and warped shutters. The boat's engine howled in his ears; the "ahoys" of angered gondoliers echoed in his head. Three stories up, between the eaves to either side, he could see the sky, a milky river of light mirroring the path of the canal.

The motorboat swept into a long bend, and when its course

straightened, Vihari saw the Grand Canal two hundred yards ahead. Thank God!

He glanced at Godessohn, who looked as if he were sitting on his 1200 horse bulldozer plowing a trench through the veld. What a maniac! He seemed to be taking gigantic risks. But was he? Or had everything been set up in advance to make this seemingly harrowing ride as safe as a steamship outing on Lake Tugela?

Knowing what he now knew about Godessohn, Vihari concluded it was the latter – and instantly relaxed. Ah, yes, to be certain he passed all future tests, he would have to ignore appearances and trust completely in his boss. If he did this, he could keep his fears under control; his fears, those aggravating emotions that had held him back from the threshold of greatness.

The speedboat roared into the Grand Canal and headed east toward the Adriatic. They sped across the Lagoon, overtaking a majestic white 100-meter yacht, and entered the Adriatic Sea through the Giudecca Inlet.

"Would you like to take the wheel now, Vihari? I have some business down below I must attend to."

"Yes, sir. Certainly, sir. But where am I going?"

"Don't worry about that, Vihari. The boat will go where it is supposed to go regardless of your input."

"I . . . see."

Godessohn's face was whipped to a splotchy pink by the sea breeze. He smiled, then disappeared down the spiral stairway to the lower level.

Two hours later, he returned. "We're there," he said. He reached over Vihari's shoulder and pushed a button on the control panel. The boat slowed to a stop, then came half way around and began automatically fine-tuning its position.

"Dynamic guidance via satellite," Godessohn explained. "The craft will hold the coordinates I have programmed, correcting as need be for water currents and wind every tenth of a second. Why have I chosen this particular spot, you will be asking yourself? The answer is simple. From where we wait, Vihari, we are going to witness a critical moment in the voyage of my steel fish."

Godessohn glanced at his watch. "The Event will take place in twenty minutes. I must return to my preparations. Please feel free to come below deck whenever you wish. I'll show you the underwater surveillance equipment."

"Thank you, sir. I'll be right down."

Vihari loved the sea. Before leaving his post at the helm, he took one last look at the water. Ah, how splendid, how beautiful. The Adriatic stretched in all directions to the horizon, an emerald jewel shaded with distant bands of blue.

Water, he thought – on earth there was water everywhere. But if Godessohn's plan succeeded, 100 million people in the breadbasket of world's most powerful nation would soon forget what water was.

A tremor of pleasure rippled through Vihari's intestines. Having so much power over the lives of others – or serving someone who did – changed the way you felt about things. He would have expected, in circumstances like these, to become sick with guilt. But that had not happened. Instead he was experiencing great bursts of exhilaration. And a persistent hot tingle, dormant since the rigors of graduate school at Harvard, had inexplicably returned to his loins.

Well, enough musing. He'd better go see what Godessohn was doing. He headed for the stairway to the lower deck, aware of a new buoyancy in his stride.

*   *   *

Godessohn worked at a keyboard, which was embedded in a desk at the center of the teak-paneled surveillance room.

"Look at Screen A, Vihari. What you see is taking place right now on our aft deck."

Vihari scanned the dozen television screens lining the starboard wall. Some were identified with letters, others with numbers. On Screen A he watched a crane-like arm pivot out over the water. A glass and metal orb constructed of flat octagonal panels dangled from its end.

Godessohn typed some more and the orb plummeted into the sea, spinning rubber-coated cable off an electric reel as it sank.

A few minutes later the viewing station was in place, its powerful lights illuminating the depths through which the fish was supposed swim.

The boat rocked lazily on the swells; the motor kept up its soft drone, holding the craft's navigational coordinates constant.

Motion negating motion, thought Vihari. You could move forever out here and never move an inch. His life had felt that way until a few days ago. No longer. He was definitely going somewhere now, though he wasn't sure where.

The numbered screens flickered to life, all seven of them, projecting images transmitted by the orb's various cameras.

"We'll make films of the Event," Godessohn explained. "As everything will happen fast, we'll want to watch it all again in less harried circumstances later. Now, Vihari, we still have sixteen minutes. I would like you return to the cabin and relax. There are some final preparations I wish to undertake on my own. You'll find field glasses in the compartment beneath the wheel, should you wish to observe the marine traffic in the area. Don't worry, you won't miss anything. I'll call you the instant I have the fish on sonar."

* * *

"Signora, are you sure your boat phone is working?"

Graziella Calvino jangled her gold bracelets and fixed Luigi with a ball-shriveling stare. "My dear man, the Altel GC 12 Boat phone does not malfunction. Of the thirty thousand units sold to date, we've had only twenty-nine thousand complaints – all of them, no doubt, the work of CRC propagandists attempting to undermine our corporate morale."

Luigi gazed longingly at his helicopter, which he had tied down on the yacht's enormous aft deck. He'd tied it down good, too: that chopper was his ticket to freedom. He was out of here the instant Dante gave him the green light to leave.

He hoped and prayed he would receive that permission before the Altel helicopters bearing their battalions of Graziella Calvino clones touched down. Forget the 58-megaton bomb they had on the yacht's towing line. A bomb he could handle. It was the thought of 50 Graziellas, all hungry to participate in adjusting his attitude toward women, that made him shudder in holy terror and cross his wrists in front of his sacred appendage. Who could say for sure none of these man-eaters would get carried away and propose some kind of castration ceremony?

Dante would understand. Dante wouldn't make his trusted friend and servant suffer through such intolerable anxiety. And if CRC absolutely *had* to have someone on board the yacht, there was always Kiyo.

He gathered his courage and spoke. "It just doesn't make sense, Signora Calvino. It's not like the Signore. Why would he tell me to call and then refuse to answer his phone?"

"My dear little man, you saw how exhausted he was. He has obviously fallen asleep. What of it? There's nothing to report yet anyway."

"Signora . . . Signora, is it my imagination, or are we accelerating?"

Graziella took a deep breath and stood tall at the wheel, her long chestnut hair wild in the rising wind. "Our fish must have felt the hook. He's speeded up. Look at the cable. He's actually pulling us. How far off shore are we?"

"Fifty-four miles."

"Good. We're outside the danger zone. We'll let him wear

himself out."

"Wear himself out?"

"Precisely, Pygmy Pecker. Don't look so alarmed. How long do you think that little sausage-shaped thing can pull this great white goddess of the seas? I know, I know, you believe his shape affords him special powers. Give up your childish male myths and join the twenty-first century. He's not going far with my yacht."

"Signora, we're traveling thirty knots. Thirty-five! Forty! Signora, we're hydroplaning!"

"Very well, we're hydroplaning. He's coming on strong, got a lot to prove to Mamma. But he'll expend himself as I'm sure you do – prematurely."

"We're going sixty knots! Listen to those noises! Signora, your ship's about to disintegrate. We must cut the cable!"

"At ease, little man. You're not working for faint-hearted men today. We'll ride out this brief and pathetic demonstration of machismo. As soon as he goes limp, we'll haul him on deck and eviscerate him."

"I've got to call Dante!" shouted Luigi above the creaking of the yacht's bones and the roar of the wind and sea. "Excuse me, I've got to try again."

"Forget it, Peckerino. Your people were right. The Altel GC 12 Boat phone is a piece of shit. Mine's broken, too. I'll have my technicians repair it when they arrive. For now you'll just have to sit tight."

"You knew! You knew it was broken! You didn't want Dante informed! You deceived him!"

"He is my competitor."

"Sig . . . nor . . . a!"

"Speak up! Spit it out! What's on your tongue?"

"Up there in front of us! A boat! We're being pulled into another boat! At sixty knots! I'm going to cut the cable before there's a horrible accident!"

"You're going to stay where you are. Stop squawking and look at me."

Luigi did, and found himself staring into the barrel of Graziella Calvino's gold Beretta.

* * *

Godessohn's voice rang loud and clear through the intercom. "Come below now, Vihari. I've picked up the fish on sonar."

"Sir! Just a moment, sir. There's something very strange going on up here. I've sighted a ship through my field glasses, a big white yacht. It looks like the same yacht we saw this morning in the Lagoon. It's about three miles to the north and closing fast. I don't know how this can be, sir, but it seems to be coming right at us, as though it's holding an intentional ram course."

"I asked you to come to the viewing room, Vihari. Forget about the yacht. After we have seen the Event, we shall study your sighting."

"But, sir! You don't understand! This yacht is moving very fast. In fact, it appears to be hydroplaning!"

"You sound agitated, Vihari. Why?"

"Sir, for God's sake, listen to me! We must take evasive action. We must . . ."

He realized with a pit in his stomach that Godessohn had switched off the intercom. What now? Should he stay where he was? Should he take the initiative and drive the boat out of harm's way?

But what was he thinking? He couldn't move the boat! It was locked in place by that damn satellite guidance system.

It flashed through his mind that this might be a test, but he quickly discarded the notion as ridiculous. The yacht was going to slam into their boat, and that was that. He could hear the dreadful crack, could see the gruesome mass of twisted teak, bone splinters and burst organs – his own among them.

An idea blazed through his confusion. He would go down

and convince Godessohn face-to-face that something was wrong . . . convince him calmly, coolly, rationally.

He raised his field glasses for one last look, just to be sure he wasn't hallucinating.

Impossible! This could not be! There was some sort of a cable protruding from the yacht's bow. The cable was slicing through the water ahead of the ship.

No! NO! This was disaster! The yacht had somehow managed to latch on to the fish! Godessohn had been outsmarted!

He ran down the stairs to the surveillance room, struggling to appear calm, and found Godessohn staring impassively at the first of the seven numbered screens.

"Sir! You must listen to me! We must talk about what I have observed."

"In less than two minutes, Vihari, the long-range camera projecting on the screen in front of you will pick her up."

"Sir! I fear we've been thwarted! Someone has snagged the fish! Sir, why won't you listen to me? That yacht we passed on our way out of the Lagoon has your fish on the end of a cable! The yacht is being towed into us. You are going to be destroyed by your own creation!"

Godessohn looked coldly at Vihari. "Have you so little faith in me that you have already forgotten our conversation of this morning? Be quiet and watch – or it's the elevator."

A test, it *was* a test, it had to be a test! And if it wasn't, so what? He would rather die a hundred times in boat collisions than be placed in front of those elevator doors again.

"Okay," mumbled Vihari, wrestling with his fear. "Okay, I have spoken my part. I have informed you of what I saw. You do not think it is a problem. I have absolute faith in you. I shall watch."

"Of course you'll watch. There she is, Vihari, left center of the screen coming toward us. Step closer. CLOSER! When she passes from this screen, she'll appear on Screen Two. Be ready to shuffle sideways."

He saw the fish. It looked like a black-nosed torpedo bearing down on them with ill intent. It *was* bearing down with ill intent. It was heading directly at them, dragging a huge yacht behind it at 60 knots!

He felt a sharp jerk on his arm as Godessohn yanked him in front of Screen 2. The fish was bigger now. Vihari could see its fins. He caught a glimpse of the cable trailing behind it as Godessohn shoved him in front of Screen 3.

"Did you see it!" cried Vihari. "It was there, the cable! Right there in your picture. Did you see it?"

"Yes, Vihari. One can see it even better here."

Something exploded, their motorboat heaved, Vihari almost bit through his tongue. Godessohn grabbed Vihari's turban in both hands and pointed his head at Screen 4. A cloud of white water erupted, obscuring his view of the fish.

Godessohn heaved him in front of Screen 5. From the swirling cloud Vihari saw a leaner, shorter fish emerge. It darted across Screens 6 and 7 and was gone.

"Pay attention," Godessohn ordered.

Vihari, mouth agape, watched the spent titanium shell of the original fish, its nose cone blown away, drift out of the debris. The cable, limp now, was still attached to the tail.

The fish had shed its skin! The snaggers were going to come up empty-handed!

Godessohn leaned over the keyboard and typed a code. The engine of the cabin cruiser came to life and the boat, released from its dynamic hold position, began to plow to the east.

Vihari dropped into a chair, breathing hard. "Well, sir, that was really something. Are you going to explain the details of what I have just observed?"

"Of course, Vihari. The fish consists of three stages, the

latter two concealed inside the first. I designed stage one to bring the payload to this point. The critical separation I came here to watch was a success. The rest of the voyage will be easy sailing.

"The second stage will take the payload through the Straits of Gibraltar and into the deep water of the Atlantic at a speed of one hundred ten knots. The third stage will ferry it very slowly along the ocean floor to its destination."

"Most impressive, sir, most impressive. But why, sir, if I might ask, did you decide to use stages?"

"The Adriatic and the Mediterranean, Vihari, are relatively shallow. I could not ignore the possibility that the fish might encounter impediments before reaching safe water."

"Very . . . farsighted, sir."

"Thank you, Vihari. Let's talk about you. You passed your test, though just barely. You're going to have to do better in the future."

"Yes, sir. Certainly, sir. I shall, sir. But . . . sir . . ."

"What is it, Vihari?"

"May I ask you another question?"

"Yes."

"How did you know the fish had been snagged? Did you see the yacht being towed?"

"No, Vihari. Cameras in the fish recorded the entire episode. I was below deck when it happened. I watched the snagger – our friend Passoni – conduct a most amusing balancing act on the screw. I could have cut him to shreds right there, Vihari, but that would have been inconsistent with my goal."

"Your . . . goal? But, sir, I do not understand. The goal is to deliver the payload to a carefully determined point beneath the South Pacific. This man Passoni is becoming quite a nuisance. I can't see why would you spare him and risk further complications."

"I shall explain to you again, Vihari, what should by now be obvious. I spared him because a game without complications is like a boxing match without an opponent; it is *boring*. The objective of my activities is not to achieve boredom but to escape it."

"But – "

"No more questions. We're going up to the cabin now to observe developments on board the yacht. I'm sure they'll be rich in entertainment value."

CHAPTER EIGHTEEN

Dante woke with a start. For an instant he didn't know where he was, but when he saw Gina standing at the balcony doors with her back to him, he remembered: he was on the living room sofa of the Senatorial Suite, where he had stretched out, exhausted, upon his arrival at the Zitti.

Luigi hadn't called yet, so Graziella Calvino evidently had the crisis in the Adriatic under control. Dante was pleased with the way he had used this lull in the action, remaining available for emergencies while catching up on his rest. If something went wrong now, he would at least be able to think clearly.

A breath of wind blew in from the canal, tousling Gina's hair and ruffling her white silk dress. She was awe-inspiring, he thought, a goddess preserved by fate for some fortunate man. He found himself wanting her as he had not wanted a woman for many years.

But this was *unacceptable*! He concentrated on his aching muscles and throbbing joints, trying to extinguish his desire. No luck. He lashed himself with all the guilt and self-loathing he could muster – which wasn't much. He resorted in desperation to his sense of decency, which seemed to help: he had *absolutely* no right to think of Gina in sexual terms. She had risked her life to do him a favor. She was young enough to be his daughter. To take advantage of her would be a sin. In five years, perhaps, when she had been out in the world and learned to cope, when she was capable of making her own decisions. But now? Forget it.

"Gina," he said softly.

She came and sat beside him. "Are you all right, Dante? You slept so hard I was beginning to worry."

"I'm fine, thank you. A little beat up but fine. Thank God you made it out of the villa. I was worried my rope bridge would give you trouble."

"I didn't use it."

"Excuse me?"

"I went out the front gate. I just couldn't bring myself to leave Bruno behind. Giorgio hadn't come home from work yet, so I simply walked out."

"Where is the dog now?"

"I took him to Piero, the trainer in Noale. That turned out well, too. Piero drove me to the gondola docks – on the condition that I pick up Bruno today. Dante, do you think you could help me get him?"

"After what you did for me? Most certainly. I'll have my associate send for him. My grandfather's farm is near Noale. He can stay there as long as need be."

"Oh, Dante, that's very kind. Perhaps he could even come to the hotel when it's convenient."

"Perhaps."

The phone rang.

Dante reached for it.

Gina screamed and wrapped her arms around him. "NO! Dante, no! You can't answer it! The phones here can kill. I saw it happen last night!"

He subdued her as gently as he could and held the receiver to his ear. "Hello, Luigi?"

"Yes, Signore, it's me at last. I have good news for you, very good news. Relax, Signore, sit back as though you're on holiday and listen to my report. Good news, very good news – and one minor request to make of you."

As Dante listened he watched Gina, thoroughly perplexed by her reaction. She sat trembling with her hand over her mouth. Tears streamed down her cheeks. He tried to assure her with his smile that everything was fine. It didn't help.

Well, he thought, one mustn't forget everything she's been through these last days. She'd probably convinced herself without realizing it that the call would be from Puzzo or the Sheik or the man she called the Presence. The ring must have plunged her into a panic. He reached out and touched her hand.

"So, Luigi, you say the fish suffered a drive line failure and is dead in the water? Seventy well-equipped Altel technicians and disarming experts have been shuttled to the yacht by helicopter? All of this has already happened, and you call me only now?"

"Signore," Luigi whispered, "the boat phone was broken. The technicians have just repaired it. It was broken, Signore, and Signora Altel knew that it was broken. She had no intention of letting me communicate with you until she had subdued the fish on her own.

"Anyway, Signore, she got lucky and the job is done. They have started the gasoline motor on the winch and are hauling the bugger in right now. It will take a long time – five, six, ten hours, I don't know. But the cable is strong and the gear ratio on the winch is favorable. Also, I have forced myself for the sake of your peace of mind to speak with the disarming people. Not to worry, Signore. The Israelis use them, so they must know what they're doing.

"Another thing, Signore. Kiyo keeps calling out here, trying to badger me into revealing your whereabouts. Under the circumstances, I of course held my tongue."

"What does she want?"

"She has some new thoughts on who killed Vittorio – nothing, I'm sure, that can't wait. She would like you to get in touch with her."

"All right, Luigi. If she calls back, tell her I'll see her at Giuseppe's later this afternoon."

"I'll tell her, Signore. And now that you have my assurance that all is well, will you hear the minor request I mentioned at the start of our conversation?"

"What is it?"

"Can I leave, Signore? These women have nothing to do until the fish is hoisted aboard. They have no one to pick on except *me*. I'm frightened, Signore. They're planning to 'adjust' my attitude toward women which, just between you and me, is becoming more medieval by the moment. I have a premonition, Signore, that this 'adjustment' could turn into some sort of tribal rite. You understand me, do you not, Signore? I fear for my sacred *parts*!"

"You mean to tell me, Luigi, that while you are reeling in a fifty-eight megaton *armed* warhead, you are thinking *not* about the well-being of Italy and *not* about your own survival as a member of the human race, but about the fate of your unit?"

"Signore! What has happened to you? You are talking like Signora Altel herself! Signore, please! Stand by your fellow males! May I leave this dangerous lair?"

"Of course not, Luigi. You are CRC's only participant in the most important antiterrorist operation in history. You will stay where you are, monitoring all developments and keeping me perfectly informed until the fish is on board *and* disarmed. Is that clear, Luigi?"

"But . . . but, Signore, you've said yourself never to minimize the danger of a pack of – "

"Luigi, I'm sorry but I must go. Call me back when you have something of relevance to report."

"Relevance. RELEVANCE! I don't believe my ears. Are you claiming that the sword and cymbals of my manhood are not – "

"Good-bye, Luigi."

Dante hung up and took Gina in his arms. "Are you all right?"

She held him tightly; she was still trembling. "Oh, Dante, I thought they would kill you when you answered. Forgive me for being such a coward, but I thought you would die. That's what happened to the poor old clerk last night – someone killed him with the telephone."

"Gina . . . "

"Don't look at me like that, Dante. I *saw* it. He picked up his phone at the reception desk, put it to his ear and collapsed. I ran to him. I tried to help him. When I felt his head, I had to withdraw my hand to keep from burning it. Dante, you must believe me. His head was as hot as an iron skillet. You must stop using the phones. The phones here can kill you – and there will soon be plenty of people trying to do just that."

He stroked her lovely hair and tried to comfort her. "Gina, the man you saw collapse had a stroke or a coronary or some such thing. It's terrible to see, I know. Perhaps his head felt hot to you because you had just experienced the trauma of seeing him stricken. Perhaps it felt hot because you were under tremendous stress yourself. Stress can cause one's nervous system to short-circuit and send false signals to the brain. It is also quite possible, Gina, that the man had a high fever. In any case, you must stop worrying. The call I just received was very positive. The men you fear will soon be rendered harmless."

She was near desperation. "Dante, no Dante, I beg you to listen to me. Even if you don't want to believe me, at least do me a favor."

"Which would be?"

"Stop using the phones in this hotel."

"I'm sorry, Gina, but I can't do that."

When she started to object, he brushed a finger across her lips. "Shhh. I'm going to call a clothing shop and have a few items sent over, and I'm going to order us lunch. The phone is our life line."

Smiling, he lifted the receiver and dialed. "And while they're preparing lunch, I'm going to take a long, hot bath. Then, Gina, we'll relax together and have a good meal."

* * *

She hadn't realized how famished Dante was until he began to eat. He sucked down three dozen oysters and let the shells fall where they might. He inhaled an enormous plate of seafood pasta, spattering the linen tablecloth with showers of red sauce. He devoured a thick *bistecca alla fiorentina*, ate an entire Swiss chard casserole, potatoes, cheeses, a side dish of porcini mushrooms, two baskets of bread and several salads, pausing only to refill his wine glass.

She stared at the table in disbelief. It had been so neat and elegant when she arranged the serving dishes. Now, with the tablecloth ruined and the jagged T-bone protruding from a chaos of oyster shells, it looked like a battlefield strewn with the remnants of plunder and carnage.

She snuck a glance at him, sitting across from her in his terry cloth hotel robe wiping his lips with his napkin, and felt herself growing weak. Something was terribly wrong. It was as if all the horrors of these last weeks had accumulated in the pit of her stomach – and then changed into an equally powerful but very different sensation.

She waited for the strange sensation to go away. Instead, it became more intense and began spreading to other parts of her body, traveling downward through her lower abdomen and along her legs, and upward, through her breasts and out her arms.

She looked at Dante again. He smiled at her, a kind, intelligent, devastatingly handsome smile. She averted her eyes. Desire was a mysterious thing to her, and now it was starting to burn out of control.

She felt breathless, faint. She had never been with a man before, had never wanted to be – until now. She was not long for this earth. She might as well face it. Giorgio and his friends would find her and dispose of her. She was being granted a last chance to know carnal love before she was snatched away from this earth. She must not let the chance elude her. She must be brave and decisive. She must tell him what she wanted.

She reached over the battlefield and grasped both his hands.

"Dante," she whispered, "Dante . . . will you make love to me?"

"What?"

"Dante, listen. You mustn't think I'm crazy. It's just that . . . I've never been with a man before. Dante! They're going to kill me! I don't want to die without having loved. Dante, please. Don't say anything. Don't make this complicated. Just make love to me."

He leaned forward, his elbows resting on oyster shells and empty plates, and took her face in his hands. "Gina, they are not going to kill you."

"Dante, please! Just make love to me!"

"You're positive it's what you want?"

"Yes!"

She began unbuttoning the top button on her dress. Very gently he removed her hand. "Let me," he said.

Her heart was racing. Her dress fell open. She held out her arms to him. He stood up, slipped off his robe and came to her.

Gina's eyes grew large with horror. Why did everything in her life go badly? He was beautiful, yes – hard and muscular, bruised but intact, his stomach flat, his chest and limbs chiseled like a marble statue. But there was a problem with a certain part of him. How could she ever take something *that* enormous inside her? It would split her open like a young spring lamb being skewered.

She closed her eyes, pressed her eyelids tightly together. She could not understand why she still burned for him after what she had seen, why her legs were parting of their own accord, why she was fumbling with the last buttons of her dress.

She heard him whisper again, "Let me."

Still in her chair, she slid forward, her heels digging into the carpet, her hands clutching the chair back so she didn't end up on the floor.

His lips brushed her hand, the hand that was again groping to unbutton her dress. He kissed it lightly as he took over the unbuttoning job.

When she opened her eyes, her dress was on the floor and she was almost horizontal in her chair. Looking between her breasts, she could see his head and thick black hair by her feet, miles away.

Whatever was he doing?

She didn't care, she didn't care. The part of him that had shocked her was hidden from view.

He began unlacing her boots, kissing her calves as he worked, pulling softly at her flesh with his lips.

She thought of the oysters. He had eaten them the same way.

Her toes curled, and she felt new muscles in her stomach and groin tighten in agonizingly wonderful new ways.

His hands came up the insides of her thighs, sending waves of pleasure to the crazy spot at the epicenter of her fire that still seemed to think it could accommodate him.

She felt his fingers run beneath the band of her panties. She arched her back and moaned.

What now?

Oh, God, he was sliding her panties down her legs.

He kissed her thighs – Allah, he could not be doing this – came higher with his kisses, brushed past her burning black triangle with the crazy ambitions.

She squirmed, and strange noises she couldn't stop escaped from her throat.

He kissed her ears and forehead, kissed her mouth for a long time, then worked his way down her torso again, stopping at her breasts, his tongue circling her nipples, his teeth playing with them, and his hands – where were his hands?

She saw his head moving again, moving down below her breasts and across her belly. She felt his fingers on her thighs, felt his tongue near her navel.

What was he doing now?

He could not be doing this!

He was!

She heard herself cry out from another world where voices were muffled and nothing made sense. Her fingers twined in his hair, she tried to push him away and pull him closer in the same motion.

He lifted her on to the oriental carpet. His lips found her neck, he was talking to her! He said beautiful things about how special she was and how he wanted her to stay with him.

And then she felt the huge thing splitting her in half. She shrieked, sank her teeth into his shoulder and wrapped her legs around his butt. Soon after that it happened, something primal and earthshaking and of such overwhelming pleasure she thought she would pass out.

She knew she was sobbing as he carried her to the sofa; she could not hear herself but she knew. She clung to him, her nails buried in his back so he could not slip away, her lips silently repeating his name.

Twenty-three years of suffering, she thought. If that was the price for an hour in paradise, it was worth it.

PART III

CHAPTER NINETEEN

Godessohn laughed. "When I told you there would be entertainment value, I underestimated the amount. This is a *spettacolo*."

Vihari was still glued to his field glasses. "Indeed, sir, a spectacle in any language. But I must say, I'm not sure I understand its significance."

Godessohn had seen enough; he wasn't watching any more. His field glasses dangled high on his chest, their strap shortened by his bull neck.

After viewing the Event, they had sailed the cabin cruiser slowly and unobtrusively three miles away from the yacht, where they had set up an observation post. They'd scarcely had time to focus their binoculars when seven large helicopters appeared from the west and unloaded their passengers – all well-dressed women of stunning good looks.

The yacht's male crew, scurrying about like obedient mice, kept their distance, all except one small nervous man with a Van Dyke whom Vihari had sized up as the boss woman's lackey.

This mighty contingent of female splendor, its jewels sparkling in the sunlight and hair waving in the breeze, listened attentively to the boss woman's speech. Soon thereafter a few of the scurrying males started the gasoline engine, and the pathetic little winch began to reel in the towing cable.

Now, a quarter hour later, most of the women had gone below. Vihari could understand why: the winch's rate of haul was slow, and many hours would pass before they landed their catch.

But the boss woman and her lackey did not go below. He was content to hover around the helicopter on the aft deck, and she stood over the winch, threatening it with the strangest hand gestures Vihari had ever seen.

Godessohn said, "Perhaps you do not understand the significance of what is going on because you do not recognize the woman in charge."

Vihari entrusted his field glasses to their strap. They ended up below his belt. "Should I recognize her?"

"Yes, Vihari. Her name is Graziella Calvino. She is the C.E.O. of Altel, one of the most inventive high-tech corporations in Europe."

"I know of Altel, sir. My wife bought one of their products recently – some sort of ingenious solar-powered muscle massaging machine."

"She bought a solar vibrator, Vihari."

"WHAT? A vibrator? Why does she need a vibrator? I'm going to have a talk with her when I return home."

"You will not be returning home, Vihari, if you do not begin to focus on the issues before you. Altel and CRC, Passoni's firm, are staunch competitors. They collaborate only on matters of great importance. Which means, Vihari, that they know about the bomb. This is why seventy Altel employees are on the yacht. They are expecting to dredge up an armed warhead that must be put out of commission."

Though the sea was calm Vihari's, stomach felt as if the boat had plunged into a deep trough. This was not good. The list of enemies stacking up against them had grown too long.

He said, "You don't mean, sir, that these two giants of high technology have *teamed up against us*?"

"I mean exactly that, Vihari. Does this upset you?"

"That would be a correct description of my emotional state, sir. Just think about it. No one was supposed to know of your fish, and look what has happened. Your fish has not only been discovered but hooked. And now . . . now, sir, you tell me that we have a coalition of high-tech firms pursuing us. It would appear that you enjoy courting disaster. Frankly, sir, it seems to me that if we are not careful, we could lose this game."

"Vihari, have we not spoken endlessly of the boredom of

conquest when there is no credible adversary? My game *requires* the possibility of losing. This is what makes it interesting. Which computer games do you play, Vihari? Ones which you win each and every time?"

"No! Of course not. But if you lose a computer game, you do not die or go to jail."

"And if you win, Vihari, you have nothing to show for it. My games are played for high stakes on both the winning and the losing sides. That is their beauty. I had hoped to find in you an associate who could appreciate a challenge."

"But . . . it's not that. I *like* challenges."

"Then what, Vihari, is your problem?"

"I . . . maybe, sir, it is an accumulation of things. Maybe I am upset because you have not told me how we are going to deal with any of this – not the girl in the next room, not Dante Passoni and CRC, not this newcomer firm."

"I have not told you, Vihari, because I thought I would let you take charge. Get us out of this mess, Vihari. You're on your own."

"But . . . what? . . . but . . . up to me? Sir, SIR! This is a mistake! Why are you doing this? Why now, of all times?"

"Stand down, Vihari. I promised you a test of your competence. Here it is. There are other reasons as well. You've come along on an interesting journey. I would like you to take some responsibility for seeing that it ends well. Also, Vihari, if I am to be honest, I must admit that I enjoy watching people perform under pressure."

"But . . . where do I begin?"

"With the girl, I should think. She is your link to Dante Passoni."

"But . . . but these Altel women? Shouldn't I deal with them first. They're all together. They're vulnerable. We could use the battleship New Jersey again. Or call in an air strike from the carrier Vincennes. The planes would arrive in minutes – if you haven't sent them all to Baghdad."

"If you wish, Vihari, you may begin in that fashion. I'll show you how to program such a strike. But it would be a stupid mistake. If you do not wait until the spent shell of the fish is aboard the yacht, you will be leaving it intact beneath the water where it can be discovered. In addition, Vihari, it would be a shame to relinquish the entertainment plum that will be ours if you time the destruction of the yacht properly."

"I don't understand, sir. The part about letting them bring up the shell so we can destroy it along with the yacht, yes. But an 'entertainment plum?' What is that?"

"By letting them bring the empty fish skin aboard, Vihari, you let them know before you dispose of them that they've been humiliated, tricked and outsmarted. And we'll be in a position to watch their reactions. When we depart for Venice, we'll leave behind the communications orb that recorded the Event. It has many capabilities we haven't used. It will float, it will swim, it will approach the yacht and photograph the faces of the Altel women staring dumbfounded into the carapace of stage one. And it will continue to photograph their faces as they see their own death approaching with terrible swiftness. Italian television is not very good, Vihari. We'll watch this drama instead. In our hotel room, on our TV screen."

"All right," stuttered Vihari. "All right, I'll wait. What now?"

"Now, Vihari, I'm going let the dynamic guidance system take us back to Venice. You have work to do at the computer that will demand all of your concentration, and I would like to watch your progress over your shoulder."

"Yes, sir, all right, sir, I'll do my best, sir."

"I'm sure you will. Stay here and compose yourself. When you're ready to get started, join me down below."

"Yes, sir. Fine, sir."

Stunned, Vihari stared at the water, which had gone from azure to steely gray. To the west, a bank of heavy clouds had formed, promising an end to the short spell of good weather.

He supposed he had passed another test by not going completely to pieces. But he didn't feel well. In fact, he felt sick. He had this terrifying premonition he might pass all of his tests – and then botch the final exam.

* * *

"Dante, it's about time!" cried Kiyo, pulling him in out of the rain. "I'm so furious at Luigi I could skin him. He refused to tell me where you were. Dante, *where* have you been?"

"At the Zitti Palace. I needed some rest. I *still* need some rest."

"Rest? After this morning's headlines?"

"I haven't seen a newspaper yet, Kiyo. What are you talking about?"

She kissed him on both cheeks. "Dante. Oh, Dante. I'm so relieved. This explains everything. Come. Let's go to my work station. I'll bring you up to date."

She took him by the arm and led him through Grandfather Giuseppe's creaking farmhouse to the room where she had set up her equipment. He watched her sit at the keyboard, lithe as a ballerina.

It was late, after five in the evening, and Dante was in urgent need of something to pick him up. He hadn't been able to tear himself away from Gina until he made love to her two more times. His body still tingled pleasantly, but his mind was half asleep. He stretched out in a comfortable armchair and opened the bottle of Cabernet Kiyo had put out, hoping it would revive him as effectively as a good Chianti.

The rain came down hard. It pattered on the roof, obscuring the sounds of Kiyo's typing.

She said, "Go on, look at the paper. It's over there beside the wine."

He stared at the first page, dumbstruck. VENICE SAVED. What was that supposed to mean?

He stood and read, pacing back and forth.

The great South African philanthropist, Pieter Godessohn, made his historic announcement at Marco Polo Airport last night.

A gift of 65 billion, no strings attached . . .

Billions for Venice because one man was outraged by the response of world's richest corporations to Vittorio Passoni's murder . . .

A gift of 65 billion because Venice – man's most beautiful artifact – must never be allowed to die . . .

And who, sir, will head the new International Commission?

Why, I wouldn't presume to dictate that choice to the Italian people.

But you must have a personal recommendation.

Yes.

And who might that be?

Senator Passoni's nephew, an Italian who has demonstrated an ability to organize and complete large projects.

Dante Passoni?

None other . . .

Dante turned the page. The article became more enthusiastic with each paragraph.

How great this Pieter Godessohn is. A man of heart, a man of vision!

A white South African who deplores racism! A foreigner who speaks our language with native fluency.

Yes, indeed. While the world's corporations pull out of the Save Venice Movement, the great Godessohn keeps the faith, for the great Godessohn understands that the death of our city – our priceless monument to the human spirit – would presage the spiritual death of mankind . . .

Dante slammed the paper down. While Kiyo let him stew, his thoughts swept back through time, settling on an autumn morning in Fiesole.

It had been a Sunday in late September. He had received a call from his uncle, a lunch invitation, and had driven south to dine in Vittorio's garden.

Easy grace and elegant charm; food, wine and children; and conversations flowing like languid water toward the warm, cloud-streaked evening.

Yes, Dante, Vittorio said, I have finally hit upon the means of achieving my lifelong goal; I have finally figured out how to save Venice. I am going to form an International Commission that will raise billions from the world's richest corporations.

Ah, Uncle, you are truly a great philanthropist.

I? No, Dante, you are wrong. I am doing this because I love Venice. I am doing it for my own satisfaction. There is only one genuine philanthropist in the world today, and you know who he is: the South African, Pieter Godessohn.

Have you contacted him yet, Uncle? He is a corporation in his own right, richer than most. I'm sure he'll want to contribute to your noble cause.

Memories, still coming, dazzling now, so bright they hurt.

Vittorio turns his head so that the shadow from his panama slides across his tan face with the crow's feet wrinkling around his eyes.

Indeed, Dante, he was among the first I asked. It was odd. He turned me down cold. He said Venice was a playground for the rich. He sounded almost angry with me for approaching him.

Dante stiffened, as if frozen by his own thought. Was it possible that Godessohn *had* been angry with Vittorio?

"Are you ready to go to work now?" Kiyo asked.

Dante shook his head, incredulous. "Most bizarre. This is

most bizarre. What do you make of it, Kiyo?" He dropped into his chair, feeling awake but dazed, and poured himself another glass of wine.

Kiyo said, "I don't know if you recall, Dante, but Pieter Godessohn did not become a public figure until nineteen ninety-one. That was the year South African billionaire C. P. Wittersand died. Godessohn inherited his entire fortune after a long court battle."

"I vaguely remember. There was some kind of scandal, wasn't there?"

"Yes. Godessohn was a complete unknown, and his past was very murky. He contested the will, which gave everything to the Order of White Knights, by claiming that he was a living blood relation of Wittersand. The wording of the will gave him a good case, provided he could prove that he was really who he said he was.

"The Order of course argued that Godessohn was an impostor. The Order lost, Godessohn won and he used his mega-inheritance to found his philanthropy. But the controversy over whether or not this man was an impostor raged for years. And, Dante, after what I've learned today, I think he was an impostor. I also think he could be the person behind the murder of your uncle."

Dante looked at her for a long time. He could see uncanny intelligence in her eyes, and feel the razor-edged sharpness of her thoughts.

"Go on, Kiyo. I'm listening. Let's take this systematically. Why do you believe he was an impostor?"

"One reason, Dante, is that in the months before Wittersand's death, the four heirs who stood to inherit his fortune all perished in very bizarre ways. It seems to me that Godessohn could have murdered these heirs, changed his identity to get his hands on the money, and then set up his charitable foundation as an unassailable symbol of his goodness.

"And, Dante, it's not as if the philanthropy has cost him anything. He's been a very shrewd businessman. Even with the billions he's given to charity, his net worth has increased many times over."

Dante swished his wine around in his glass, still feeling mentally slow. He decided not to drink anymore: the grapes of the Veneto, unlike their Tuscan cousins, lacked the stimulus he needed.

"Interesting," he said. "And whether or not Godessohn is an impostor, the fact remains that he refused my uncle's request for Venice aid. Now, suddenly, he's willing to put up a much larger sum for the same 'unworthy' cause. Suspect, all of it."

Kiyo nodded. "It is equally suspect that Godessohn wants *you* to lead *his* Commission, and that he is here in Venice on the very day the nuclear warhead left the refinery. The elements of a cat and mouse game are certainly present."

The wind was blowing harder. Rain hammered the windows and thunder shook the earth.

Dante said, "So you think he's engaged a group of scientists brilliant and evil enough to construct this enormous warhead and ingenious transporter?"

"I think that's one possibility. The other, more likely possibility is that Godessohn directed the work himself."

"Kiyo, Godessohn is not a scientist. He's an administrator, a businessman . . . a philanthropist."

"I'm afraid you're not thinking clearly, my dear Dante, and I could probably guess why. If Godessohn is an impostor, we do not know *who* he is. Therefore we cannot rule out the possibility that he *is* a scientist capable of organizing such enterprises."

"That's right, Kiyo. But if he is one of the few scientists in the world capable of such feats, what happened to his alter ego? Wouldn't that scientist have to disappear before his new incarnation could step up to claim Wittersand's inheritance."

"Yes, Dante. I believe that's exactly what happened."

"Excuse me?"

"Think back: the Nobel Prize for Physics, nineteen eighty-nine . . . the incorporation of light and gravity into the general theory of relativity . . . ."

"Laar?" said Dante. "You're talking about Nils Laar?"

"Yes! *South African* physicist, Nils Laar. South African, Dante."

"But Nils Laar died in plane crash on Mont Blanc. No one ever disputed *his* death."

"I dispute it. Look at the screen. This is the Courmayeur newspaper from the day after the crash."

Dante read the article. Near the end of the story, he came to the passage that must have caught Kiyo's attention. It was the eyewitness account of a man and a woman, presumably lovers, who had been in a sleeping bag in the snow when the plane struck the mountain. They heard the explosion. They watched in horror as Mont Blanc, wreathed in cloud, appeared in silhouette against an incandescent sky. While they were watching, a parafoil opened above them. It floated to a soft landing not twenty yards away. They lay still, not wanting to be seen. The man, who was wearing street clothes and a black bodysuit hood, hurried to a car parked nearby.

Why had the couple waited until the next day to tell anyone?

Well, it all happened so fast. They wanted to sleep on what they had seen. It was probably just a coincidence anyway, some mountain-climbing buff getting his night kicks above town when NTR Flight 31 slammed into Mont Blanc.

Dante said, "I assume these two lovers were questioned by the police?"

"Yes, Dante, and I've read the report. But I think you'll find the next day's newspaper headlines more helpful."

She typed.

On the screen, he read, "Couple Claiming Parafoil Sighting

Killed in Auto Crash."

"All right, Kiyo, let's get busy. Have you had photographs of Laar and Godessohn transmitted here for comparison."

"They're on the table beside you."

Dante opened the folder marked "Laar."

There he was, an unforgettable presence: blond hair parted in the middle and slicked straight back; a predator's beak for a nose; blue eyes, piercing even in photographs; high cheekbones, a thin face, a broadening of the cranium between the ears, as if to make room for an oversized brain.

"Ugly bugger," Dante said.

He opened the second folder and leafed through the photos of the Philanthropist. To his aggravation, the two men had nothing of significance in common – and not only because one had hair and the other didn't. Godessohn's nose was pudgy. His face was flat and broad. His eyes were set far back in their sockets – blue like Laar's, yes, but veiled in deep shadow.

Dante put away the pictures. "I don't see how it could be him, Kiyo. The physiologies of these men are entirely different. Laar is slender, the bony type – an ectomorph. Godessohn is your classic endomorph."

"Dante, you of all people are talking as if plastic surgery and steroids were yet to be invented." She picked up a sheaf of printouts, found the one she was looking for.

"Listen to this. Dr. Heinz von Leitsch – you remember him, the plastic surgeon who worked for the Red Brigades – was murdered in Rome six months after the NTR crash. Doesn't that suggest anything to you? And, Dante, another item to add to the growing list of coincidences: a year after von Leitsch died, Wilhelm Langfels, an Olympic weight lifting trainer and pioneer in the use of anabolic steroids, was found in Barbados with his throat slit."

"Kiyo, I see where you're going. But I don't believe all the steroids and plastic surgery in the world could effect a change in appearance that great. I could be wrong, of course. What I'd like to do is have a close look at Godessohn in person. I can't see his eyes very well in the photographs. If it turns out that he's got Nils Laar's eyes, we're on to something. Is he still in town?"

"I assume so, but I haven't been able to find out where he's staying. No one seems to know, not even the mayor."

"The city government officials must be keeping him under wraps. I can't say I blame them. If he's going to pour that much money into Venice, he's the most valuable resource they'll ever see."

He glanced at his watch: 8:40. "Keep trying to locate him, Kiyo. I've got to go."

"Go *where*, Dante? We shouldn't lose contact again."

"It will only be for a short time. Puzzo's girl from the refinery is in Venice. I want to get her out of the city before we start snooping around."

He didn't tell Kiyo about the promises he had made that afternoon. The first was that he would pick up Gina's dog, Bruno, before the trainer closed shop at nine o'clock. The second was that he would bring Bruno with him when he returned to the hotel later that night.

Dante was determined to keep these promises, even though Gina would be leaving the Zitti. He knew the gesture would delight her, and picking up the dog would only add a few minutes to his trip back into Venice.

No, he did not tell Kiyo these things because Kiyo would not have understood. She would have called the brief detour to pick up a dog "ridiculous;" she might even have accused him of falling in love.

So he hugged her instead, and kissed her on both cheeks, and hurried out into the storm.

CHAPTER TWENTY

Night had fallen an hour ago. An ill wind blew inland from the Adriatic, the scirocco. Heavy clouds, their bellies tinted rose by the glow of the city, swooped low, engulfing the great white dome of Santa Maria della Salute. Rain exploded in silver showers around the canal lights, and black gondolas tugged wildly at their moorings.

Vihari stood at a window of the Presidential Suite, his gut in knots and his shirt drenched with sweat. His scalp itched beneath his turban, and icy chills ran down his spine. Peering into this night of vague medieval shapes made him think of death – his own. He had failed his test of competence; Godessohn had been forced to take charge again.

Godessohn burst out of the toilet with the energy of a wild boar. Vihari froze, unable to look at him. Godessohn came near, his steps surprisingly light. "It is handled, Vihari, so I would appreciate it if you relaxed. The game is over. We have won."

"But . . . but . . ."

"Sit down. You look terrible."

Godessohn pointed to a chair. Vihari dropped into it, his chin trembling uncontrollably. "We . . . we have won? But it has only been five minutes since I confessed my failure."

"That's right, Vihari. The time it took to set things straight was brief because the tasks involved were trivial. Six French submarines on permanent patrol beneath the Adriatic have received their orders from Paris. Presently they are sailing at full speed toward the yacht. They have been instructed to form a noose around the suspicious vessel. I'll give them the green light to fire their torpedoes as soon as the fish has been hoisted aboard – and we've seen enough of the theater on deck."

"But . . . the refinery? What about the refinery? You have left all sorts of evidence in the refinery. The corpse of Puzzo, the bomb plant, the – "

"Nothing will remain. At the same time that the French

submarines are receiving their orders to destroy the yacht, the fighter-bombers of the 93rd Wing, Italian Air Force, will be ordered airborne on a fully armed combat drill. Imagine the dismay of the pilots, Vihari, when they realize they are locked on a target near Venice. Which brings us to Dante Passoni. I'll have the girl next door over for a visit. I think I can convince her to be of assistance in finding him, don't you?"

"Ugh . . . yes . . . yes, sir, most certainly, sir. But what about me? I failed my test. Does this . . . mean the elevator, sir?"

Godessohn laughed. "No, Vihari. You tried your best. I had forgotten what a handicap a one-hundred-eighty I.Q. is. As long as you remain loyal, as long as you have absolute faith in me and continue to do your best work, nothing need change."

Vihari felt a tidal wave of relief, tinged by anger. "You knew, sir. You knew, didn't you? You made me attempt things I could not possibly do – and you did this just to see me sweat."

Godessohn shrugged his shoulders. "What difference does it make, Vihari? You're still alive. Have a beer while I fetch the girl."

* * *

Gina was in awe of the spectacular fruit basket the hotel had sent up to her suite. She had had the courteous boy in the brass-buttoned tunic place it on her coffee table. Now, waking from her nap, all she could do was look at it: grapes and oranges, bananas and pears, figs and mangos, exotic fruits she had never seen before and, at its center, a smooth, succulent melon.

She was hungry, ravenous, in fact. She hadn't eaten since lunch, it was now nearly nine o'clock, and a lot had happened between then and now!

The basket was so perfect she hated to disturb it. But disturb it she must: Dante had ordered her not to leave the room, and she wasn't brave enough to use the telephone to call for dinner.

Still wearing the light gown she had worn all afternoon, she sat on the sofa and peeled a pear with her knife. She was about to take her first bite when a voice startled her.

"Good evening, Signora Passoni. Thank you kindly for your invitation."

She gasped and jerked her head up. A huge man was sitting in the flowered armchair across the room, his face lost in the shadows. The glow of the canal lights outside her balcony door shone on his massive bald pate.

Gina opened her mouth, but nothing came out. Was this it? Had Giorgio's people found her? Had the end she knew was coming come already?

The man seemed oblivious to her terror. "Signora Passoni, am I to take it you do not recognize me?"

"I . . . I . . . no," she stammered, "I do not know who you are and I did not invite you here. Please leave."

"Leave? That's hardly the sort of hospitality I've become accustomed to in this wonderful city." He stood and walked toward her. Though he was smiling, the air around him seemed charged with malevolence.

She slid to the corner of the sofa, trying not to cower, trying to believe this was not the end she feared.

He stopped beside the coffee table, gestured with his hand. "A lovely selection of fruits," he said, picking up a bunch of purple grapes.

Her heart was thumping so loudly she imagined he could hear it. "Signore, please leave . . . Signore, what are you doing in my suite? You can see that I was not expecting anyone. I did not invite you, and I do *not* know who you are."

He tossed down the grapes and sat beside her. He was so heavy he made a deep indentation in the sofa, and she felt herself sliding across the smooth leather toward him. She grabbed the sofa arm to stop herself.

He said, "Certainly, Signora Passoni, you do not expect me

to believe that you do not know who I am."

"But . . . but I *do not* know. Now, please. Go away. You had no right to come in here like this. If you do not go at once, I shall call the desk."

She reached for the telephone – what did it matter now? – but his powerful hand grasped her forearm and guided it to her lap.

She glanced at his face and wished she hadn't. His eyes burned with a fierce, almost otherworldly intensity, and his smile was a slice of evil.

He said, "My visit is not a mistake. You made a foolish attempt to meddle in my affairs. That, my dear girl, was an invitation for me to come."

She gasped. She could not make him leave. All she could do was try to stall and hope Dante came back in time to help her. "But . . ." she stammered, "but how did you get in?"

He smiled solicitously. "I entered by way of the twelfth-century passage linking our two suites. I am a student of this hotel. If it interests you, the passage was built by the great Sienese lover, Count Lorenzo Battola. Count Battola, it is said, made many a blond princess of the north ecstatic with his nocturnal calls, often while the husband slumbered unsuspectingly in the same bed."

She could think of nothing to say. How could she stall if she couldn't talk? He loomed huge and silent on the sofa beside her, waiting. He was giving her the opportunity to speak. She mustn't squander it.

"I . . . Signore, I am not an educated person. I did not know the story of Count Battola. These passages, it surprises me that they still exist."

"It shouldn't surprise you. You've been in Italy quite long enough to know how things function here. The job of closing the passages, a job that would take any other people a few days to complete, takes the Italians eight centuries – and it's still not finished! Why is Venice crumbling? The reason, Signora, is the glaring incompetence of an entire nation. But let us not be too hard on these noisy, good-natured asses. To sit here with you, I needed only remove a few unmortared stones."

"But . . . but *why* did you come?"

"Don't play the fool with me, Gina. You are working for Dante Passoni. You are supposed to be working for my people, Puzzo and the Sheik. You've switched sides. Now you're going to have to switch back again."

She saw the syringe coming, but she could not move. He sank the needle into her thigh. The ceiling spun slowly out of focus, a merry-go-round of crystal chandeliers and gilded cherubs.

The Presence! He had come for her! She had known all along something horrible awaited her. She saw him spinning above her, spinning with the chandeliers and cherubs, his broad face splotched with pink. She saw him take a bite out of a pear. And then he disappeared in a cloud of misty gray.

* * *

When she awoke, she was sprawled across a large bed. Her skirt was above her knees. His leering nut-brown servant, wearing a tan suit and maroon turban, rubbed a pin prick on her thigh, gesticulating with a syringe as he chattered. She had seen him before – in the lobby when the night clerk collapsed, if she wasn't mistaken. She brushed his hand away and pulled her skirt down. Using the ornate wooden headboard for support, she managed to sit up.

Her mind cleared quickly; she emerged from her stupor with her memory – and her terror – intact. She had been abducted by the man Giorgio called the Presence! The servant had evidently used another drug to wake her up. And now . . . they were going to make her talk about Dante. If they would just kill her, kill her and end her tortured life, it would be so much easier. She was prepared to die; she was *not* prepared to betray her only friend.

The servant sounded like an agitated monkey, but he wasn't

talking to her. He was talking to the Presence, who sat in an armchair beside the fire, ablaze in an enormous stone hearth. He was watching TV, and his thick features danced in the light of the flames. On the screen she could make out a deck party on board a yacht.

When she felt steady enough to climb down from the bed, she swung a leg over the side.

"Stay there," Godessohn said in Italian. He left his armchair and stood over her. She cowered, and the carved wooden figurines on the headboard cut into her back.

He said, "I would like to take up where we left off a short time ago. If you will recall, you were going to answer my questions regarding Dante Passoni.

"Now, Signorina, you may either cooperate with me, in which case this interrogation will be brief and painless, or you may resist me, in which case you will force me to hurt you. Whatever you choose, I assure you the outcome will be the same. Tell me when and where you met Passoni."

She turned away, refusing to speak.

He leaned over the bed until his face was inches from hers. She felt the hair rising on her neck.

He said, "Give up trying to resist, Gina. This suite is a soundproof chamber, designed to protect Presidents from the indiscretions of their women. Your screams, should you resort to them, will not be heard. Do you see the hearth? Do you see the poker hanging above it? I am a man of technical sophistication, Signorina, but I sometimes find enjoyment in the use of primitive techniques. That poker will be a splendid device for making you talk. Fourteenth-century iron dull with age. Heated red-hot and jammed into your eyes, I think it should suffice to loosen your tongue. Imagine the smell of burning flesh, Gina, and the hiss of your tears going up in steam. We needn't belabor the point by discussing pain."

He leaned so close she felt she was suffocating in the wash of his breath. "You will be a gruesome sight. The beggars at the train station will look away when you pass. And Dante Passoni . . . how do you think he will react to your new appearance?"

He slapped the bed and called to his servant in English.

The servant stuck the poker into the fire and began fanning the coals with an ancient leather bellows. The blaze crackled with fresh life.

"Vihari!" barked Godessohn.

The servant pulled out the poker and held it up. The tip glowed orange.

Gina looked down at the bedspread to escape the intensity of Godessohn's stare. She saw her fingers kneading the quilt, working mindlessly, detached from her will. Her hair fell forward over her eyes. She wanted to hide behind that black veil until she woke in Dante's arms and discovered this was nothing but a hideous dream.

She said, "Dante Passoni and I are having an affair. He is gone. I don't know when I'll see him again."

Godessohn straightened up and sighed. He said something in English. The servant started the bellows wheezing. The fire leaped and flared.

"You are a very bad liar, Gina." Godessohn smiled ominously, and she saw a scrap of pear peeling lodged between his teeth. "You shouldn't have done what you did – is this what you wish to say? Manfred, the Sheik and Puzzo were sorry, too. They wisely repented and saved themselves a lot of unnecessary suffering. I executed them painlessly today."

"Giorgio . . . is . . . dead?"

"Yes. I disposed of the nervous little rat by telephone."

"By . . . telephone?"

Godessohn chuckled. "An elementary exercise in microwave transmission."

The telephone!

Gina listened to the bellows sigh and the fire crackle and the servant's knees pop when he stood. She listened; and fought not to panic. God, she had been right. The phones here could kill! And Dante would soon be returning to the room next door. He wouldn't be worried about answering the phone because he had refused to listen to her! Whatever happened, Godessohn must not find out that Dante was coming back to the Zitti . . .

The servant began to chatter more loudly. He left his post at the hearth and scurried to the television, waving frantically at Godessohn.

"One moment," Godessohn said. He ambled over to join the servant in front of the TV. The two men fell silent as they watched.

Between them, Gina could see the picture. The crowd of women on the yacht's deck had all moved to one side. They were peering over the railing at a long gray cylinder with tail fins, which was being hoisted out of the water.

Godessohn, laughing to himself, returned to the bed and sat down beside her, making a deep crater like the one he had made in her sofa. He picked up the telephone on the antique night table beside the bed.

She could not stop herself, she slid down the incline toward him. Her thigh bumped against his rock-hard butt. She was near him, she was touching him. Something moved her to grab his huge arm. Hot tears came streaming down her face. He must have a grain of humanity buried somewhere inside him! Everyone did, even pigs like Giorgio. She shook him. She would uncover that grain of humanity! She must uncover it! She would tell him about her feelings for Dante. How could he not be moved by her simple story of love?

"Please," she whispered. "Please, Signore, I will tell you how I met Dante Passoni. But it is not what you think. We did not come here to look for you. Giorgio was angry with me. Dante Passoni rescued me from Giorgio. We are . . . in love."

"Be quiet," Godessohn growled. He detached her hands from his arm and pushed her roughly away. "Can't you see that I'm busy."

She watched, trembling, as he put the receiver down and hammered on the touch-tone buttons. The beeps rang senselessly in her ears, a chaos of insane chirping.

Godessohn hung up. He was staring at her. She shivered. She had been wrong about his humanity. He was like a bank of cold fog, no warm center.

The servant, still in front of the television, began to cackle.

Godessohn said, "We have haven't much more time, Gina. I've begun to tie up loose ends. In eight minutes the French Navy will sink the yacht you see on television. In twenty-six minutes the Italian Air Force will destroy Puzzo's refinery. The sinking of the yacht will be your deadline, as I wish to watch the air show undisturbed.

"Therefore, you are going to answer my questions about Passoni quickly and truthfully. One more lie, even a little one, and I shall burn your eyes out."

Defiance stirred deep inside her, as new and powerful as the sexual feelings Dante had unleashed. It chased away her fear and filled her heart with resolve. She would accept the poker in her eyes! She would accept the agony, the stench, the hissing – and she would spit in Godessohn's face! Her entire life she had been a slave of evil men. Then Dante had come and shown her kindness. She could not, she *would* not, betray him.

She bit deep into her lip. She willed her sobbing to stop. She said, "Tell your servant to come with his poker. I have said all that I am going to say."

Godessohn laughed. "How naive you are, Gina. You didn't think I was actually going to smell up this fine suite with your burning flesh, did you? I was passing time, trying to entertain myself during our vigil. While you were under Sodium Pentothal, you told me everything I needed to know. We – you and I – are presently waiting for Dante Passoni to return to your suite, as you assured me he would."

"He is not returning!" cried Gina. "He is not coming back. You are lying! I never said that!"

Godessohn smiled thinly. "Please excuse me. The segment of the television program that interests me is about to begin."

* * *

She heard a strange and delicate noise, like a miniature music box. She stiffened. She had resisted the fierce urge to curl up in the fetal position and weep, telling herself again and again that it might be a bluff, that she might not have talked under the drug.

Godessohn walked toward her, bringing the noise with him. He sat on the bed; she bounced and slid toward him. He pulled the chiming object from his pocket. She couldn't see it very well, but it looked like an old-fashioned watch.

He pushed a tiny button. The gold cover popped up, and he held the watch in her direction.

It wasn't a watch at all, but a bright liquid crystal display that reminded her of a miniature flow diagram. A wavering yellow line snaked across its face.

Godessohn turned off the chime and dropped the device back into his pocket. "My seismograph informs me that you have a visitor next door."

His hand moved toward the telephone.

He knew; it had not been a bluff.

She threw herself at him, screaming at the top of her lungs. He pushed her away and laughed. He seemed to be having fun!

She came at him again, broke her nails, jammed her fingers, bit her tongue as she flailed at this unyielding wall of muscle.

All the while, the image of the stricken night clerk swam before her, his temples bulging like eggs as he dropped the receiver and collapsed.

Now it was Dante answering the phone. She could see him as clearly as if he were standing before her, could see his handsome face, his eyes, his hair, gray around the temples, gray marking the spots where his perfect head would bulge.

Godessohn shoved her against the headboard. She felt a prick on her thigh. The servant had snuck up on her and given her another injection!

Godessohn started speaking English, and his voice sounded like an echo in a cave. The servant smiled, his teeth sparkling like pearls.

A micro syringe lay on the quilt beside her, its plunger all the way down. Yes, another injection. She felt the drug coming on, but it wasn't the same drug Godessohn had used on her for the abduction. The room was not spinning, and she was still alert.

She tried to turn her head, but her neck refused to move. She watched the servant pick up the empty syringe and put it in its plastic container, then stare shamelessly at her crotch. She tried to say something. She could not open her mouth. She could not make a sound.

Her back began to slide across the headboard, the sharp little figurines clawing at her flesh. Godessohn propped her up with pillows.

"The drug will last only a few minutes," he said, "long enough for me to deal with your friend."

She watched in helpless agony as he lifted the receiver and hammered the touch-tone buttons. Dante was going to die. Her vision of his head exploding had been a glimpse into the future. And she in her naïveté had mistaken this for the happiest day of her life!

She screamed from the depths of her soul as Godessohn picked up the receiver and spoke, a silent scream that tore her heart.

Oh, God, she could hear them talking . . .

"Good evening, Signor Passoni. This is Pieter Godessohn.

I'm in the suite next door. I hope I'm not disturbing . . . "

Smiling, he held the receiver away from his head so that she could hear Dante's voice. She *could* hear it, faint but unmistakable.

He said, "As a matter of fact, Signor Godessohn, I tried to reach you earlier to congratulate you on your magnificent act of philanthropy . . . "

Godessohn looked at his watch, smiled.

He said, "I am here with your lovely wife and several . . . "

He stopped talking and stretched the receiver in Gina's direction.

A wet, muffled pop came out the earpiece, followed by the sounds of a body crashing into furniture. As Dante expired, she heard him make a noise like a whimpering wolfhound, a pathetic death rattle.

Godessohn laughed and hung up. "Now, Vihari, after the yacht show, I'm going up to the Presidential Patio to watch the air raid. From the roof one has a fine view across the Lagoon toward the refinery."

He took a tiny plastic handgun from his pocket and gave it to his servant. "You will accompany Gina to her suite, where you will reunite her in death with her lover. When you are finished, join me upstairs."

* * *

A throaty female cheer rose from the deck of the yacht when the tail fins of the fish broke water. Luigi, wedged at the rail between two rain-slickered Altel women, struggled to get a better view.

It had become a nasty night. Lightning flashed nearby and hail raked the deck. Appropriate weather, he thought, for the fishing story of the millennium. He had to hand it to Graziella Calvino: she'd made the catch in conditions that would have deterred many a brave man.

Or had she?

The nose of the fish was emerging now, and it was as blunt as the top of a soup can. How could something with a blunt nose travel at 60 knots under water?

As the fish swung over the deck, Luigi saw that the lunker had no innards! It was nothing but an empty shell! Madonna, he had known it all along: this job was too big for anyone but Dante Passoni.

He heard Graziella's distraught voice. He watched, stunned, as the crew and technicians attached the fish to the stands they had set up for it. He slithered through the rain-slickered crowd for a better view – and found himself staring down a hollow tube lined with polished tracks. Near the back of the long cylinder was a steel plate blackened by three burn spots.

Stages! A rocket had gone off to separate a smaller fish from its mother and send it shooting forward. Graziella Calvino and her women had landed a shell containing an expended first-stage power plant. The cargo was still en route to wherever it was going.

He had to inform Dante immediately!

Should he ask Graziella Calvino to use the boat phone?

No. She would not be in the mood to admit defeat. He had one option: the helicopter.

He pulled his hood over his head and started toward the aft deck, moving like a pickpocket through groups of grumbling, frustrated women.

Every few steps he glanced at Graziella Calvino, who stood in the glare of bright lights in front of the gutted fish lecturing her employees.

So far, so good. She didn't seem to suspect a mutiny.

He climbed aboard the helicopter, shut the door as quietly as he could and started the engines. The blades began to clatter and whir, foaming the puddles on deck.

Luigi kept one eye trained on Graziella, the other on his

gauges. "Spin, you slow dog. Spin!"

She looked in his direction. Then, without a moment's hesitation, she bolted toward him.

He gave full throttle. She was too late; for once in her life, she was too late!

The chopper tilted forward, the wheels left the yawing deck, the tail came about 45 degrees.

He couldn't see her now, she had run beneath him.

Up we go, throttle still buried. Altitude ten feet, out of harm's way.

He blasted the shipload of women with his pecking gesture.

So long, Graziella. So long, all of you. I'm at twenty feet, doubly out of harm's way. Dante will be coming soon, the man you all need.

Up, up, up. Two hundred feet, almost in the clouds. Rain still falling, wintery squalls. The overcast opened in a jagged tear, admitting the pale light of the moon. The sea came alive, a great jeweled supine beast.

And then he saw them: six churning alabaster torpedo trails heading for the yacht.

The first torpedo struck with a dazzling flash just as the helicopter entered the clouds. Five more flashes came in quick sequence, explosions so violent he felt their shock waves. Burning debris ripped past him like streaking shards of flak and fell slowly in blazing orbs, just missing his blades.

Christ in a Knocking Shop, what was that noise? Dammit, he had spoken too soon. A horrible banging echoed up through the cargo hold. He'd been hit, hit bad! He'd never heard such an awful sound. Engine damage! Shaft bearings! Blade missing a chunk, completely out of balance.

He checked his gauges. Strange. No leaks and no loss of power. He cut back on the throttle to see if the horrible noise would diminish. It grew louder.

Holy Madonna, how was he going to take the right emergency action when he didn't know what the problem was? He'd better put her on automatic hover and check things out visually.

He climbed into the cargo bay, opened the doors and turned on his spotlight. A high-heeled shoe whistled by his ear.

Graziella released the wheel strut from which she hung, grabbed his pant legs and hoisted herself aboard. Her gold Beretta appeared before he could move.

"Back to the cockpit, Peanut Peg! You will fly me directly to Dante Passoni. He's destroyed the top echelons of my company with his monstrous male trick. He's gone too far."

CHAPTER TWENTY-ONE

"No barking," said Dante, arriving at Gina's door after a long climb up the service stairs. He inserted the hotel key in the lock. "No barking, *capisc*? She might already have gone to bed."

Bruno whimpered and wagged his tail.

Dante opened. The Senatorial Suite was deathly quiet. In the bedroom, where he expected to find her asleep, the lights still burned.

The bathroom was empty. He quickened his pace. Bruno lagged behind, sniffing out familiar smells.

The dining room was empty. It bore no trace of their lunch or lovemaking.

He stepped into the living room, softly calling her name. He saw a gigantic fruit basket on the coffee table. A pear had been taken from it and peeled with a knife and fork. It lay uneaten on a china plate.

Bruno sniffed his pant leg, and he irritably ordered the dog to lie down. Had she ignored his instructions and gone out?

He returned his attention to the basket. The large smooth melon at its center was undisturbed, but one of the remaining pears seemed out of place, lying among the grapes. When he picked it up, he noticed that a large bite was missing from its flank.

The world was divided into two types of people: those who peeled their pears and those who did not. Both a peeler and a non-peeler had been in the Senatorial Suite since he had left. Gina had had a visitor.

He closed his eyes. What if her fears had been justified and he had been wrong? What if they *had* found her?

Rain lashed the windows. A sharp gust of wind shook the balcony door.

The balcony! He hadn't checked it yet. He had a horrible vision of Gina's body lying out there in the night.

He looked. Nothing but the cold sheen of ceramic tiles,

slick in the rain.

He stared at the oily black water three stories down. A few boats still plowed the canal, their deck lights glowing dimly in the mist.

He suddenly wished he had a gun, but this was Italy and the nearest gun was an hour away at his grandfather's farmhouse. He wasn't going to talk down America anymore. You might not be able to get wine with your fast-food hamburger, but you *could* pick up a weapon at the discount store across the street.

Dammit, his thoughts were becoming muddled. He needed an espresso. He would call the kitchen to see who had ordered the fruit basket – and have them send up a pot worthy of Puzzo.

He walked to the end table beside the sofa and reached for the telephone. In the same instant, it rang.

He took a deep breath and answered. "Hello."

"Good evening, Signor Passoni. This is Pieter Godessohn. I am presently in the suite next door . . ."

Dante felt a pleasant tingle near the center of his brain. His muddled thoughts were instantly clear.

The telephone!

His mind charged ahead at a dizzy pace. If Kiyo was right, if Godessohn was Nils Laar, he would be capable of transforming anything into a murder weapon – even a telephone.

How had Gina described the death of the night clerk?

Temples bulging, forehead too hot to touch. Holy Madonna, it sounded like microwaves. Get the receiver off your ear! Get it off but keep talking! If this is a murder attempt, the killer must believe he's succeeded. You've got no gun. It's your only chance.

GET THAT RECEIVER OFF YOUR EAR.

He twisted it so that the earpiece was pointing away from him.

He could still hear Godessohn's businesslike voice. "I hope I'm not disturbing . . ."

Dante's eyes settled on the fruit basket, his mind whirred like a CRC mainframe.

How could he determine if the phone was lethal?

How could he simulate his own death if it was?

The melon!

He placed the earpiece of the receiver against the melon's smooth white skin. He bent over and craned his neck at a weird angle so that he could speak into the mouthpiece while staying out of the path of any possible microwave stream. He increased the volume of his voice to make up for the distance.

A steely calm came over him.

He said, "As a matter of fact, Signor Godessohn, I tried to reach you earlier to congratulate you on your magnificent act of philanthropy . . ."

He could feel the guts of the melon coming to a boil.

Godessohn's muffled voice leaked out the gap between the earpiece and the melon skin. "I am here with your lovely wife and several . . ."

Godessohn stopped talking.

A microsecond later, the melon exploded in a bomb burst of sizzling green slime.

Dante dropped the phone and crashed on to the coffee table.

Bruno whimpered and fled in panic.

Though his head still echoed from the explosion, Dante could hear hateful laughter coming over the line. There was a click as Godessohn hung up.

The Zitti's Presidential Suite! Of course that's where this supposed Savior of Venice would be staying!

Dante wiped the steaming melon innards from his face and hauled himself to his feet.

Bruno was in hiding. No time to go looking for him now: the damned dog had already cost Dante enough time. His advantage, if he had one, wouldn't last forever. He had to *move*!

Move, yes, but which way?

Godessohn's balcony was 20 feet from his. Perhaps he could tie a couple of sheets into a makeshift rope and use coat hangers to fashion hooks.

No good. There was still boat traffic on the canal. Some late-night skipper would see him dangling above the water on his way to the balcony of the Presidential Suite. *He* would be taken for an assailant. The fog horns would go off, the spotlights would come on, Godessohn would be alerted.

So what were his options short of involving the carabinieri, the ultimate guarantee of failure? He knew from his uncle that there was a secret Passage of Presidential Mistresses, but that was all he knew. He would need hours to locate the entrance and crack the heavy locks.

No good.

He felt as if he were driving his Lamborghini on a perfect stretch of highway with a thousand Fiats blocking the left lane.

He thought he saw something move off to his left. He jerked his head around. His imagination.

He went back to his brainstorming. Again, he thought he saw something move.

Was there a *mouse* in the hearth?

Yes, a mouse. He heard it now, scratching away as though it was trying to tell him something.

The hearth! It was enormous. With any luck he could climb up the inside of the chimney to the hotel roof. He wouldn't be able to break into Godessohn's suite through the Presidential Patio. Altel had outfitted the patio access with an impenetrable system of doors and locks. But the *chimney* of the Presidential Suite? Italians did not consider chimneys security risks because Italian crooks did not like to get dirty.

Yes, that was it: Godessohn's suite would be accessible through the chimney. Godessohn took him for dead. If Dante could get in through the chimney – and if Godessohn was where he said he was – Dante could take him by surprise. Even if Godessohn was armed, a good blow to the back of his neck would neutralize his advantage.

Dante felt a glimmer of encouragement: he had a plan.

He stuck his head into the medieval hearth, opened the long iron damper, and looked up at the inside walls of the chimney. Plenty of room, firm handholds in the craggy stonework. A short simple climb. God the Florentine was watching after him, helping him to correct the horrible mistake he had made in leaving Gina alone.

He reached the top easily, worked the heavy ceramic chimney cap off its mounts and slid it to the side. Squeezing out into the rainy night, he let himself down on the gently sloping tile roof.

The sight of smoke curling from Godessohn's chimney stunned him. He had been so sure he would get his break on the roof. He was not mentally prepared for a dead end.

Feeling sick, Dante gazed at the mist-enshrouded lights of the sleeping city. Cold rain washed the soot from his face and carried it into his mouth. It tasted bitter, like defeat.

An earsplitting howl brought him out of his torpor. He dove instinctively on to his stomach, glancing up just in time to see a wedge of supersonic fighter-bombers break out of the overcast above his head. He followed the fires of their exhausts as they roared across the Lagoon.

The pride of the Italian Air Force! The hotshots of the 93rd Wing! The daring rolls, the sound of those turbines! But what were they doing over Venice?

Seconds later the first bombs hit the refinery. Gasoline storage tanks erupted like Vesuvius in '44, lighting up the heavy night sky. Red tile roofs and rain-dimpled canals emerged from the darkness, giving Venice the look of a city under siege.

As Dante clambered to his feet, another wave of attacking aircraft howled toward their blazing target. He scarcely noticed them; nothing surprised him anymore. He would have to leave the Zitti, that much was clear. He would have to approach Godessohn through the Passage of Presidential Mistresses after all.

But what were his chances of success? Fortunately, he knew the favorite mistress of the President very well. Unfortunately, he had not been receptive to her advances.

After a third wave of jets swept overhead, there was a lull in the attack. He took a deep breath, shook his head, grimaced. He could only hope that Godessohn would still be in the suite when he finally got there.

And that Gina would still be alive.

Hope, how he hated the word! He had always considered hope the last resort of mediocre men.

As he turned toward the chimney, he heard his name spoken in the same businesslike voice that had come to him over the telephone. He lifted his eyes to the flat rectangular summit of the roof and saw a great hulk of a man standing beneath the canopy that spanned the Presidential Patio. The man was holding something that looked like a miniature video camera.

"Good evening, Signor Passoni. I've been watching your antics. Most entertaining. A Christ-like rise from the tomb, a perfect belly landing. I must say, you've added a fine operatic touch to my air show. Come join me for a drink, won't you?"

Godessohn pointed the camera-like device at Dante and conducted a thorough scan. Dante recognized the device as CRC's new antiterrorist probe, a long-range, portable weapons and explosives detector.

Godessohn said, "A wise addition to the Presidential Patio, wouldn't you agree? Good not only for visiting presidents but for the two of us as well. Without it, fear and suspicion might prevent us from sitting down with one another for a civilized chat. That would be a shame, Signor Passoni. We have so many things in common, and so many things to discuss."

Smiling, Godessohn pushed the device on to the inclined roof. It slid down a gully between the tiles in a torrent of rainwater. Dante caught it and aimed it at Godessohn. The light on its console blinked green.

Dante had absolute confidence in the new CRC unit. It was shockproof, tamper proof, waterproof and foolproof. It picked up metal, gunpowder, plastique explosives and the chemical compounds used in the new Customs Buster plastic guns. Godessohn might have weapons stashed somewhere up there on the patio – Dante would keep a wary eye on him – but he carried nothing on his person.

Dante threw the detector off the roof.

Godessohn said, "Extraordinary, isn't it, Signor Passoni. We meet at last, and neither of us is armed. You look in need of a drink, and I would like to enjoy this historic evening in the company of a man able to appreciate its significance. Won't you join me?"

"Yes," Dante said, "I would be happy to join you."

The rain pelted him, the jets resumed their attack on the refinery.

He started up the roof toward the top.

He had a fighting chance, he thought. No man had a right to ask for more.

* * *

"Come on, come on," chattered Vihari impatiently. "A few steps and we're there."

He knew she couldn't understand a word he said, but he could not stop talking. He was aroused, and whenever he was aroused, his mouth moved like a high-pitched little motor.

He could hear the first wave of jets hurtling toward the refinery. Bugger the air show. Forget joining Godessohn up on the roof. He had more interesting things to do in the Senatorial Suite.

Ah, yes, thought Vihari, much more interesting. His job was to make it appear that this girl had been involved in a lovers' murder-suicide. He wore surgical gloves, he carried condoms in his wallet. Why shouldn't he supply the missing element, the lust?

He chuckled to himself. Someone had to do it, and Passoni was dead.

Vihari held her under her arm. She was limp. She felt as though she might fall. He jerked her upright.

In the dim light, he finally found what he had been looking for, the rusty spoked wheel he was supposed to turn. He took it in one hand, and keeping his grip on Gina with the other, cranked it around.

Ah, yes, just as that bastard Godessohn had said. He could see it now: the stone hearth of the Senatorial Suite doubled as a secret entrance. It was on tracks and it moved a half inch or so with each revolution of the wheel. Soon, very soon, they would step from this dank passage into the girl's comfortable quarters.

Ah, yes, the sliver of light was widening nicely. He could see into the room now, could see the balcony door and the amber lights of canal below.

Widening, widening. He bit Gina's ear and pinched her on the breast. She stiffened and hissed at him.

Ah, yes, he thought, alive and well. She would fight when he ripped off her clothes. She would fight when he gave her the gift of his smooth brown cobra. This was good. After ten years of Tamina lying under him like something dead, he was going to enjoy any kind of movement.

Cranking, sweating, breathing harder, Vihari could scarcely control his lust. He began rubbing up and down against her, like a dog. She took a swing at him. He laughed. Godessohn was a bastard, but Godessohn had shown him a thing or two about having fun.

He gave the wheel two more turns . . . there, there, that

should do it.

He shoved Gina through the opening. She tripped and fell face down. Stay right there, he thought, lie right there on that fine oriental carpet. I'll take you Indian-style from behind – for a start.

He turned the wheel once more and squeezed himself inside. Standing over her, he listened to the next wave of jets bearing down on the refinery.

He looked around the living room.

No Passoni here, he must have answered one of the other telephones. But . . . what was this? The phone on the end table by the sofa was off the hook. The receiver lay on the floor amid a heap of spilled fruit.

"Get up," he shrieked at Gina, yanking her fiercely to her feet. "What's all that fruit doing on the floor?"

He hurled her down on the sofa, picked up the receiver and examined it. He thought he heard her make a sound – a squeak or a laugh.

She was mocking him! He stared at her. She had her hand over her mouth. She laughed some more – nervously, childishly. She looked at him as if he had put his palm in pigeon shit again.

This was unforgivable. This was outrageous. She was about to be raped and killed and she was laughing at him! What did she need before she took him seriously? His cobra between her legs? His two-shot plastic gun barking at her breasts? He was feeling different about himself after this last encounter with Godessohn. The days when Vihari allowed women, or anyone else, to make fun of him were over.

He raised his hand to strike her. In that instant he saw a misshapen melon with a huge gash in its side lying on the floor.

Vihari dropped his hand and took a closer look at the corner of the living room where he stood.

This could not be! Pale green melon guts were everywhere – befouling paintings, dangling from chandeliers, bespattering the cherubs on the domed ceiling.

Godessohn had microwaved a melon!

He took a deep breath. This was his test by fire, his ultimate test of competence. Passoni was not dead! Passoni might be in this very suite! He drew his pistol, backed against the wall and listened for the sound of footsteps. Nothing. Cautiously, he moved in the direction of the dining room.

She came off the sofa shrieking like a wildcat and grabbed him around the legs. "No!" she screamed. "Dante, *attenzione!*"

He sent her sprawling on the floor with a knee to the side of her head.

Ah, yes, Dante Passoni *is* here, thought Vihari. She had called his name. Of course he is here: the Italian male flees only in groups. Alone, he fights to the death.

Vihari chuckled to himself. This pathetic fool Passoni must not be armed or he would already have attacked. Ah, yes, he is defenseless. He is here, but he is defenseless. Killing him is just a matter of hunting him down.

He heard faint footsteps in some distant room of the suite.

Good, good, they were light footsteps. Dante Passoni must be small, not some fear-making giant like Godessohn. No reason to doubt the gun's ability to do the job.

Now there were lots of these light footsteps. Good, very good. Further proof Passoni was small. That many of Godessohn's footsteps would have sounded like a division of soldiers marching across a bridge.

Vihari smiled at Gina, who was still writhing in pain on the floor. He could hardly contain his elation. Godessohn had been tricked! Godessohn was fallible. Vihari was going to save him and harvest his eternal gratitude! No more humiliations at the hands of his boss, not after this!

Gina got to all fours and tried to tackle him. Vihari yanked his leg loose and kicked her in the stomach. She rolled over, gasping.

The footsteps were approaching.

He raised his gun.

She screamed.

Come on, Dante Passoni, he thought, keep running this way. The instant you turn that corner, you're dead.

Footsteps growing louder, accelerating, some kind of futile Latin charge. Vihari was awash in the sweat of eager anticipation. It poured into his eyes and ran like cold water down his hairless chest.

A mango hit him in the side of the head. He did not look around. His association with the Philanthropist had taught him to look out for cheap tricks.

The footsteps were very close now, a couple of yards away. He drew his lips tight and squinted to stabilize the room. He steadied his gun with both hands, like he had seen them do on TV.

Dante Passoni exploded into his field of vision, not at all what he was expecting, but a giant airborne dog with lips curled back to reveal rows of long pointed teeth.

Steady! Pull the trigger!

He did, but a chair hit him in the arm and sent the bullet into the ceiling. He heard chandelier glass raining down with the music of wind chimes. And then a fury of claws and teeth was upon him. The dog seemed to know what a gun was: it clamped his wrist firmly in its jaws. It was a brute, a monster; it dragged him down on the floor.

But he still had the gun, and he hung on to it though canine teeth pierced his flesh to the bone. He had one shot left, he'd damned well better make it count.

He was being dragged in circles now, whirled so viciously he felt the heat burning through his trousers. Gina stood over him, pelting him with ripe fruits. He thought he heard her mocking him.

He managed to transfer the gun to his other hand.

The dog did not notice! It was twirling him around by the same wrist! Soon he would have a shot.

But what was this? The girl had somehow managed to climb on to his back!

Take care of the dog first! He aimed, but before he could fire she pulled his turban over his eyes. When he yanked it off, she grabbed the gun, two hands to his one, and squeezed the finger he held on the trigger. Nothing. She wasn't strong enough. He spun on his knees. She fell hard but continued to cling to the gun, squeezing, squeezing, his finger growing tired now, it wasn't made to push out. He rolled on top of her and cursed in wild frustration when the gun went off and he heard the bullet ricochet over by the hearth.

She screamed. The dog didn't like that at all. It let go of his wrist and went for his neck. The girl urged the beast on in that frenzied language of hers. Its ferocious growling filled his ears.

Vihari rolled on his stomach and wrapped his arms around his head. He felt teeth sink into the scruff of his neck. And then he was being pushed forward by the dog, pushed like a body sled at a belly-scorching speed. He stuck his hands out in front of him to brake the slide, and put his butt in the air in a frantic attempt to clamber to his feet.

It was then that he felt the dog's pelvis banging against him.

No, no, anything but this! It would look to the girl as if he were being sodomized by a dog! Terminal humiliation!

He thought he heard her howl with laughter, then realized he was listening to his own howls. He rolled on his back and kicked wildly, the way he used to kick in schoolyard fights.

A break at last: he scored a direct hit on the dog's flank, a blow so hard it nearly broke Vihari's toes.

The dog yelped and backed off. But the girl let out another scream, and the dog recovered, and low ugly growling sounds began to come from deep in its throat.

He'd better get out of here while he could. He bolted for the balcony, flung open the glass door and held it shut with both hands when he was outside.

The rain beat down on him, stinging his bites. The jets roared overhead, rattling his brain. He saw his nemesis inside, petting the dog. She walked to the hearth and took down the poker.

He glanced over his shoulder at the Grand Canal. It was a long way down, and the water was filthy. But if she came for him with that killer dog and that instrument of karma she was wielding, he had an escape route. He would jump, of course he would jump.

Ah, yes, the landing would hurt: it would feel like a huge body slap. He would lie stunned for a few seconds in the water. But as soon as he recovered, he would swim to safety. He could swim to the ends of the earth. The day he'd had an argument with his father on the family boat, he'd swum eight miles to shore.

Decided then: he would flee if he she came for him, defeated not by his own incompetence but because the infallible Godessohn had microwaved a melon instead of Dante Passoni's head.

CHAPTER TWENTY-TWO

The jets had stopped attacking, but the rainy December night was nonetheless full of noise. Sirens wailed on the mainland, and the sporadic thunder of refinery explosions rumbled across the Lagoon.

Dante reached the flat summit of the roof and stepped over the low wrought-iron fence surrounding the Presidential Patio. He felt as if he had entered a heated bubble: the patio's great transparent canopy shielded him from the rain, and vents in the floor blew warm air into his sodden pant legs.

He had been worried his cold, wet muscles would cramp, but in this sauna-like place, he knew they would be all right. He could now concentrate on more important things – such as how he was going to slay the bull-necked Goliath waiting for him not 20 feet away.

Godessohn stood beside a gargantuan crescent-shaped marble bar that must have weighed tons. He sipped his drink and ignored Dante's arrival. His attention seemed focused on a fire boat that was plowing a slow, smoky course along the Grand Canal. His expression as he watched the Mussolini-era coal steamer was brimming with contempt.

Not the type, thought Dante, to appreciate the Old Italy. A Savior of Venice he was definitely not.

Godessohn wore a sport coat and a white shirt with an open collar. His big bald head, touched by the glow of the red, white and green patio lights, shone with the colors of the Republic.

This was a good omen, thought Dante. It was as if the Italy Godessohn detested, the old Italy of incomparable charm, secret passages and byzantine byways, had seen through his bogus savior act and marked him with Her colors for death.

To either side of the bar were thickly padded chairs and glass tables. Potted geraniums and neatly arranged clusters of miniature pines created the ambiance of an expensive outdoor café. There was a charming antique dumb waiter – the very old in the midst of the very new – and toward the northwest corner, a raised bandstand with a small decorative canopy from which hung four unlit spotlights.

Godessohn turned slowly toward Dante. His face and eyes were wreathed in shadow. He shook his head. The red, white and green reflection clung to his scalp like a birthmark.

He smiled.

"A thoroughly ridiculous country yours is, Signor Passoni. Your national antics bring such amusement to the foreign visitor. The air attack was a special delight. I have no doubt that the world would again live in fear of Rome if you people ever learned to fight your enemies with the same ferocity that you reserve for each other."

He laughed.

He seemed to be having fun.

Dante stripped off his wet sooty jacket and tossed it aside. It landed with a splat on the tile floor. "I would like to know what you have done with Gina."

Godessohn raised his eyebrows. "Gina? Oh, yes, that dreary concubine of Puzzo's. Perhaps we should discuss more important things first, such as what you wish to drink."

Dante fought back his rage. He must not respond to this vile man's provocations, must not allow himself to be baited into an all-out war until he was ready. *He* would choose the moment to strike.

He scrutinized Godessohn's face for signs of fear or tension. There were none, only the same haughty smile. Godessohn evidently didn't consider him a threat.

Dante swallowed his pride. He needed to keep cool. If Gina was not in immediate danger, he would string things out, try to lull Godessohn into complacency.

He said, "Give me your assurance that Gina is safe, and we can discuss whatever you wish."

Godessohn chuckled. "I'm very sorry, Signor Passoni, but I

cannot provide you with that assurance. I have given her my gun, which is why I am unarmed. She believes that you are dead. For some reason, she is heartbroken. Not because she has lost you, I would presume, but because she has lost her charwoman's ticket to wealth and status, the things to which whores worldwide aspire. For all I know, she might shoot herself. I have no control over her actions while I'm here with you on the roof."

"Gina will not shoot herself."

"Then she is safe, Signor Passoni. You can relax and enjoy our extraordinary encounter. You can relish the irony of it all. You like irony, don't you, Signor Passoni? I'm sure you do. It is common knowledge that intelligent men like irony.

"Think about it, Signor Passoni. Here we stand, two prophets of high technology, each with the capacity to destroy entire nations. Yet you, in a fine Italian display of emotion, have been climbing up chimneys and diving on to wet roof tiles. You come to this meeting of technical titans looking like a bum who sleeps in the rail yard. And I, your adversary, am unarmed, having given my pistol to a suicidal slut.

"And the irony continues, Signor Passoni. You and I have a score to settle. But the battle, when we get around to it, will not be fought with the tools of the twenty-first century. It is as if we harbingers of the future have fallen into a time warp and emerged before the dawn of civilization. We are stripped of our technologies and must fight like savages. I must say, Signor Passoni, I find this a thrilling prospect."

"You won't when I'm finished with you."

"Ah, Signor Passoni, what an exemplary Italian male you are! What bravado! What bluster! While we await the proper moment to discover if there's anything behind your marvelous facade, let me again offer you a drink. As I'm sure you know, the Zitti Palace has one of the Continent's premier wine cellars."

Dante reflected a moment. His faith in wine was somewhat

shaken after his experience at the farmhouse. But he must not forget that the wine Kiyo had served him was a Venetian Cabernet. Good Chianti always sharpened his wits and never dulled his reflexes.

He said, "Very well, Mr. Godessohn. Brunello di Montalcino Riserva, Biondi e Santi, 'Eighty-nine."

"Of course, Signor Passoni. I like your choice of years. Nineteen eighty-nine is a year I remember with great fondness."

Godessohn jotted down Dante's order, placed the note in the antique dumb waiter and pulled the bell cord to the kitchen. A groaning system of pulleys responded, and the cumbersome device began a slow, clattering descent.

Dante noticed a switch on one of the main canopy supports. He flicked it on. An oval of white light flooded the bandstand.

Godessohn did not flinch. "How, Signor Passoni, am I to interpret your childlike fascination with lights? Did you wish to have a better look at me?"

Dante took a step toward Godessohn. "Yes."

Godessohn shrugged his shoulders. "You might have asked." He strode to the bandstand with his hands clasped behind his back and stepped into the light.

When he looked up, his smile had vanished, and the shadows were gone from his face. His eyes bored into Dante like blue lasers.

Dante conjured up Nils Laar's face from the photographs Kiyo had given him: high cheekbones, blond hair slicked straight back, a hawk nose that gave him the look of a bird of prey coming right at you – and those unforgettable, piercing blue eyes.

The face had been changed, the eyes had not. Dante could no longer duck the truth: he was up against the greatest mind of the century.

Lest he falter and show the fear he could not help but feel, he thought about his Uncle Vittorio, brutally strangled with his own medallion; and about Gina, lost and alone. His anger came bubbling to the surface like hot lava. He was still afraid – what mortal would not have been? – but he was not intimidated. Those cold, fierce, intelligent eyes would get nothing back from him but a stare of iron defiance.

Godessohn bent down and picked up the middle segment of the heavy black electrical cord that ran to the spotlights. "Seen enough, Signor Passoni?"

"More than enough."

"Good. The lights detract from the atmosphere of this lovely patio."

He unplugged the cord at both ends. When the lights went out, his eyes retreated into shadow, and his contemptuous smile returned. He began pulling the cord through his hands, measuring off three-foot lengths like a rope vendor. The cord fell at his feet, neatly coiled.

"Well, Signor Passoni, what did you learn from your observations?

"What I already suspected. Your name is Nils Laar. A few days after you won the Nobel Prize for Physics, you murdered your family – and everyone else aboard NTR Flight Thirty-One to Rome. That was nineteen eighty-nine . . ."

Eighty-nine! He wished he had chosen a different vintage Chianti. A bad omen? Perhaps, but there was nothing to do now but keep on talking. He said, "I don't know how many thousands you've murdered since, or how many millions you were planning to murder with your refinery project. But you made a fatal mistake when you killed my uncle. Anyone who murders a Passoni signs his own death warrant."

Godessohn laughed jovially. "Ah, Signor Passoni, I can see you now on the stage of the Verona Opera. What a soul-stirring *spettacolo*! Your bravado would capture the hearts of your countrymen as surely as did Mussolini's. Too bad Mussolini had to go to war or he'd still be swaggering around Rome. Too bad that *you* must go to war, Signor Passoni."

Godessohn held up a large noose he had tied at the end of the cord. "My one-way slip knot, Signor Passoni – my boyhood solution to a problem in physics. You can tighten it but you can't loosen it. Watch."

He made an effort to tug it open with his thick fingers and huge arms. It did not budge. He pulled it gently in the other direction. The noose drew smaller.

"When you get this thing around your neck, Signor Passoni, you'll feel as though you've been transferred from the opera to the circus. It makes men behave in amusing ways – especially, I should think, Italian men."

Smiling pleasantly, Godessohn hung the noose over an arm of the musicians' coat rack. He picked up the other end of the long cord, carried it to the wrought-iron fence that formed the boundary of the patio and secured it to one of the sturdy, spiked posts.

"Seventy feet of cord, Signor Passoni. Ten feet I've used for my knot and noose, forty feet will be taken up getting you over the edge of the roof, the final twenty feet will allow you to accelerate nicely before you hit the end of the line. As an Italian male, you'll no doubt enjoy the acceleration."

Dante was silent, and full of hatred. No way this *stronzo* was going to get a noose over his head.

Rain beat on the canopy, and harsh chemical odors from the refinery fire reached his nostrils. He wondered what Gina was doing.

Godessohn sat down in a comfortable chaise longue.

"Really, Signor Passoni, I must thank you. You have been most entertaining. I'll be sorry to see you go, and not only because I have enjoyed your antics. I have enjoyed you as an adversary, too. It is difficult to find men who love the game sufficiently, and have sufficient mental skills, to step into the ring with me. You have not only stepped into the ring; you have survived for several rounds. I compliment you."

Godessohn yawned and stretched, as if he were contemplating a nap. "But now, regrettably, I must use you in another role. You, Signor Passoni, are an indispensable element in a murder-suicide I must stage. When your slut has shot herself and I have strangled you with my noose, I am going to haul you down to the Senatorial Suite. You'll be with her – in a sense. You see, I'm going to dangle you by the cord around your neck from the rail of her balcony.

"So, Signor Passoni, I shall soon be saying good-bye to you and to Italy. But we still have a little time. If there are questions you wish me to answer about myself, I would be happy to answer them. In fact, Signor Passoni, it would be a pleasure. I don't often have the occasion to speak freely of my achievements – my real achievements, that is."

The antique dumb waiter clanked up its shaft like a bucket being drawn up a well. When it came to a stop, Dante walked to it and opened the little brass gate. He read the apologetic note from the kitchen – no more '89, we hope this '87 will meet with your approval . . .

The bad omen had been banished. Dante opened the '87 and poured himself a glass. A long, appreciative swallow sent the life force of Italy pulsing through his veins. He leaned against the smooth marble bar.

"I have just one question, Mr. Godessohn. What were you planning to do with the thermonuclear device you built in Puzzo's refinery?"

"*Were* planning, Signor Passoni? The device is on its way to a carefully chosen point below the South Pacific, where it will be detonated near the end of a bad El Niño year. The further warming of the ocean's surface just when it should be cooling down will have a radical effect on global weather conditions. As a well-read man, you know the relationship between wind currents and climate. By mid-August, after severe spring flooding, the central portion of the United States will be hit by a drought of African proportions. Not a drop of rain will fall, and daytime temperatures will reach one hundred thirty degrees Fahrenheit. One will speak of the American breadbasket in the past tense for decades to come."

Dante felt a tiny twinge of satisfaction. Even if his undependable ally, God the Florentine, should forsake him, even if he should die tonight on a rooftop terrace in Venice, he had still managed to derail Godessohn's diabolical plan, a plan which would have killed millions. He could not help smile as he poured himself another glass of the velvety Chianti.

He said, "You evidently don't know, Mr. Godessohn, that I snagged your transporter sub with a towing cable as it backed out of the refinery. Your sub is presently dead in the water fifty miles from here. It is being taken aboard a yacht, where Altel experts are waiting to disarm the warhead."

Godessohn erupted with booming laughter. He slapped his thighs, and the sturdy chaise longue on which he sat shuddered like a frail auditorium chair. "What a sad day for you, Signor Passoni! First a series of small defeats. Then death."

His smile vanished, his voice was suddenly menacing. "You snagged the *first stage* of my fish. The second stage of the fish is back on schedule after the slight delay caused by your intervention. It will pass through the Straits of Gibraltar at dawn. From there it will go deep, too deep for detection by submarine or satellite. The third stage will ferry the warhead along the bottom of the seas the remaining eighteen thousand miles to its destination. Your yacht, by the way, was sunk by French torpedoes. There are no survivors. When you challenge me, Signor Passoni, there is a price to pay."

Dante fought off visions of Luigi and Graziella on a burning ship. "I refuse to believe that."

Godessohn's smile returned. He stood up, kicked his chaise

longue aside and made a sweeping gesture toward the great orange blaze across the Lagoon.

"Even after watching your own Air Force obliterate Puzzo's refinery? Signor Passoni, there are many things you do not know. I have built a communications system beneath the South African veld. Using low-frequency electronic waves which pass through the earth and cannot be traced back to their origin, I am able to penetrate the sacred temples of the world's military giants.

"Let me give you several examples. I ordered French defense contractors to build me my fish; I ordered nuclear power plants around the globe to deliver their plutonium waste products to my receptacles; I ordered a Pakistani engineering firm to build me one of the most powerful warheads ever assembled.

"To have the Italian Air Force take out an Italian refinery, to order the French Submarine Fleet to destroy an unarmed yacht, these are deeds which I can only characterize as trivial. It is time, Signor Passoni, that you face the facts. For an Italian, you are a remarkably competent man. Nonetheless, you are in way over your head."

Dante winced. Luigi! Grief sapped his strength like an onslaught of nausea. He had done his best, yet his heroics in the refinery and in the Lagoon had accomplished little – other than getting those he loved killed.

When he looked up from his wine, Godessohn was coming toward him slowly, like a steam locomotive leaving the station. An ugly scowl contorted his orange-tinted face.

The bastard, thought Dante, had seen his moment of weakness. He had decided to exploit it.

Dante grabbed the Chianti bottle and retreated. He wished the confrontation had come earlier, when he had felt better. He circled behind a cluster of miniature pines, struggling to regain his will to fight.

Godessohn stalked, sucking Dante into the magnetic field of

his malice. He spoke in low, ominous tones. "I did not like your telephone trick, Passoni, whatever it was. People do not play tricks on me. You are going to pay dearly for your moment of fun. I am going to hurt you so badly you will beg me to deliver you into death. Do you hear me, Passoni? You will beg me to kill you."

Godessohn took off his sport coat and tossed it aside. His chest was so big his shirt bulged open between the buttons. He speeded up his pursuit.

A gunshot rang out, clear and brittle against the muffled noises of the night. Dante stopped in his tracks. Gina! This monster had forced Gina to kill herself!

His grief momentarily retreated behind some stone wall in his heart. His crisis of confidence vanished. He felt just one emotion now – rage – and that rage was building force like a turbine howling toward peak power.

A second shot went off. It was not a suicide! Godessohn had someone working for him, someone with a gun, someone who would soon be joining his boss on the patio! Things were looking bad. God the Florentine was keeping His distance, not wishing to sully His reputation through involvement in a losing cause.

Dante put his odds of winning this fight at zero. But his broken heart told him something else: it told him that in his anguish he had become invincible.

CHAPTER TWENTY-THREE

"Don't take it so hard, Passoni. She was a nobody, not your type at all."

Godessohn stopped beside the black cord noose which hung from the musicians' coat tree. He gave it a push. The noose swung back and forth, the trailing length of cord writhing like a snake.

Dante's ears rang with the rising howl of his rage. He stared at Godessohn's massive dome, which still reflected the colors of the Republic. In a bold, swift move, he hurled the Chianti bottle at Godessohn's head.

Dante was in tunnel-driving mode the instant he made his throw. His perception became so keen everything appeared to him in slow motion. He watched the bottle spin end over end, spewing a cartwheel of wine. It was on target and closing, the bottom coming round to crash into Godessohn's skull like the rock from David's sling.

But what was this? At the last instant, Godessohn lifted his gigantic forearm and deflected the bottle. It sailed away and shattered harmlessly on the tile roof.

The big man's voice when he spoke was full of scorn.

"I'm old, Passoni, fifties, but you shouldn't be misled by age." Godessohn picked up a chair and flung it as if it were a small toy. Dante watched it tumble toward him. He sidestepped it easily and glanced around for a weapon of his own.

Pines? No, too soft and clumsy.

Geranium pots? No, too heavy.

He had his fists, that was it.

His fists and his rage.

Godessohn was coming at him now, stalking him, his huge rounded shoulders hunched, his bull neck and great bald head thrust forward.

Dante raised his fists.

Godessohn stopped and straightened up. Dante watched an

enormous foot loop in slow motion toward his solar plexus. He dodged it gracefully, but found himself in the path of a left hook. He ducked in the nick of time; the fierce blow split the air beside his ear. Another foot came at him out of nowhere, grazing his ribs.

Too close, too damn close. Fighting a man who used his feet was like driving in a foreign country.

Godessohn spun, still in slow motion, and lashed out with a whipping back kick that brushed Dante's thigh and snapped a spray of water from his pant leg.

His reflexes, Dante knew, were the only thing keeping him alive. But they wouldn't keep him alive forever. He had to do some damage of his own before Godessohn connected.

He moved in closer, dodging huge fists and the dangerous thrust of Godessohn's knee.

The big man spun again. A treacherous back kick came at Dante's mouth straight and true.

Dante ducked, hurling himself at Godessohn's planted leg while Godessohn's kicking leg was still in the air. Godessohn went down with a roof-jarring thud.

Dante rolled out of the way and sprang to his feet. The big bald head was right in front of his foot, a red, white and green soccer ball. Dante unleashed a quick, short kick, the kind that had scored him 27 goals the season he'd played for Juventus.

Godessohn hauled himself angrily to his haunches. Dante could see red displacing the white and green on top of his head. Goal 28. First blood. Go for the kill – before the bastard who shot Gina gets up here.

Dante grabbed an umbrella from one of the tables and rushed forward, hoping to joust Godessohn on to his back. No luck. He felt as if he had collided with a truck. Godessohn wrenched the pole away from him and tossed it aside, then came forward in a crouch. He was no longer smiling.

Stay with him, sting him and don't get hit. Sting him a

hundred times, a thousand times. And *don't get hit.*

The kicks were more dangerous now, low, aimed at Dante's shins. They hissed like a scythe slicing through wheat, forcing Dante to leap backwards before he could throw a punch. Let them come, feel their rhythm, counter with a rhythm of your own.

Back!

Godessohn takes three kicks, then unloads a big punch.

Duck and go after him!

Dante dishes out two sharp lefts that send blood spurting from Godessohn's broad flat nose.

Don't get cocky. Don't get hit. BACK!

It's the scythe again, snarling hungrily at Dante's shins . . . Back, back, Godessohn's straight right thunders through his wet hair, back, back, the scythe, no time to watch what's behind you.

Godessohn seems to stumble. Dante takes a chance, lunges forward, nails him with an overhand right to his jaw that sounds like a cleaver coming down on a chicken . . . and . . . and the punch brings Godessohn's smile back!

What's the bastard smiling about? Is he hurt? Is he trying to bluff?

No time for questions. Godessohn's hands are low, he is vulnerable. Dante's knows he must take advantage of every opportunity. But it's strange, disconcerting. Godessohn is laughing!

Dante loads up and unleashes a left uppercut. A solid, devastating punch; he feels it in his arm like he's socked the window ledge of a granite building. His knuckles shatter, his shoulder nearly flies out of joint – and Godessohn shakes his big bald head as if to say, Passoni, you fool.

Dante throws his best punch, a straight right aimed at the center of Godessohn's face. Godessohn dips his chin slightly so the fist crashes into the hard bone of his forehead.

The knuckles on Dante's right hand shatter, his elbow jams.

He picks up the pace, hits Godessohn again and again, never mind the pain to his fists, pummels him, socks the bull neck to spare his knuckles, feels he's whacking at a truck tire. Fall, you son of a bitch! Dante's hands feel like they've been trampled under a Cossack dance, his arms are weary, and still Godessohn stands.

Stands and laughs and shakes his head.

The kicks! What happened to those scythe-like kicks? Dante realizes he has gotten carried away with his offensive. He has completely forgotten about the kicks. He is standing this very instant in a spot where one kick would snap his tibia like a dry branch. So why isn't Godessohn kicking? What is going on?

Maybe Godessohn's hurt, he must be hurt or he'd be fighting. That's it, THAT'S IT! He's about to drop.

Dante fires off another salvo of punches. But his force is gone, he sees he is doing no damage.

Godessohn has a few cuts, but he looks as fresh as he did when they started. And now he's doing something bizarre. He's sucking in his huge chest, drawing his great rounded shoulders forward until his chest is concave.

Now Dante understands: Godessohn wants to hit him with a chest blow!

No problem, take it easy. He's slow, he can't hit you that way. Back up, he's making a mistake, he'll exhaust himself trying to unload his chest. Retreat, recover, tire him out! He'll drop like a carcass when he's tired.

Godessohn steps forward and unloads his chest. It comes at Dante like a side of beef swinging on a chain. He follows his plan, retreating swiftly, agilely, until the marble bar hits him in the small of his back and stops him cold. He doesn't need to look, he knows what's happened. The crescent-shaped bar is huge. He is trapped.

He tries to drop low, but a knee between his legs lifts him with perverse gentleness off his feet. And then the chest is coming again. It hits him with a dull thud, a chest twice the size of his own, and a hundred times more powerful. It crushes the wind from his lungs, and bends his back so violently over the edge of the bar he expects to hear it snap.

No wind, all knocked out of him, he can't even wheeze, and the big knee is still there between his legs, not hammering but lifting him gently as Godessohn now takes his turn at the punching bag.

A right slams into Dante's solar plexus just when he has sucked in his first breath. A left pulverizes his rib cage, and the heavy blows begin rising in systematic fury toward his head. He sees them floating toward him like .50 caliber tracers in war footage. But they get there soon enough, and Dante can't do a thing to avoid them.

He holds up his fists for protection. They don't help. A crushing blow knocks his jaw out of joint, a nasty shot to the center of his forehead makes him see a crazy starburst of colors. He can't get air. Every time he starts to recover and wheezes, Godessohn hits him in the solar plexus. He feels consciousness slowly slipping away.

And then the truth hits him, the hardest punch of all.

Madonna, he is going to hang! He struggles not to pass out. Stay conscious, stay conscious! Think! That big knee is still lifting him by the crotch, lifting him as if to say, you know what I could do to you, but I won't. Won't because I'd rather watch you on the end of a noose.

Whack! A terrible left hook crashes into the side of his head. Whack. Another hits him square on the chin. Godessohn steps back now, laughing quietly, and Dante falls face down on the floor.

He can't move, he's beaten to a pulp, his arms and legs are paralyzed, his lungs are full of hot blood, his head throbs with searing pain.

He's aware of being kicked over on to his back like a dead

dog and dragged by one foot across the patio. He sees tables and chairs whizzing by, as though he's driving and they're beside the road. Through the transparent canopy, he sees the shaggy orange sky. It's alive, swooping down at him.

Godessohn lets go of his ankle. His foot hits the floor like a shoe tossed across the room. But he's breathing again, sucking in air, coughing.

How long till his strength returns? He tries to move a toe. Nothing. He tries to lift an arm. Nothing. He closes his eyes, hears the sound of surf on a distant beach, sees Gina smiling at him across a table heaped with oyster shells.

In that moment, he feels it, the cord being slipped around his neck – gently, like the knee in his groin.

He hears Godessohn's laughter, and footsteps trailing off.

His legs spasm, his feet move, his head begins to clear. He opens his eyes and grabs the noose. It isn't tight, he can slide both swollen hands under it. But when he tries to raise it over his head, he discovers that it won't quite clear his chin.

He is stronger now, strong enough to feel a stab of panic. He tries to pull the noose open, pulls till his arms shake. He needs another half inch to get the thing over his chin and off his neck, but the cord will not stretch and the knot won't budge.

Is it really a one-way knot? He gives the cord a tiny tug in the other direction. The knot slides like it's greased, and the noose now fits more tightly.

* * *

After a dizzy spell and two violent bouts of nausea, Dante tried to get his bearings. The cord running from the noose lay in big black coils beside him. The other end was still tied to the wrought-iron fence surrounding the patio.

Godessohn stood beside the fence rubbing the cord like a pet. When he saw Dante look at him, he turned off the patio lights. The red, white and green reflection disappeared from his dome.

Dante felt as if the Republic had abandoned him. He knew what darkness meant: Godessohn was ready to move in for the kill.

Think!

If he could get out on to the roof, perhaps he could find a piece of the broken Chianti bottle and use it to cut through the cord.

He moved his stiff, swollen fingers. They would rise to the occasion, but would Godessohn give him the minute or so he'd need to saw through rubber and copper? Not likely. If the slicing of the cord was going to work, it would have to be instantaneous.

What else could he cut it with? A broken roof tile? The jagged stonework of a chimney? Maybe, but he would have the same time problem. Godessohn would either jerk the cord or come down and batter him before he could get the job done. Which meant he would have to fight with the cord around his neck.

Godessohn clapped his hands like a seal trainer. "Get up, Passoni. Up! Up! Your mediocre performance is beginning to bore me. I'll bet the folks at Verona expect more."

Dante pretended to be groggier than he was. He struggled to his knees and toppled over on his side. As he floundered around on all fours, he formed a mental picture of the Zitti's facade.

He didn't like what he saw. The eaves stuck out a good five feet from the vertical wall. If Godessohn allowed him to flee, he could let himself down over the edge of the roof by gripping the cord like a climbing rope.

But what would he do after he got over the edge? The eaves would hold him too far away from the wall to reach a window. To make matters worse, the only windows on the third floor were his and Godessohn's. Even if he managed to get someone's attention, it would be the attention of the man who had just shot Gina. He could forget about working the walls.

"Well, Passoni," Godessohn boomed, "I was hoping you would come up with some sort of interesting attempt to save yourself. I didn't let you live so that you could lie around like a dead man. I'm going to count to ten. If you haven't started to fight by then, I'm going to dispose of you where you lie.

"I know, Passoni, I know. You're upset about your tough situation. If you let go of the cord to fight back, I strangle you with a single jerk. If you hang on to the cord to save your neck, I simply kick you to death. You're a big disappointment, Passoni. From you I had expected a modicum of opposition."

Dante crawled around some more, like a hurt fighter trying to beat the count. Godessohn had said he would fall 20 feet from the edge of the roof before he came to the end of his tether. Looking at the cord, Dante estimated that this was more or less correct. Which meant he would have 20 feet of rope to work with once he started down over the edge.

"Three," said Godessohn, who had been counting in a jovial voice.

No good, no good. Dante's frustration came on strong, eclipsing his fear and pain. The roof, dammit, the roof was at least 30 feet above the third-story balconies. If he lowered himself as skillfully as Reinhold Messner, he would still end up dangling too high to touch a balcony railing with his foot.

"Five."

That's what Godessohn really wanted, Dante thought. He wanted him to go over the edge of the roof and hang on to the cord until his hands cramped and his arms gave out and the noose did its job. The degradation, the panic, the pain . . . this horrible man knew no limits.

"Seven."

Dante started shakily to get to his feet. Nothing else to do but to grab the coil of cord beside him and charge Godessohn. If he could somehow get him wrapped up in that cord long enough to unload a kick of his own, if he could somehow get the cord untied from the fence post, maybe . . . maybe . . .

"Nine!"

Dante was on his feet, wobbling like a drunk. A beautiful brass lion kept growling through his awareness.

Then, suddenly, he remembered.

The Zitti lion!

Madonna, had God the Florentine decided to help him after all? Three days ago, the lion had been temporarily moved from the southwest corner of the hotel, where it had been protecting the Zitti from evil spirits for 600 years, to a point just under the eaves midway between the Presidential and Senatorial Suites. Though Dante hadn't yet seen the lion in its temporary position, he knew all about the mount: CRC had received the contract for the structural buttressing. The famous lion's move had gotten very little coverage in the press. After all, the original mount was to be ready for its return in 15 days. Which meant that if Godessohn had not had the opportunity to study the facade of the hotel, he might not know where the lion was!

Dante was instantly consumed with one goal: get to that lion. She had protected the Zitti from harm for six centuries; would she not protect this loyal son of Italy for a few seconds?

"Ten!"

He grabbed the cord and wrapped it around his right forearm, leaving plenty of slack between his arm and the noose. He picked up the coil of cord beside him and broke into a dead run. His body was a pulsing mass of pain, but his mind was working again.

He was not beaten yet.

He jumped the patio fence, dropped the coil of cord, came down on his side and rolled on to his back. He was beyond the canopy now, on the gently sloping roof tiles. The cold rain felt like boiling oil in his wounds.

He looked at Godessohn. The big man was reeling in slack cord, arm over arm. A game, thought Dante, for him it was all a game . . .

He got to his feet and ran, wrapping the cord around both arms. When the slack gave out, he knew he was going to receive a nasty jerk.

He ran in the same direction as the rainwater, which churned in foaming streams down the gullies between the long humped rows of tile. He could see the Grand Canal beyond the roof, asleep in the misty night. He oriented himself by the chimneys of the two suites, trying to stay roughly the same distance from each. It wouldn't do him any good to sail over the edge and find the lion way off to one side.

He was running down the incline at top speed when he hit the end of his line. The jerk pulled him off his feet and spun him around in midair. He crashed to the tiles, belly down, his arms stretched out in front of him, his head pointing toward the Presidential Patio. He did not like the feel of the cord: the water was making it slippery.

Cursing under his breath, the gully streams splattering his face, Dante squirmed and struggled like a fish on a line.

Godessohn laughed. With the strength of a diesel winch, he started pulling Dante back up the incline. Godessohn was playing with him!

"How does it feel?" Godessohn chided. "How does it feel, Passoni, to be hooked in the same way you hooked my fish? Too bad you're not built in stages. Too bad you can't shed your skin and swim away. Careful, Passoni. Better hold on tighter. The cord's slipping through your hands."

Godessohn gave a ferocious yank, then threw Dante some more slack. "What's your plan, Passoni? I'm curious to see how you intend to proceed."

He laughed some more: he was having fun.

Blood rushed into Dante's hands. Good, they weren't numb yet. He got to knees. He was about to resume his rush to the edge of the roof when he had a horrible thought: if Godessohn saw how badly he wanted off the roof, Godessohn would likely become suspicious.

No good!

He had to make Godessohn knock him off the edge, had to make Godessohn believe he was doing everything in his power to stay *on* the roof.

Then why had he run all the way down here?

The chimney, of course!

He grabbed the slack Godessohn had thrown him and sprinted horizontally across the roof toward Gina's chimney. Godessohn tried to steer him, but Dante fed him back his slack and stayed on course. He circled Gina's chimney, let the cord dig into the stones and grip, began rubbing a length of cord close to his hands back and forth on a jagged rock.

Godessohn took the bait. He came thundering down the roof, gripping the cord and growling insults. In the weak light, Dante could see the rain pelting his bare head and running down into his collar.

Now Dante laughed – defiantly. If nothing else, he'd gotten the bastard wet.

Godessohn came around the chimney after him, yanking on the cord like someone trying to train a dog. Dante managed to unload a soccer kick to Godessohn's shin before Godessohn's fist sent him sprawling.

Dante curled into the fetal position, arms around his head. Godessohn's slow motion kicks dug into his legs and ribs. Dante squirmed and slithered, tried to flee.

Godessohn hauled back on the cord. Dante cried out in pain, crawling with legs splayed, choking on rainwater. He took a kick square in the butt that knocked him on his face and made him mad enough to go for a shot of his own. He spun on to his back at lightning speed, rolled into the big man's legs and upended him.

Dante paid the price with a rabbit punch and an elbow to the side of the head that brought back the stars.

No more of that! No more! You've got to be all there when you sail into space.

He glanced left and right. He had worked himself between the two chimneys, more or less the same distance from each. He was where he wanted to be when he went over the edge, no use waiting any longer. He got to his feet, looked quickly over his shoulder and feigned shudder of dread when he saw that he was two body lengths from the end of the roof.

Godessohn, on his feet now, smiled at Dante's apparent fear. "How long, Passoni? How long can you hang on to that cord with your hands and arms? How long until you become just another whimpering coward on the end of a line? How long till you let go and hang yourself? I'm going to stand up here and count for you. I doubt you'll make it for a minute. *Arrivederci*, Passoni. It's been good fun."

Godessohn sucked in his chest and hunched his shoulders. The chest blow! The last time it had pinned Dante against the marble bar. This time it would free him.

Godessohn pulled Dante fiercely toward him in order to bring him in range, then threw down the cord, stepped forward and unsprang his mighty chest. Dante turned to the side so that the impact of the blow wouldn't knock the wind out of him. The chest smashed into his shoulder and sent him careening backwards. As he stumbled, he hauled in some of the slack that had been left when Godessohn threw down the cord. He wanted to fall, but not 20 feet!

He pretended to trip. His feet flew out from under him, he landed on to his back. He was sliding down in a torrent of rain water, he had no way to stop himself.

He heard Godessohn's uproarious laughter, but the laughter came from a distance. The big man was evidently not going to follow him to the edge.

Dante was still on his back, head toward the canal, when he

slid into space. He fell five feet before the cord, tied at its other end to the rock-solid wrought-iron fence post, jerked him upright. He cried out in pain as the cord cut into his wrists and forearms. But when he twirled to face the hotel, he forgot his troubles: he was staring right into the open mouth of the Zitti lion.

Careful, now, careful. Everything depends on the quality of your deception. You are not out of danger by a long shot; you still have that godforsaken one-way knot around your neck.

He vented a litany of agonizing groans as waited for his twirling to slow. He used the time to unwrap the cord from his forearms and wrists so that his hands would not go to sleep. He needed those poor battered hands to function perfectly if he was going to climb back up the cord to the roof.

What temptation, dangling in agony in front of this stout, beautiful lion, to latch on to it for support. But no! Dante could not permit himself to take that risk. He was fighting a man of utter precision. He must keep *exactly* the right tension on the cord. Who was to say that Godessohn wouldn't reach down and pluck the cord like a harp string. Who was to say that he wouldn't pick up on a minor irregularity. The lion would be called into service, but not yet.

He began to make his way slowly up the cord, hand over hand, dangling and still groaning. The lion nuzzled him in the chest, poked him in the stomach, sniffed his crotch. The cold rain fell on his shattered finger joints. Hot oil, good that it's hot. It will ward off your new enemy number one – cramps.

Godessohn was talking to him now, mocking him. "How much longer, Passoni? How much longer?"

Dante continued up the cord, hand over hand, arms shaking badly, eyes burning now, stomach in knots. This was when they gave up on the vertical ascents, he thought, the climbers who had taken on too much mountain. This was when Dante got his second wind.

The hot oil rain was warming his fingers, memories of Gina were stoking his rage, grief over Luigi and, yes, even over Graziella Calvino, were keeping him as keen as an attacking animal.

The lion is sniffing his shins now, his shins and not his crotch, because Dante has raised himself all the way up to where he can reach the edge of the roof with one hand when he's ready.

He's ceased to hurt. He realizes he's forgotten to groan, so he croaks out something that sounds like a death rattle.

Still dangling, his two hands a couple inches below the edge of the roof, he lifts his legs and slips both feet into the mouth of the lion. No weight on those feet, not yet. But when he lets go of the cord, he'll have a solid place to stand.

He takes a deep breath. This is it. Godessohn had better play along.

He lets out a desperation grunt and, holding himself by one hand, he lifts his other hand over the edge of the roof. With his swollen fingers, the bait, he digs the cord out of the gully between the tiles and grabs on to it.

Nothing. He waits, his heart sinking. He's still got the noose around his neck. What does he do if Godessohn doesn't bite? What does he do if Godessohn pulls him up on the roof again?

Madonna, has God the Florentine gone to dinner?

He feels a tremor in the cord. He knows what's happening: Godessohn is leaning down, checking the tension. A bite!

And now he's coming, Dante can hear him, can feel his steps on the roof, he's coming like a bull, coming to have some fun, he can't resist it, the fun of stepping on Dante's hand.

Come on, son of a bitch, come on.

Footsteps moving closer, sloshing, and tile vibrating under Dante's hand.

And then the footsteps stop, and the night is silent, like a forest in a rainstorm.

Godessohn is feeling the cord again, twanging it. Dante's

hands are finally cramping, his forearms are cramping, and still Godessohn is playing with the cord.

Madonna, how much longer?

Dante squeezes his eyes shut, the world spins in unhealthy colors behind his lids. Then, suddenly, he hears a great laugh. He can feel weight shifting above him. He can read the sounds.

Now! Dante lowers his feet until they're resting firmly on the lower jaw of the lion. He straightens his bent legs so that he is standing up. His head appears above the edge of the roof. Godessohn glimpses him while his foot is still in the air. His mouth falls open in shock.

Dante lets go of the cord. He moves his endangered hand and lunges, wrapping both arms around Godessohn's planted leg. He gives a single sharp pull.

Godessohn goes down hard. He scrambles to his knees, but Dante snares him by the belt. Godessohn's got no traction up there, his weight's a disadvantage.

Dante climbs up on to the lion and wraps his legs around its torso like a man on a runaway horse. He's got leverage, he leans back on the lion's upturned snout and heaves with all his might on Godessohn's fat belt.

Godessohn comes sliding off the roof like a log in a chute. Dante ducks and Godessohn sails over his head, on his way to the Grand Canal.

CHAPTER TWENTY-FOUR

Vihari crouched low, his weight against the bottom of the balcony door. No problem, he could survive out here until Godessohn came to his rescue.

The crazed girl inside had knocked out all nine squares of door glass with the poker, but she still wasn't able to get a clean poke at him. The squares were too high and too small, so small her sodomizing dog couldn't open his snout after he'd jammed it through.

Vihari was safe for the moment. And as soon as Godessohn finished his business on the roof, Vihari would be back inside the Senatorial Suite, taking care of the girl and her perverted animal.

He had heard Godessohn's laugh, heard him call out the name "Passoni," heard the unmistakable sounds of a philanthropic torture session.

Ah, yes, Godessohn had fucked up. He'd microwaved a melon and let Passoni escape. But he'd recovered. He'd gotten lucky and lured Passoni up on the roof, and Passoni would soon be dead. After this small glitch was handled, the night could proceed as planned: the staging of the passion murder here in the Senatorial Suite, a little TV, with Godessohn translating, to hear what the Italians were saying about the performance of their Air Force, a good sleep, breakfast, a meeting with the press to announce that Godessohn was withdrawing his pledge to save Venice.

Yes, yes, Vihari was sure he would withdraw it. Now that he had seen off his fish and disposed of his enemies, Godessohn had no reason for throwing away his money. The Save Venice farce had been a cover, a smoke screen . . .

The poker grazed his ear. "Just wait," Vihari hissed. "You haven't seen the last of me."

He looked in the direction of the muffled sounds of fighting that spilled toward the edge of the roof. Ah, yes, he thought, wiping the rain from his eyes with his sleeve, Passoni would be trying to jump into the canal, and Godessohn would be making damn sure he didn't. They needed Passoni's corpse for their passion murder.

But what was this? What was going on? Here came Passoni sliding head-first over the edge clutching a cord in both hands. He fell a few feet, hit the end of his tether, stopped with a jerk and dangled there, spinning lazily.

The poker shot through the windowless door at a new angle, just missing Vihari's nose. He grumbled and cursed but kept his eyes on the strange drama unfolding beneath the eaves. Why was Passoni hanging on to the cord? Didn't he want to fall into the canal and escape? What was he trying to do? Return to the roof and continue the fight with Godessohn?

Vihari dodged the poker again and gaped in disbelief as Passoni, looking like a ragged bum, started back up the cord, hand over hand, groaning as if he wanted to die.

And then Vihari saw the black noose around Passoni's neck, and the big black knot under his chin. No wonder he hadn't let go! He would have hung himself!

Ah, yes, things *were* back on track again. The little glitch caused by Godessohn's misdirected microwaves had not hurt them at all.

The poker caught him on side of the forehead, inflicting a shallow cut. He reached up and grabbed it, tore it from Gina's grasp, pitched it over the balcony railing and returned his eyes to the roof.

What was this, what was this? Vihari hadn't noticed it before. Some sort of snarling gargoyle was up there, a lion, jutting from the wall just under the eaves!

Should Vihari call out and try to alert Godessohn? No, of course not. Godessohn would know how to deal with the situation. Godessohn would know the lion was there. In fact, Godessohn had probably put it there!

Passoni was getting close to the edge of the roof now,

preparing to put a hand up over the eaves.

What if Godessohn *did not* know the lion was there? What if Passoni, by some incredible quirk of fate, took him by surprise and killed him?

Vihari felt a huge smug smile creasing his face. What of it? What of it? Vihari had read Godessohn's will. He could almost see the small gray safe in Godessohn's office where it was kept.

If Godessohn died, Vihari would be the richest man in South Africa, the next Philanthropist. And Vihari knew how to run the communications system – sort of. Once he figured out how to stop the fish, he would harvest rewards worth billions! And he would become a Champion of Humanity on a par with Mahatma Gandhi and Martin Luther King!

What was going on up there now? Ah, yes, it was clear. Passoni was pretending to hang by the cord, but he was really standing on the gargoyle. He lifted a hand up over the roof. Godessohn raised a foot to smash that hand. But Passoni stood straight up, his feet in the lion's mouth, grabbed Godessohn's planted leg and jerked it out from under him. Godessohn fell hard, landing near the edge of the roof. With a move so swift Vihari almost missed it, Passoni caught him by the belt, sat down on the gargoyle and gave a yank. And there went Godessohn, bald dome out front like a flying monk, sailing through space on his way to the canal!

Vihari hesitated. Goddammit, goddammit, *this* was nothing to rejoice over. Godessohn was not going to die. No, no, he would swim to safety, find a phone and order his cabin cruiser to pick him up!

Godessohn was going to escape to South Africa while Vihari got his ass tossed into some dank Italian dungeon!

Godessohn might even try to lay the blame for his crimes on Vihari!

No thank you. He and Godessohn were in this together, and

they were going to depart together.

He left the balcony door and ran. The door flew open and the sodomizer came tearing after him. As the dog leaped for his back, Vihari hurtled the balcony rail.

He hit the canal, touched the slimy bottom and started back up. By the time he surfaced, he had stripped to his shorts and money belt. The water was cold but he was all right; he could swim forever.

Vihari spotted Godessohn some 20 yards away, bellowing and beating furiously at the water. Strange. He was behaving like a huge, violent, frustrated beast. His rage at having been tricked not once but twice by Passoni had turned him into a madman! His head bobbed strangely, disappearing beneath the waves only to pop up again in a different spot.

What waves they were! Waves from this enormous outburst, oily waves pulsing outward in concentric circles, as if a meteor had smacked into the canal.

But really, thought Vihari, treading water with efficient strokes, Godessohn's behavior was becoming ridiculous. Worse: it was becoming dangerous. They didn't need someone venturing out here to rescue them. They needed to *escape*, to swim quietly up dark side canals until they could find a telephone.

A great gurgling filled his ears, a garbage barge. A bright light lit up a swath of the canal.

Time to go underwater! Time to dive like a sub! Time to get out of here! Even a man handicapped by a 180 I.Q. could see that.

But Godessohn did not dive. No! He continued to thrash and bellow, almost as if he wanted to get caught. The barge sloshed by. No one had seen them. But next time?

What was wrong with Godessohn? thought Vihari, swimming toward him. Had he snapped? Had he lost his mind in the fall? Vihari stopped ten feet away so that he didn't get swamped.

"Sir," he called, "it's me, Vihari. Keep quiet! Someone will hear you!"

Godessohn thrashed even more violently. His big bald head moved haltingly toward Vihari, like a beach ball in the surf.

Godessohn tried to say something, but he went under instead. He came up choking and sputtering and bleating miserably.

"Quiet!" Vihari hissed. "Be quiet!"

Godessohn was five feet away now, and he looked like a wild-eyed maniac. "Vihari," he choked. "Vihari . . ."

"What, dammit?"

He went under again, stayed down for several seconds, then broke water like a surfacing whale. He opened his mouth and let out a loud grisly burp, followed by a stream of water.

"Vihari! I . . . can't . . . swim!"

He gave a mighty heave, as if he were trying to fly, but his head stayed where it was.

"Save me!" he gasped. He went down, came up, beat the water into a churning white cataract.

Vihari finned away, keeping a safe distance. He felt his smile coming on now and twisting his face, coming irresistibly, like an orgasm. There could be no sweeter ending to their association than this.

Godessohn began to sink. His mouth went under, his nose and eyes went under, the roily black water closed over his glistening dome.

Ah, yes, Passoni would be on the loose soon, and everyone would be searching for Godessohn. They would find his corpse. They would not find Vihari. Nor would they bother to look for him too hard. After all, what had he done? What crimes had he committed? He'd fired two shots at a dog trying to sodomize him. What court would lock him up for that? None – especially if he had 300 billion dollars to spend on legal fees. All he had to do was make it back to South Africa and the world was his.

In the distance he could see the rhythmic sloshing of a gondola. Time to disappear.

He swam under water, hugging the buildings along the dark side of the canal. He turned into the first tiny side canal he came to, then into another.

Ah, yes, it was pitch black in here. He could swim on the surface without fear of being seen, swim farther and farther into this labyrinth of small canals while he formulated his plan for getting home.

* * *

Dante clung weakly to the lion, fighting not to lose consciousness. When he had heaved Godessohn over the edge of the roof, his cord had received an unintentional jerk. Now the one-way slip knot held the noose around his neck so tightly that he could scarcely breathe and could not utter a sound.

As the world of his vision spun slowly in and out of focus, he watched the bizarre phenomenon unfolding in the canal below. A man was in the water with Godessohn, and Godessohn seemed to be drowning. The man started to help him, then suddenly backed off, as if he had had second thoughts.

A garbage barge plowed by, lighting up the other side of the canal. After it passed, Godessohn went under and the other man swam away.

Dead, drowned. An insignificant consolation for the losses Dante had suffered. Vittorio, Gina, Luigi, Graziella . . . His heart ached even more than his body. And the crisis was still not over. Godessohn's deadly cargo continued on route, heading to some unknown place, a messenger of death that could kill millions of innocent, unsuspecting people, the vile legacy of the world's most evil man.

But . . . but what was this? Old Ugo, the Zitti's night gondolier, was poling with powerful strokes toward the spot where

Godessohn had gone under. Dante watched with glazed eyes. When Ugo was close to the spot, he yanked his pole from the water and let the gondola glide closer of its own momentum. He quickly attached his rescue hook to the end of the pole and began probing the depths for the sunken man.

Not ten seconds later he was straining to hoist something to the surface. Dante's heart sank when he saw Godessohn's big bald dome break the surface. Ugo bent down, grabbed the hulking man by the collar and struck his back. Fortunately, Godessohn did not move. He was dead.

Dante was about to close his eyes in relief when he saw a thick stream of water erupt from Godessohn's mouth. His head quivered and jerked, he seemed to be choking. Yet more water sprayed and dribbled from his mouth, he threw up, and then his hands climbed the side of the gondola and latched on.

Dante shuddered with dread. The cord around his neck seemed to have grown tighter, though he hadn't moved. His mind must be playing tricks on him again, he thought. He forced himself to concentrate on his breathing, to keep it even, not to panic, to remain conscious on the tiny wisps of air he could suck past the noose into his lungs.

Godessohn was alive, but he wasn't going anywhere. He was too sick, he would have to be taken to a hospital. Any minute now, someone would see Dante up on the gargoyle and help him to get down. Dante would make sure Godessohn ended up in a secure prison where he could be forced to reveal the destination of his fish, and what could be done to stop it.

But . . . but what was he doing now? Still clinging to the side of the gondola with one hand, Godessohn had taken something from an underwater pocket that looked like a remote control unit. Moments later, the roar of a speed boat pierced the night. A large cabin cruiser swept out of a side canal and came bearing down on the gondola at awesome speed.

Godessohn hoisted himself into the gondola, a wet, dripping corpse who had returned to life with more of his strength intact than seemed possible. Ugo reached down to help him. Godessohn caught the old man by the arm and pitched him into the canal like a toy soldier.

The cabin cruiser slowed, came around like a docking craft, bumped its side against the gondola and held position. Godessohn shakily climbed the boat's ladder as a silent scream tore through Dante's lungs. Seconds later, the marine engine's high-pitched roar again shattered the night. The cabin cruiser surged ahead in a fury of white wake. Before Ugo could climb back aboard his gondola, Godessohn's rescue boat had disappeared from view.

Lost. Everything was lost. Dante laid his head down on the lion's nape and watched the moon emerge from behind a heavy bank of clouds. He followed its flaxen light to the balcony of the Senatorial Suite. What he saw convinced him that he had already died and been transported by God the Florentine to that gentle place called Paradise. Gina stood with Bruno at the railing, looking up at him. A breath of wind tousled her blue-back hair. It tumbled forward over her eyes. She brushed it back, and lifted her hand in a timid wave.

Moments later, the clatter of a helicopter filled the night. He closed his eyes and waited, not knowing if it was friend or foe. The helicopter stabilized above him. He hugged the lion as the swirling down draft buffeted him. Mingled somewhere in the jet exhaust, he smelled a vaguely familiar perfume.

Wet hair brushed his battered face, and a hand with long fingernails studied the noose around his neck.

"Bull Balls, is that you?"

He opened his eyes. Graziella Calvino hung from the cargo sling of the chopper, looking as though she had been through a hell as bad as his. He tried to see the chopper, but he couldn't turn his head far enough.

"Be still," Graziella said. "It's Luigi, he's all right. Be still, I said. I've got a knife. I'll cut you free."

And he was still. Very still. For he had finally passed out.

CHAPTER TWENTY-FIVE

Vihari made it back to Johannesburg in nine days. He'd swum the Lagoon and stowed away on a tanker that took him non-stop to Djibouti. On board, he'd found safari clothes in an empty cabin and a gun he hoped he wouldn't need. He bought false papers in Addis Abbaba and hired a seat on a private plane to Kasanga.

From Kasanga, he traveled south by rail to Bulawayo, where he joined a sightseeing herd of pink, overweight German tourists. He left the air-conditioned bus in Beitbridge near the South African border and, lest police and customs officials be looking for him, he waited until the dead of night to swim the Limpopo River, arriving in his adopted homeland in the same soaked and battered condition in which he had left Venice.

With rising confidence, he pitched his gun into a dumpster and entered a shop in Nylstroom. He bought himself fresh underwear, reddish-brown shoes which, to his aggravation, were made in Italy, a tan summer suit just a trifle too large, and a maroon cotton scarf which he fashioned into a passable turban.

He visited a barber in Witbank who excavated his smooth, soft skin from beneath a scruffy week-long growth of beard, trimmed his parched hair and tamed it with a sweet-smelling oil as viscous as Puzzo's crude.

Friday night he repaired to a black brothel to make certain his cobra had not been damaged by the dive into the canal and the deprivations of his long trip home. A three-star performance – three times in thirty minutes – convinced him that he was in good form and ready to move ahead with his plan.

The next morning, Saturday, December 21, he spent the last of the cash from his money belt on a cab to Godessohn's downtown Johannesburg office building, which he entered warily with his own special pass key, his heart pounding in joyous anticipation.

The elevator disgorged him on the eighth floor. He gazed down the long rows of cubicles, partitioned by glass, stretching endlessly along the windowed walls. He squinted into the glare of the bright African sun. No one here. Very good. Whoever had taken over – temporarily – after Godessohn's death was continuing the Philanthropist's Saturday no work tradition.

Ah, yes, things were shaping up nicely. He took a deep breath and walked toward Godessohn's office, that thick-walled, windowless bunker he knew so well sitting like a misplaced cube smack in the center of the eighth floor. A few arrhythmias crept into his happy heartbeat when he knocked.

Silence.

Ah, yes, good, very good. Godessohn's temporary replacement, unlike Godessohn, did not work on Saturday. He would be some mediocre administrator from the ranks, perhaps the fool who had tried to take away Vihari's job. No need to worry about him now. He'd be gone by Monday night, fired, shoveled out on the street where he belonged; for by Monday night, Godessohn's will would be filed with the courts.

Once inside Godessohn's office, the rest would be – how should Vihari put it? – trivial.

Ah, yes, trivial. He knew where the safe stood, and the combination was emblazoned in his memory as indelibly as his age or telephone number.

But he had to get inside first. Fortunately, he'd thought about this. There were torches and crowbars in the maintenance shop off the parking garage. He might make a mess, but what did he care?

He'd try the door first, though. Perhaps this competitor of his, this temporary replacement who was too complacent to work on Saturdays, did not lock doors.

The big oval knob, when he twisted it, turned and the door swung easily, as if someone had opened it for him.

Ah, yes, thought Vihari, stepping inside, things had begun to go his way. He saw the little gray safe, planted beside the larger safe like some kind of mechanical offspring, sitting right where it had been the day Godessohn showed him the will.

He took a step forward, but stopped in his tracks when he heard the office door closing quietly behind him.

He spun around.

No one.

Ah, yes, what a door. He had forgotten. Two hundred pounds of Kenya hardwood, polished steel bearings in the hinges so perfect a tiny tug of wind, the wake of a walking man, would pull it shut.

He kneeled in front of the safe and clicked the cool splined knob back and forth, back and forth. He pulled. There it was, the will, lying right on top!

His heart was soaring now, soaring smooth and free, beyond arrhythmias and ungainly poundings. He rifled gleefully through the pages. They were exactly as he had seen them last! Signed and notarized, the words unequivocal, the content stupendous. It was his! All of it! The Wittersand fortune, the office buildings, the seven banks, Godessohn Resource Management, Ltd., mountains of stocks and bonds, bullion and treasury certificates.

Three hundred billion had been too modest an estimate! His head was spinning. He was euphoric. He would take Tamina from behind tonight – and divorce her on Monday!

He stuffed the will into his breast pocket, hurried to the office door and turned the stout oval handle.

Locked!

Vihari's soaring heart took a dive. His gut felt as if he had jumped off another three-story balcony. What was this? His competitor had it backwards. Doors were supposed to keep people out of your office, not trap them inside it.

Calm down, calm down! He had access to Godessohn's computer *and* to his communications system. A few minutes at the keyboard and he would figure out his exit.

He sat at his familiar mahogany desk stacked with familiar manuals, and switched on the power. The hard disk whirred to life. He heard another whirring sound in the distance, the high-tech hum of the office elevator. He stiffened his spine and craned his neck. The computer prompted him for a command. He shut it off and stood up, not knowing whether to approach the gleaming, polished steel elevator doors or back away. Who could this be? The elevator went only one place: to the gym in the basement, a very private gym.

Calm down! What was he worried about? Now that Godessohn was gone, his temporary replacement would have begun to use the gym himself to get his sluggish ass in shape. It now seemed he worked on Saturday after all: that's why the office door had been open. He had been down in Godessohn's gym, and now he was coming back.

The whirring stopped. Vihari straightened his turban and prepared his smile. This was one of those awkward situations best confronted with a little charm.

When the doors parted and Godessohn stepped toward him, an involuntary gasp escaped Vihari's throat. He tried to sit down, but he could not move. He tried to breathe, but Godessohn had already sucked up all his air. His frantic efforts at inhalation rasped in his ears like the wheezes of a dying asthmatic.

Godessohn was smiling! Tiny beads of perspiration glistened on his dome, and he smelled of post-work-out talc.

"Hello, Vihari. Why don't you have a seat?"

"I . . . I . . ."

"Sit down." Godessohn took him roughly by the arm and deposited him in his chair, then sat on the edge of the desk, looming above him like a Freudian father.

Vihari's mind hurtled back through time, to his childhood and the nurse who had bandaged his playground cuts, to his mother's lap during tea, and the fragrance of jasmine folding him in a sleepy embrace.

Back, back his memories flew, until he thought he saw his mother's womb, the dark cave whence he had come and to which he now so desperately wished to return.

"You've missed a week of work without calling in," Godessohn said. "That's not like you, Vihari."

"But . . . but . . . but . . . I thought you were . . . ugh . . . dead. I tried . . . you must believe me, sir . . . do not look at me like that, sir . . . I tried to save you. I tried to pull you out of the canal. But you flailed so violently I lost my grip on you, my grip, yes, and you went under. I dove and dove. I searched for hours in very treacherous conditions. Sir, it was night, the tide was going out, and the currents were – "

"Why, Vihari, when we both know the truth, do you stammer on like some pathetic schoolboy caught in a lie?"

"But . . . but – "

"Shut up. You failed your test of competence, and I forgave you. You failed your loyalty test, and for this I cannot forgive you. The elevator is waiting, Vihari. You have ten minutes to jump down the empty shaft to a painless death. If you prefer not to jump, you know the alternative. Need I describe the cyanide and heated meat hook again?"

"But . . . but, sir. Sir! No, sir. All right, sir, all right . . . I shall jump!"

Vihari bowed his head to conceal a glimmer of hope. Might this too be a test, a trick? Might Godessohn cleanse himself of his rage by scaring Vihari half to death – and then let him live? Yes! There was much fun to be had at Vihari's expense, fun which could not be had if Vihari were dead!

Godessohn started a timer. "Very well, then. I suppose I should ask you how you wish to spend your last nine and a half minutes."

Yes, Vihari was sure of it! He was not going to die. As

long as he feigned holy terror, he would not die!

"Sir . . . I am frightened, sir. I am too frightened to have a preference."

"Then, Vihari, why don't you spare yourself some anxiety and jump now?"

"Yes . . . yes, perhaps I will. But, sir, perhaps you, before I jump, perhaps you will tell me what is happening with your project?"

"Everything is going well, Vihari. The fish is five miles deep, on course and on schedule. Dante Passoni has not gone to the police."

"What? Not gone to the police? But he knows, does he not? He knows everything."

"Yes, Vihari, but his knowledge is useless. I have already released three billion dollars of the Save Venice money to the new International Commission. I have become an Italian national hero. If Passoni were to make outrageous charges against me, if he were to appear to aggravate me, the Venetians themselves would kill him. You see, Vihari, they're almost as anxious as you were to get their hands on my money. Passoni knows this. He is a perceptive man. Therefore he has done the only thing he can do: he has accepted the post I recommended him for, that of Chairman of the new International Commission."

"What? You . . . sir, you are actually going to pay for the rescue of Venice?"

"I can afford to, Vihari."

"But . . . but, Passoni . . . if he cannot go to the police, he will come for you privately."

"Just so, Vihari. And for this I am immensely grateful. He and I are going to have a most entertaining relationship. Sorry you won't be here to partake of the fun."

"But . . . but how did you get out of the canal?"

"My cabin cruiser, Vihari. The mini-transmitter I carry kept it informed of my position. I pressed the rescue button, and it came for me."

"But . . . but can you swim?"

"What difference does it make, Vihari? You have one minute. I suggest you position yourself for your jump."

"Yes . . . sir."

Vihari got to his feet, pretending to stagger like a newborn deer. He belched and heaved and tried to produce an eruption of vomit, but all that came up was a slender dribble of saliva.

He crossed the sea of blue-gray industrial carpet, laughing inwardly at the terror of his first trip to the elevator.

Near the doors, he smelled overheated metal, and caught a whiff of Godessohn's talc. He leaned against the wall, feigning dread, and tried to remember how it had been. The doors stayed open for three seconds, that was all. You had to throw yourself precipitously into a rectangle of black. It had been terrifying the first time, yes. And even this time, a nasty little whirlpool of fear was stirring in his gut.

Ah, yes, he was getting frightened now, just a bit uneasy. But he had a cure for his discomfort. When he saw the black rectangle yawing in front of him, he would think of it as his mother's womb. He would be going home, going all the way back, to a place safe and warm and dark, where those piercing blue eyes could not see him.

"Good-bye, Vihari," Godessohn said.

Vihari started to respond, but before he could say anything the elevator doors separated. He hurled himself through the opening with a tinsel scream on his lips, extending his arms to soften his landing on the carpeted platform.

His stomach remained on the eighth floor. His fake scream became a ghastly howl of horror. He accelerated down an empty shaft, cables humming all around him.

Ah, yes, he was going home, going all the way back, beyond

the womb to the oily bowels of the earth, from which all living things issued, and to which they all returned.

CHAPTER TWENTY-SIX

"I used to dread the arrival of each new day," Gina said. "I don't anymore."

Dante propped himself higher on his big down pillows and looked at her with adoration.

"And it's because of you, Dante."

"Me? I almost got you killed."

"You gave me something to live for."

She lowered her eyes, and a blush the color of a Venetian dawn spread across her cheeks. She had become more confident, he thought, but he was pleased to see that some of her old shyness had remained.

"Dante," she said, "I must be moving out soon. You promised to help me begin a new life, and you've certainly done that. But as Graziella Calvino said, the rest is now up to me."

"Gina . . ."

"I'll be fine, Dante, I promise. You mustn't worry about me."

He wanted to take her in his arms – this morning and every morning for the rest of his life. He'd better not, though. He knew where it would lead, and Dr. Benotto had given him a stern lecture on how his excesses were undermining his recovery. At least he would wait until the lunch hour. He spoke to his hidden computer, and the slats of his antique shutters pivoted open. Morning light flooded into the elegant bell tower flat.

She snuggled close and they gazed at Florence in the valley below. The Duomo, the Palazzo Vecchio, the Uffizzi, Santa Maria Novella – all of the fine old landmarks were visible through the winter haze. He thought of his ancestors, going all the way back to the Medicis, and thanked them once again for their spiritual assistance during his confrontation with Godessohn.

"Would you like your cappuccino now?" Gina asked.

"That would be perfect."

She flicked on the intercom, she was a quick learner. "Luigi, send up breakfast, please."

"Right away, Signorina," responded a testy, high-pitched voice. She had to smile. She could picture him 300 feet beneath them in the kitchen, his Van Dyke neatly trimmed and his ruffled silk shirt immaculate, cursing the inequities of class while he steamed their milk and laid out their pastries.

"Luigi," said Dante, leaning over Gina, "I've changed my mind. Instead of the usual breakfast, we'd like a bottle of Dom Perginon. Also, Luigi, prepare us some appropriate morning hors d'oeuvres. There's something Gina and I wish to toast, and I have lost my resolve to wait until tonight."

"As your trusted friend and servant, Signore, I must refuse your request. I heard what Dr. Benotto said. I will not hasten your moral and physical decay with champagne, pâté and caviar at this early hour."

"Luigi . . ."

"All right, all right, just forget I was trying to look after you. By the way, Signore, what is the occasion for this toast?"

"Luigi, please."

"Sorry, Signore, forgive me. I suppose I'm rather bored and lonely down here."

"Would you like me to send you to work with Kiyo in South Africa?"

"I'll prepare your order at once, Signore."

"Thank you, Luigi."

Dante switched off the intercom. Gina took his hand and examined his fingers one at a time. Some were healing faster than others. "What is Kiyo doing in South Africa?"

"Applying for a job with Godessohn's philanthropy."

"Oh, Dante, how could you let her do that?"

"It was not my idea."

"Dante! This is getting absurd. You must go to the

authorities! I do not understand why you refuse."

He put on his robe and walked to the window. In the crowded square, kids were arguing over a bicycle. A few old codgers had gathered for a morning game of *baci*, and Flavio, the baker, was singing his daily aria of love to Signora Pavese.

Dante waited for the tolling of ancient chimes to stop. "I wish it were that simple, Gina. I wish I could entrust this mess to someone else."

"Why don't you, Dante? Why don't you? When you accosted me at Giorgio's, you told me the authorities would put me in jail forever if I didn't do what you wanted. Certainly they would do the same with this awful man."

"There are no witnesses to his crimes."

Gina leaped out of bed and took him by the arm. "Dante, what are you talking about? What has gotten into you? I saw everything. The microwave killing of the old clerk, the telephone call meant for you that blew up the melon, everything."

"You, according to the records of the Italian Republic, do not even exist. There would be too much to explain. I'm afraid your testimony would not be credible."

"Then what about that repulsive nut-brown man, Godessohn's servant? Couldn't he be made to testify?"

"He was not Godessohn's servant, Gina. He was a computer expert named Vihari Hivali. Unfortunately he is no longer with us. My surveillance team reports that he committed suicide."

"Well . . . I can't say that I'm sorry. What about you, Dante? Certainly you could testify."

"Yes, but I doubt I could be effective. Now that Godessohn has appointed me head of the International Commission, he could easily depict me as a disgruntled underling. You must understand certain things, Gina. The man is spending a lot of money here. Money attracts power. If there is a public conflict, many influential interests will side with him for that reason alone. And you mustn't forget that he has become an Italian national hero."

"That's disgusting."

"There's something else, Gina. With each passing day, Godessohn's fish swims closer to its destination. Even if we succeeded in having him locked up, this would not prevent the greatest natural disaster in history. We have to find a way to recall or disarm his gift to the Americans. I'm afraid, Gina, that Godessohn is the only man alive capable of reversing the ghastly scenario he has set in motion. He is going to have to be compelled to do what we say. Our actions will have to be more drastic than those permitted under the law. I have no choice but to conduct this battle as a personal vendetta."

"That sounds like the old Italy talking."

"So be it."

"But, Dante . . . can you win?"

"I don't know."

As if in answer to her question, she glimpsed a large bald head in the square. The head was moving in a bee line toward the bell tower entrance.

It couldn't be Godessohn, she thought. Dante had promised her that he was under round-the-clock surveillance. Still, she wanted Dante to take a precautionary look. She turned to him, but he had gone to the door for the breakfast cart.

Smiling warmly, Dante motioned her to join him at the table. Gina glanced back at the square. The bald man had come so close to the base of the tower she couldn't see him anymore.

Dante looked happy, almost healthy, as if he had telescoped the remaining weeks of his recovery into a few seconds. Gina could not bring herself to darken his mood with her latest irrational fear. She must just keep reminding herself that Godessohn was in South Africa and that Dante would know the moment he left.

When they were seated, he poured champagne into slender crystal glasses.

"Gina . . ."

"Yes."

"There can be no talk of your going off on your own. I don't care what Graziella Calvino says, I want you to stay with me. Gina, will you wait for me?"

"I . . . I don't understand."

"I can hardly ask you to spend the rest of your life with me until the present conflict is resolved." He raised his glass. "But if I survive, Gina, there's only one thing I want – to settle down with you, and raise the children we will have together, and fall asleep each night with you in my arms."

There was a loud knock at the emergency door no one ever used. She gasped and put a hand over her mouth. This was it, the end. She knew as surely as she had known about the phones in the Zitti.

Dante went to open. Gina tried to cry out, to warn him of what she had seen, but her voice was frozen in her throat. She tried to stand up and throw herself in his path, but her legs would not lift her. She was paralyzed, she could not move, she watched in horror as he turned the knob.

Luigi poked his head into the room, sweating and breathing heavily. "Signorina, Signore, excuse me. Buongiorno, excuse me, I know how – "

"What the devil are you doing barging in on us? This had better be serious."

"Oh, it is, Signore, it is very serious. Flavio, the baker, is waiting downstairs. He would not let me use the intercom. He forced me to come up the stairs. I tried to reason with him but he turned vicious. I am not a fighter, Signore, and . . . "

"And *what*?"

"He demands to speak with you in person. You know he has asked Signora Pavese, the widow, to marry him every morning for the past twenty years. Well, today she accepted. The poor man is beside himself. He does not know what to do. He considers you the only person who can help him out of his dilemma. He is threatening to throw himself off the Ponte Vecchio if you do not advise him at once."

"Very well. Tell him to go back to his shop and wait for me. And tell him to continue with his baking until I arrive. There is no reason for him to ruin lunch for the entire neighborhood just because he is anticipating marital difficulties. And, Luigi . . ."

"Yes, Signore?"

"If you disturb me again for any reason, I shall send you to work for Altel. Is that clear?"

"Yes, Signore, very clear. I would rather throw myself off the bridge with my fellow male soldier, Flavio."

* * *

Gina stood at the window, trembling. Dante came up and put his arms around her. "Gina," he said tenderly, "I was asking you something when Luigi crashed in on us."

"Yes . . ."

"I was asking you to stay with me for now, and to be my wife when this ordeal is behind us."

She tensed horribly, as if she were having the same reaction as the baker to the prospect of marriage.

"Gina, what is it? Is something wrong."

"Look. Dante, look! That's him. Oh, God, it's him."

Dante saw a stout low-slung man with a big bald head cutting a swath through the crowded square. He hugged Gina more tightly.

"No, my love, the man you see is not Pieter Godessohn. It is Flavio, our visitor. Now that you mention it, though, there is an uncanny resemblance. I think shall advise Flavio to remain single. Perhaps he can be of use to us later. What about you, Gina? Do you also wish to remain single?"

A great wave of relief swept over her as she flung her arms

around Dante's neck. "No!" she cried. "Graziella Calvino be damned! I want to be yours forever. Forever."

He handed her a glass of champagne and carried her to the bed. When the intercom sounded, he switched off the volume and put a finger to her lips. "Priorities," he said. "One cannot live without them."

She wanted him to answer, just in case it was an emergency. But her ecstasy was on the rise, and she soon forgot everything except Dante and the dazzling moment they had entered together.

The End

Made in the USA
Lexington, KY
27 November 2010